W9-BJU-201

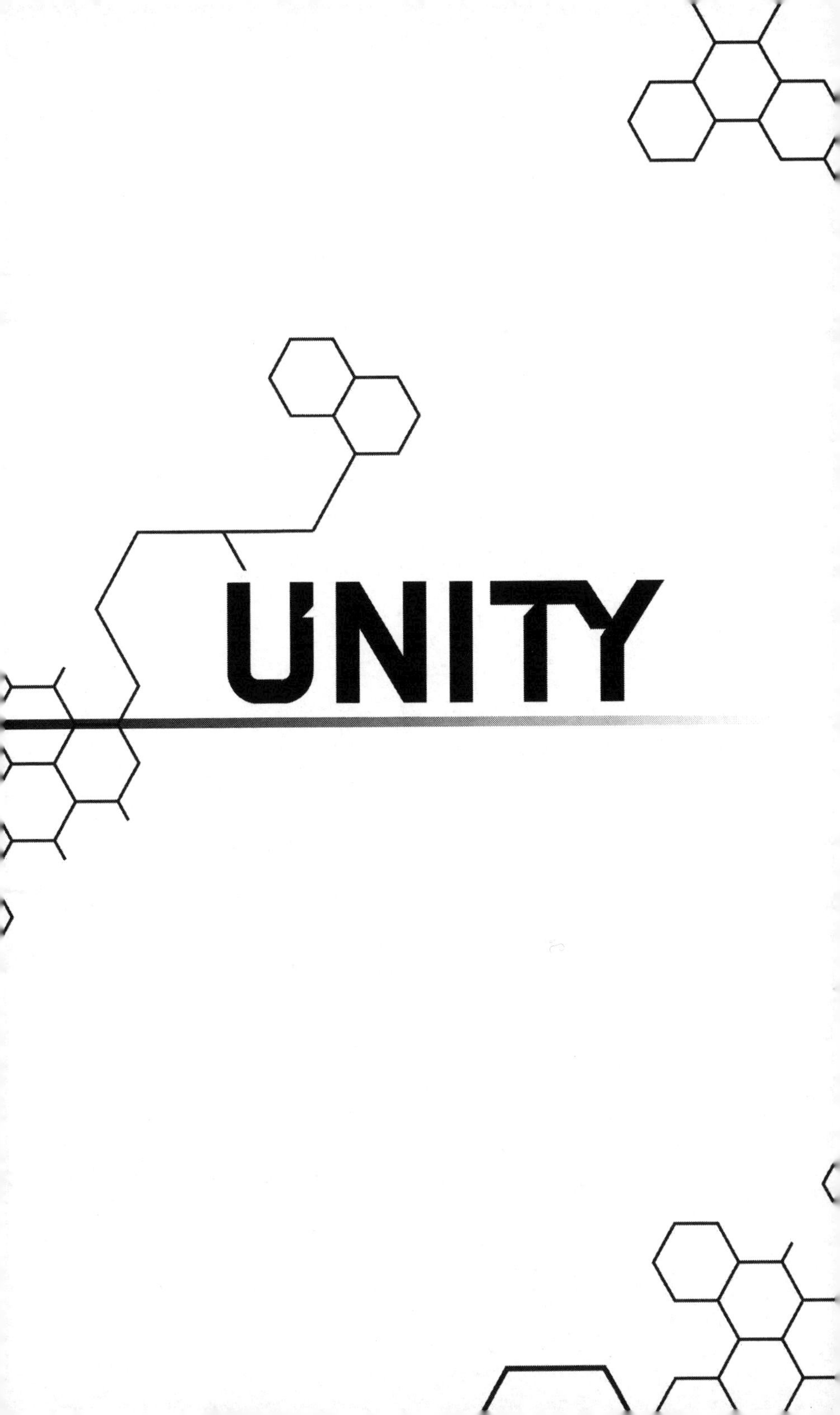
UNITY

Also by Jeremy Robinson

Standalone Novels
The Didymus Contingency
Raising The Past
Beneath
Antarktos Rising
Kronos
Xom-B
Flood Rising
MirrorWorld
Apocalypse Machine

Nemesis Saga Novels
Island 731
Project Nemesis
Project Maigo
Project 731
Project Hyperion
Project Legion (2016)

The Antarktos Saga
The Last Hunter – Descent
The Last Hunter – Pursuit
The Last Hunter – Ascent
The Last Hunter – Lament
The Last Hunter – Onslaught
The Last Hunter – Collected Edition

SecondWorld Novels
SecondWorld
Nazi Hunter: Atlantis

Cerberus Group Novels
Herculean

The Jack Sigler/Chess Team Thrillers
Prime
Pulse
Instinct
Threshold
Ragnarok
Omega
Savage
Cannibal
Empire

Jack Sigler Continuum Novels
Guardian
Patriot

Chesspocalypse Novellas
Callsign: King
Callsign: Queen
Callsign: Rook
Callsign: King 2 – Underworld
Callsign: Bishop
Callsign: Knight
Callsign: Deep Blue
Callsign: King 3 – Blackout

Chesspocalypse Novella Collections
The Brainstorm Trilogy
Callsign – Tripleshot
Callsign – Doubleshot

Writing Under Pseudonyms

Horror Fiction as Jeremy Bishop

Torment
The Sentinel
The Raven
Refuge

Post-Apoc Sci-Fi Fiction as Jeremiah Knight

Hunger
Feast
Viking Tomorrow (2016)

UNITY

JEREMY ROBINSON

BREAKNECK MEDIA

Copyright ©2016 by Jeremy Robinson

All rights reserved. No part of this book may be reproduced or transmitted in any form or by any means without written permission of the author.

This is a work of fiction. Names, characters, places, and incidents either are the product of the author's imagination or are used fictitiously. Any resemblance to actual events or locales or persons, living or dead, is entirely coincidental.

No part of this book may be used or reproduced in any manner whatsoever without written permission, except in the case of brief quotations embodied in critical articles and reviews. For information address Jeremy Robinson at jrobinsauthor@gmail.com.

Cover design copyright ©2016 by Jeremy Robinson

Visit Jeremy Robinson on the World Wide Web at:
www.bewareofmonsters.com

For Tori Paquette.

So it begins…

BASE

THE NEAR FUTURE

"Who did you leave behind?" the boy sitting across from me asks. When I offer no reply, as I'm prone to do, he asks a follow-up question, equally as nosey. "What did you bring?"

He seems like a nice kid. Kind, Asian eyes. Someone in the world we left behind adored him. Taught him to make conversation. So I acknowledge his presence for the first time in our thus-far, six-hour flight to who-knows-where. I hold up the weathered photo in my hand, the old-school printed-on-paper kind, and turn it around so he can see it.

"That's it? A *photo?*"

"Family photo," I tell him.

"You're not in it," he says. "How can it be a family photo, if you're not in it?"

I wrap a single digit around the image and tap my mother's slim stomach. She's smiling, leaning back into my father, her long brown hair curling around her neck like a scarf, her blue eyes visible even from a distance, even though the photo is faded. My father's muscular, tan arms are wrapped around her. A tropical beach in the background. "I was in there."

"That's...weird," he says, lifting his Featherlight tablet, tapping it on and scrolling through an endless stream of photos with a flick of his finger. Family. Friends. Parents. Digital years pass by. "You could have brought more than one photo, you know. The limitation was set to a 'single object weighing less than two pounds,' but data is weightless. I have movies, books, music and—"

He stops when he looks at my eyes, devoid of emotion, locked on the still scrolling images of a life I never had. His finger stops swiping. The scrolling ends on a photo of the boy, leaping into a pool, not a care in the world.

"Sorry," he says, somehow understanding that this photo in my hand is all that I have left of my family.

His sudden discomfort unnerves me. Not because I feel bad for him, but because his reaction means that I'm outwardly annoyed, and I don't like people to know how I'm feeling. Emotions are messy, and I like my world neat and tidy. All fourteen psychologists who have evaluated me over the years came to the same stunning conclusion: 'compartmentalization of emotions to avoid childhood trauma.' Bonus points for the seven-syllable word, but it's not really a revelation if it's something I *consciously* try to do. The only time a psychologist really caught me off guard was three weeks ago, when she referred to my emotional compartmentalization as an 'asset.' I never got to ask why, though the following weeks of testing seemed designed to evaluate the limits of my ability to cope with trauma. And all without me cussing. Not once.

At the request of my most recent foster-mother, who is actually kind to me, despite my frosty exterior, I agreed to temper my language. My name is Euphemia Williams, and I've punched exactly seven people for calling me by that name, including my third foster-mother. I was just six at the time, but I still managed to draw blood. That was the first time I felt my own strength—I'm talking fortitude, not muscle—and I've been relying on it since. The name that anyone with a shred of sense uses to address me, is Effie. The three times I've been in a school long enough to earn a nickname, it's been the same every time: 'Eff-Bomb'—hence foster-mom's request.

Unity was billed as a program for the gifted, but it's closer to military basic training. In the three weeks that I've been here, I've barely spoken a word, let alone dropped my nickname's namesake. So when the kid says, "You're Eff-Bomb, right?" it's like a perfectly aimed arrow through the chink in Smaug's armor. A bark of a laugh escapes my lips, the sound waves spaghettifying as they're pulled back into the black hole that has suddenly appeared at the back of my throat.

"Was that a hiccup or a laugh?" the boy asks.

I glance up, looking past the shock of orange-dye-tipped hair hanging over the left side of my face, and I meet his eyes. "Are *you* laughing?"

He is. Not loudly, but he's having a hard time containing it. My instinct is to knock the smile off his face, but the kid, who can't be older than twelve, wears adorability the way a turtle does a shell. It might protect him for another year, but when he hits puberty and his nose outgrows his face, he's going to need a new survival strategy.

"Where did you hear that name?" I ask.

"Sig," he says, sending a second arrow through the chink.

I met Sig during one of many loathsome events that make up my life. It was my first day at Brook Meadow, a school for kids who didn't fit the rigid paradigm of modern educational institutions. The school was an unusual mix of troubled and brilliant kids, whose social skills lacked refinement or conformity. The school change was the result of being deported to a new foster home. My ninth in sixteen years. Day one in a new home, at a new school, I got in a fight, earning a 'strike one' suspension. When a boy grabs your butt, you intro-duce him to your knuckles. That's a motto worth living by, I think. Except this boy had Asperger's and a complete lack of impulse control, so no one but me blamed him. I tried to argue natural consequences, but his broken jaw spoke louder than my relatively few words.

I left the building in a storm, but didn't go farther than the back of the gym; despite having a skateboard to ride, I didn't know the way home. Sig approached with the silence of a mouse, surprising me as she sat down beside me and leaned against the warm, sunlit brick wall. Through the corner of my eye, I could see her slight grin and her radiant green irises, her hair tied back in a braid. She was just eleven then, half my size, barely noticeable. But then she did the unthinkable and leaned her head on my shoulder. That ounce of affection, from a girl whose name I didn't yet know, undid me.

She's the only person to have ever seen me cry. But she made up for that by introducing me to chocolate pudding, a snack I now consider one of my more indulgent vices.

Sig is one of the few people in the world I have ever called a friend. She's now a thirteen-year-old savant who can recite the numbers of Pi until she runs out of breath or has to pee. She's quiet because most people can't understand what she says, though I seem to manage. I think of her as multilingual, her first language being numbers, and her second being computer code. English is a distant third, and a good portion of that focuses on space and its mysteries, a subject for which she's given me a greater appreciation. I think she's the only reason Brook Meadow didn't kick me out. Without me, her ideas and her voice remain locked in her head. I thought that might even be the reason I was welcomed to—forced to go to—Unity. But upon our arrival, we were separated, and I haven't seen her since.

That this boy knows her name and has communicated with Sig enough to 1) recognize me based on description, and 2) know my nickname, means that they are friends. And that means he's safe. I lean forward. "Is she okay?"

He looks confused by the question. "Why wouldn't she be?"

"She has a hard time talking to people."

"Not us," he says.

"Us, who?"

He holds up the back of his right hand, revealing a triangular tattoo—Unity's logo. The sides and tip of the outlined triangle, which come to a point between the middle and index knuckles, are black. The band across the bottom is blue. The symbol marks him as a 'Base.' I'm not entirely certain what that means, but all of the kids I've met with the Base tattoo are stupid smart.

He motions to the Unity logo on my hand. The bottom and sides are black, but the top is red. "You're a Point."

I hold up my hand, inspecting the brand, which was applied in one quick, painful stamp. We all received them on Day One. I was told it was temporary, but it hasn't faded yet. There are three stamps: Base, Point and Support—which has orange sides and a black bottom. No one ever said what they signify.

"Do you know what they're for?" I ask.

"I think they're based on personality," he says, "rather than cognitive abilities."

"Meaning what?"

The kid leans in close and whispers, like what he's about to say might get him in trouble. I'm not sure why he's bothering, since there aren't any adults in the transport's passenger seating. I'm assuming our pilots are in charge, but it's only the two of us and eight other Unity students. "I haven't seen many Points. Just a few. But from what Sig says, I think it means you're a badass."

He manages to get a second chuckle out of me, and I decide I like him. I extend my right hand toward him, making it official. "You know my name."

"*Really?*" There's a phrase for the kind of grin he has, but I really am trying to cut down on the four-letter words. According to my newest stand-in mother—her name is Judy—a vocabulary dependent on profanity, colorful and fun though it may be, is a sign of a 'dull intellect.' People can think I'm rude and standoffish all they want, but stupid? No bleeping way. Then again, research has shown that people who swear have higher IQs. Which I guess explains a lot. But I do like Judy, so I'm watching my language, for her. If the great orators of history, whom I admire, could use language in powerful ways, without cursing, so can I.

"Until I change my mind," I tell him.

He takes my hand and gives it a firm shake. "Daniel. Daniel Chen."

"Chinese?" I ask.

"Half. My father was born in America, though. My mother was white. Like yours."

I'm about to ask him how he knows that, when I remember the photo in my hand. I tuck it back into my flight suit, which is black with red racing stripes and a Point triangle badge on the front.

"Your father was—"

"From Puerto Rico," I say. Most people—foster-parents and psychologists—guess Mexican, and it's gotten annoying. It's one of the few things I know about my real parents, and I wish, for once, someone would get it right.

"So we both had short dads," he says, drawing some kind of embarrassing snort from my mouth. I gag on the laugh and cough.

Oh, man, I really like this kid.

"That's horrible," I say.

"Only if you think there's something wrong with being short, and I hope you don't. You're genetically predisposed to be short, thanks to your parents and your, umm, gender."

"I'm also genetically predisposed to kicking the butts of people who insult me."

For some reason, this gets *him* laughing. Sig must have left out my violent history. Which reminds me... "When did you last see her? Sig?"

"Before boarding the transport. It was kind of chaotic, as I'm sure you remember, but I saw her get on Transport 37."

Chaotic is an understatement. They woke us up in the middle of the night. Normally calm adults were screaming. Full-on panic mode. We grabbed our 'go-packs,' the contents of which are still a mystery, and our one item. Then we were herded onto transports. Now that we've been in the air for six hours, I've had some time to reflect. I think it was all some kind of elaborate test, to see how we cope under confusing conditions.

Daniel unbuckles his seatbelt and steps across the single aisle separating the two rows of inward-facing seats. He kneels beside me and looks out the long window lining the transport's side. He taps on the glass. "There it is."

I try to turn around, but the seatbelt, which is more like a five-point racing harness wrapping around from my shoulders, waist and crotch, holds me in place. I unbuckle and turn around.

Someone from the front says, "They told us not to unbuckle under any circumstances."

I lift my right fist, displaying my Point tattoo, but I stop short of extending my middle finger. F-Bombs in sign language count. But the raised fist is enough to silence the peanut gallery.

Outside the window are two gray transports. Like ours, they're long, clunky looking things without wings. Flying school buses. They're tough, but barely aerodynamic, and they only stay aloft thanks to the repulse engines—a kind of antigravity, I suppose. Traditional wings went out of style ten years ago, though the most maneuverable of aircraft still have them. The transport beside us, five hundred feet out, is labeled 37. Beyond it, another five hundred feet away, is 38. I suppose that makes us 36, and it inspires the question, "Where are the rest of them?"

The Unity program, up until six hours ago, was held on a retrofitted aircraft carrier. When we were prodded to the flight deck and shoved aboard the transports, there were hundreds of students and a fleet of aircraft. If 37 and 38 are as loosely packed as our transport, that leaves hundreds of students unaccounted for. Not that it's my position to do an accounting of them.

Daniel just shrugs. "Your other friend is on 38."

"Other friend?"

"Hutch."

"Ugh," I groan. Hutch is like a puppy. His orange-sided Support stamp matches the orange dye coloring the last few inches of my black hair. I made the mistake of grinning at him on Day One, when I felt out of sorts and lost, like everyone else. He took it as an invitation to follow me around. To talk to me. To befriend me. While I learned to cope with his presence, I would certainly not call him a friend. "Next subject."

"Oookay," Daniel says. "That storm looks wicked."

I look beyond the transports and realize we're descending, our long flight apparently nearing its end. We're flying low over the endless Pacific Ocean, perhaps just a few thousand feet up. The storm is coming in high, roiling in the atmosphere, spitting out bands of lightning. I don't normally apply emotions to nature, but the sky really does look angry. The band of red light where the setting sun cuts between the horizon and the storm doesn't help. It will be dark soon, and if we're not on the ground by the time the storm reaches us, it's going to be a bumpy ride.

"You're not a puker, are you?" I ask.

Daniel swallows and shrinks back from the view. *Great.*

Then his eyes widen as though we're in one of those old timey action movies where poignant moments are slowed down so the audience doesn't miss all the on-screen awesomeness. In the reflection of his wide eyes, I see a flickering orange sprite. Then another. And another.

I nearly fall from my seat as I spin around. Fireballs cut through the storm clouds, trailed by steam and then smoke. Voices rise up from the front of the transport as the others see what's happening. Some of the kids unbuckle for a better look. To my surprise, it's me who asks Daniel the obvious question, "What is it, a satellite?"

"Too big," he whispers, and he's right. The fireball at the center looks far bigger than any satellite.

"Meteor?"

"Too slow," he says, leaning forward, face nearly pressed against the glass. "I think... It looks like..."

The ball of fire erupts, the blinding light forcing us back, hands to our eyes. Shouts fill the cabin. When the light subsides, tendrils of smoke and fire drop straight down. Above the explosion, the storm clouds bend upward, propelled by the invisible shockwave.

Things are about to get rough.

I shove Daniel back across the aisle. He slams hard into his seat and looks a little wounded—emotionally—until I shout, "Everyone buckle up! Now!"

I slip back into my harness, clipping it quickly in place. Daniel tries to stow his Featherlight back in his go-pack, but his fingers slip off the magnetic strip twice, and he gives up, holding the device while he struggles with his buckles. His shaking fingers are all but useless. When I see tears squeeze from the sides of his eyes, I unbuckle and jump across the aisle.

He tries to resist for a moment, offering a brave, "I can do it!" but I quickly overpower him and fasten his harness. Not waiting for, or needing any thanks, I turn back toward my seat, but stop. What I see through the window freezes me in place. Transport 38 goes dark and drops from the sky.

Hutch...

I place my hand on the glass and say, "Sig," just before 37 loses power and falls. I dive for my seat, looping an arm beneath one of the shoulder straps, but then the transport shakes, like it's been backhanded by God. I'm thrown to the floor as we lose power and plummet downward.

The silence that follows the transport's loss of power feels like pressure on the sides of my head. Then I realize the compression is an actual pressure change, brought on by the fact that we're plummeting from the sky. The repulse discs mounted to the bottom of the transport have lost power. I glance at the Featherlight clutched in Daniel's hands. The screen is black, which means nothing, but the small LED light indicating a charge has also gone out.

As I wrestle against the shaking floor, crawling back to my seat, I run through scenarios and come to a quick conclusion. That explosion, whatever it was, generated an electromagnetic pulse that fried everything electronic inside its blast radius. Part of me wants to tell the pilots that their efforts are futile. There'll be no avoiding our fate. But I also know we weren't very high when we lost power. We're going to pancake into the ocean in just a few seconds.

"Twenty seconds!" Daniel shouts, putting a number to my fear.

But it seems wrong. The transports will fall like stones, slowed by drag perhaps, but their weight will more than make up for it.

"Hold on!" Daniel shouts, and my muscles react to his warning—fingers clutching the harness straps—before my mind decides he knows what he's talking about.

Several loud clunks boom inside the cylindrical cabin. They're followed by a hard tug on my arm, as our rate of our descent suddenly slows.

"Drag wings," Daniel shouts, over the shrill voices of our fellow freaked-out passengers. "This model of transport has several crash countermeasures. Some of them don't require power. Fifteen seconds."

With both hands wrapped around my seat's shoulder straps, I pull myself up while giving Daniel a dubious look.

"This is what I do," he says. "Trust—" His voice is cut off by a shrill whistle. His eyes go wide, and I barely hear him shout, "Hold on!" again.

This time, my muscles and mind work in tandem. Daniel seems to know a lot about the transport's systems. He's part of Unity for a reason, and he's a Base—like Sig—which means he's probably got an uncanny amount of knowledge crammed into that cute head.

The transport kicks into a high velocity spin. I'm pinned against the bottom of my seat, unable to move. The air is pushed from my lungs. Pinpoints of light spiral in my vision, like silent fireworks. There's a jarring snap and a clang that silences the whistle, but it changes our spin into a tumble. For a moment, I'm able to hold on, but the combined forces of motion and gravity conspire against me. I'm lifted from the floor and slung against the ceiling, my hands still clutching my seat straps.

I see Daniel's wide eyes looking up at me. He shouts over the roar of the wind outside and the blood surging behind my ears. "Effie!"

I'm slammed back to the floor, eliciting a rare shout of pain. I can take a lot of abuse. I've *taken* a lot—from bullies, from bad foster-parents and from foster-siblings. But the impacts wracking my body are unrestrained by the fear of being caught. One hand falls free of the strap, and I think I hear Daniel scream, "Three seconds."

There is no way I'm getting back in the chair and buckled up inside three jarring seconds. I'm surprised that my instinct, instead of fighting to the end, is to look in Daniel's eyes and see a little bit of kindness before I'm erased from the world. And sent where? Heaven? Hell? Infinite oblivion? I don't know much about the first option, but I've been told to visit the second option many times. And option three? That doesn't sound all that different from hell to me. So fingers crossed that God is as merciful as they say.

A high pitched voice cuts through the chaos and prevents me from reaching out to a higher power in my last moments. It's Daniel's voice. Repeating something. I focus past the roar, and the words work their way into my ears. "Let go!"

My fingers snap open as I'm thrashed back up to the ceiling. Held in place, I look down at Daniel, and he's still shouting at me. "Hold your breath!"

As my lungs fill to capacity, Daniel's words run through my mind. *'This model of transport has several crash countermeasures. Some of them don't require power.'*

What do you know, Daniel?

A hiss fills the cabin, building to a sudden intensity. As I'm tossed back toward the floor, I catch sight of gray, liquid streaks jutting from every side of the cabin. There's a fraction of a moment when I think the liquid is expanding, but then it and the rest of the world is consumed. I feel nothing but tightness all around me.

I hear nothing.

See nothing.

I can't breathe.

And then my insides shift downward. I can feel my guts push on my bladder. My head aches, as my brain bounces against my skull. My compressed lungs try to cough out air, but there's no escape—

Something is in my nose!

A second impact pushes everything in the other direction. The force is less intense, but the pain is absolute. And then, it gets worse. I need to exhale. The pressure around me builds, pushing on my lungs, as if they were too-full balloons.

Stillness surrounds me. I can feel my heart struggling to beat inside a confined chest. People weren't meant to feel their own heartbeats. It's a clear sign of wrongness. And it only gets worse, as the world compresses itself into my very pores, pushing past my clenched eyelids.

I've been trapped inside a human-sized blood-pressure cuff.

And then, like at the doctor's, it releases.

Blood flows first, reaching my brain and clearing the lights from my vision.

My body decompresses, lungs expanding to a more natural position.

But the air still needs a release.

I still need to breathe!

The material clogging my nostrils turns to a warm, pungent liquid and drools out. I feel warmth all around me, and then nothing. I'm released.

And dropped.

The air in my lungs coughs out, as I hit the floor. I'm wracked by heaving gasps, my body curling in on itself like a terrified pill bug. Pain screams through my body, and I swear I feel an organ slip back into place. The image of my twisted insides fills me with nausea. Or is that the concussion, which I definitely have?

As confusion subsides, I'm struck by the realization that I'm alive.

And trapped in a fetid, infinite darkness. This can't be oblivion. It smells horrible. Chemical. And while I'm in pain, I don't think it's quite bad enough to be hell.

Alive, I decide. *Now, think.*

"Daniel?" I ask, my voice sounding flat, like the sound is being absorbed. I move a hand across the floor—which is covered in several inches of goo—trying to find my bearings. But in the center aisle, where there should be a straight, flat surface, I find a lump.

A light.

We're upside down. I'm on the *ceiling.*

"Daniel. Are you alive?"

A gentle coughing replies, and I know it's Daniel because the sound is close, and above me. "Effie?"

"I'm here."

"My head..."

"You're upside down."

"Oh."

"What was that stuff?"

"It's an REF safety system. Rapid Expanding Foam. Most new military aircraft have it for when ejecting isn't possible. The whole system is mechanical, relying on air pressure. A sudden decrease in external pressure opens the valves, and air pressure moves the foam. When it contacts open air, well, you saw what happened. Or at least you felt it."

"It nearly killed me."

"Thirty-seven percent of the people it's supposed to save are killed by it. That's why it's not in civilian vehicles. Even though sixty-three percent of people are saved, the manufacturer would be held responsible for the thirty-seven percent it didn't save, because the REF would be the official cause of death, not the crash."

That Daniel can not only assemble multiple sentences right now, but can also recall this kind of detailed information, is impressive. But it's also a distraction. There were ten kids on board our transport. According to Daniel's numbers, at least three of them are dead. Likely four.

"I need light," I say, as groans and coughing from the front end make the hairs on my arms stand on end.

"Above my—below my head. There's a cabinet."

I find the small door, but I can't find a handle.

"Push it in," Daniel says. "There should be a first aid kit. Inside that you'll find four chemical glow-sticks."

I push on the door, and it pops open. A plastic box the size of a small briefcase slides out. "How do you know all this?"

"I was on the design team. Two years ago. I was working for a private firm until Unity recruited me."

I open the first aid kit and feel around. The case is full of unidentifiable packages, bottles and tools. "Recruited you?"

"I couldn't turn them down when they doubled my fee."

"Your *what?* You're being paid?" Between crunchy packages that must be bandages, I find four plastic-wrapped cylinders.

"You're not?"

"I wasn't given a choice. It was this or a life wallowing in self-pity."

"That's still a choice," he points out.

"Yeah, well, it's not much of one." I bend one of the glowsticks without unwrapping it. There's a moment of resistance before the small glass cylinder inside it breaks. A dull green light emerges as the two chemical liquids inside make contact. The light grows even brighter when I shake the tube.

Daniel's face is lit in green light. He looks far more strained than his voice let on. There are wet streaks from his eyes to his hairline.

"Hey," someone from the front says. The voice is feminine and terrified. "Help us!"

I put the glowstick on top of the first aid kit, which is resting on the gelatinous bed of what was, just moments ago, a cabin full of rock-hard foam. It's slippery beneath my feet, but I manage to stand

and get a shoulder underneath Daniel's legs. "Hold on to my waist."

He wraps his small arms around my waist, while I support his body with one hand and fumble with his seatbelt clip with the other. When I find the triangular button and push it, his weight is transferred to me. We nearly topple over together, but we both release in time to shift the momentum to Daniel's body. He flops over my arms and lands on his feet.

"That was surprisingly graceful," I say, and I bend down to the first aid kit, recovering the three unused glowsticks. "You know how to get out of here?"

"The rear hatch can operate manually," he says.

"Get it open," I say, cracking a fresh glowstick and heading for the front of the transport, where several small, whimpering voices, and at least a few dead bodies, await.

I wince as the smell of blood mingles with the chemical odor left behind by the foam. The ceiling-turned-floor is slick beneath my feet, the sludge congealing to something resembling kid's gooey gunk. I cling to the seats above my head and notice our go-packs, which had been stored beneath us, are now stowed in a more traditional location.

When we were shoved on board, we were given simple instructions. Put your go-pack beneath your seat. Buckle up. And do not unbuckle until you are on the ground. The words were shouted at us. Rushed and angry. Then the hatch closed, and the transport lifted off.

There's no one here to tell us what to do now. If the pilots survived the crash, they're probably still trying to recover. For now, we're on our own.

"Hurry up," a girl I can't see says, sounding a little more pushy than I appreciate. Given the circumstances, I can't blame her, so I refrain from commenting. What I don't do is hurry. I'm one misplaced slippery step from toppling over, and the way my head feels, another good clunk to my melon might undo me.

A pair of dangling arms glow green in the light as I approach. I freeze for a moment, unsettled by the limbs' stillness. *There are eight people hanging upside down,* I tell myself. *And you're the only one who can get them down. Move!*

I reach out and take hold of the wrist, below which is a Support brand. The temperature of the skin is the first sign of something wrong. Then the lack of a pulse. And then, I turn my head up to the face of a young girl, her eyes locked open, staring down at nothing.

"Is she dead?" someone asks. A boy, I think.

"I think Nick is, too," says the more impatient feminine voice.

The arm swings slowly when I let go, moving in the slow circles of a pendulum before coming to a stop. Gasping in a quick breath and setting my compartmentalization ability to full power, I move across the upside-down aisle and encounter my second ever corpse. As I reel back from the sight of a body whose ribs have been compressed from the foam's pressure, I bump into a hand that fumbles across my head and through my hair like a scurrying mouse. Without thinking, I duck and spin. My feet squeak against the slick metal ceiling and then seem to launch out like there are little rockets attached to my heels.

My breath catches as I reach out, finding a hand, and I catch hold. My fall turns into a slide, stopping beneath the upside down person who caught me. Only she didn't catch me. She had nothing to do with it. In the dull light provided by the glowstick now embedded in the slime beneath me, I see a dead girl's eyes looking down at me.

A second hand reaches out of the gloom. "Here." It's the impatient one.

I take her hand, noting another Support brand, and I manage to not topple over. The girl is strong and hoists me to my feet so that our eyes—mine dark brown, her's light blue—are inches apart, though rotated 180 degrees. Her long wavy hair hangs like a golden curtain. "Get. Me. Down."

Without a word, I comply with the girl's request. Working together, she's on her feet beside me in seconds. "I'll check the front," she says. "Help Gizmo."

Gizmo? A nickname, I decide, and I look for the person whose mousey hand ran through my hair. I find the boy behind me, his face bloodied, his chest rising and falling in quick but labored breaths. Kid's not doing well.

"Gizmo," I say, taking his warm hand.

He says nothing. Just stares at me with crazy wide eyes, the white orbs accentuated by his dark skin. He's terrified. A dying animal. Perhaps literally. But his silence might not be from fear. Unity, like Brook Meadow, is comprised mostly of kids whose minds are unique. Like Sig, Gizmo might just not talk.

"I'm going to get you down now, okay?" When he doesn't offer a reply or show any sign of apprehension, I reach up and unbuckle him. He slides into my arms, and I have no trouble spinning the boy's skin-and-bones frame right-side-up. To my relief, Gizmo shakes his head gently and remains standing. I crack a fresh light stick and crouch beside him.

"Do you know Daniel?"

He nods.

I point to the rear end of the transport, some twenty feet away, where Daniel's silhouette can be seen in the light of his glowstick, which he's wedged into something on the wall. I can hear him grunting with exertion. The hatch's manual operation is giving him some trouble.

"That's him. He's getting the door open." I bend down and pick up Gizmo's go-pack. He takes the pack and nods when I say, "See if you can help Daniel." Then he's off, pack over his shoulder like it's the first day of school.

I turn toward the front of the transport and take a few steps before coming across another set of dangling arms. *That's four, Daniel,* I think. An even 40%, which is close enough to 37%.

I nearly scream when the blonde Support girl steps into the dull sphere of light around the glowstick still embedded in the floor behind me. She's got another girl, unconscious, in her arms. The girl's body is as limp as the dead, but her small chest is rising and falling.

"Let's go," the Support girl says.

I shake my head. "There should be one more."

"That would be Owen," she says, and I think the tone of her voice is meant to remind me that while I don't really know anyone on this transport, she considers them friends, whom she would never leave behind unless there was no choice. Owen, it would seem, is dead, too.

Fifty percent, Daniel. My anger is squelched by the knowledge that it could have been one hundred percent.

I'm about to lead the way to the back of the transport when the blonde says, "Get our go-packs."

"We don't even know what's in them," I say, my reaction born from a strong sense of don't-tell-me-what-to-do.

"Rations, survival gear, clothing." Before I can ask, she lifts the girl up so I can see her Support brand, like it's supposed to mean something. Then she squints at me. "How long have you been with Unity?"

"Three weeks."

She deflates a little.

"How long have you been with Unity?" I ask.

"Three months." She motions to the girl in her arms. "This is Mandi. She's been with Unity for a year. My name is Gwen, and if you need my assistance, I'll be—"

"I got this," I say. I step around her and pull a go-pack out, my rapid action fueled by my embarrassment over being kept in the dark. When I turn for the next bag, I see that Gwen hasn't left my side.

"That they put you in the field after three weeks says a lot for your strength of will. It means they think you can handle this." Her confidence wavers a little. "Whatever *this* is."

At least she doesn't know everything.

"I'll meet you at the back," I say. She nods and leaves, and I go back to collecting go-packs. They're a little smaller than standard school backpacks—jet black, and packed tight. Each weighs about three pounds. With my left arm loaded with four packs, I work up the nerve to steal two more from the dead, but that's all I can manage. I head toward the back, pausing for a moment to recover my own mystery go-pack, which I notice weighs three times as much as the others.

"C'mon," Gwen says, as I approach the still-closed back hatch. I'm about to lose my patience again, when I realize she's not talking to me. She's talking to Daniel, who is straining to turn the handle of a lock, high above his head. It looks like something he might struggle to do normally, but with the transport upside down, the mechanism is nearly out of his reach. He doesn't have the leverage to turn it.

I approach the scene, lit in dull green, and I hand two of the go-packs to Gizmo. When he takes them, I hand over another two to Daniel. He already has his around his shoulders, but he has no trouble with another two. I put the last two by my feet and mine on my back. "We're upside down, so the hatch is going to open up, not down, and there's a chance it won't stay open, once it's up. Don't hang around to have a conversation."

I take their lack of audible replies to be compliance, and then I take hold of the lever Daniel couldn't move. I give it a tug, and when it doesn't budge, I pull myself up, clinging to the handle like a monkey bar. I place my feet against one of two metal rails stretching down the hatch. Pushing with my legs and pulling with my torso and arms, the lever slides ten inches and then clunks into place.

When I release the handle and drop to my feet, there are three sets of glowing green and impressed eyes looking at me. "It's called leverage," I say, uncomfortable with their attention.

"We understand the concept," Daniel explains. "We just couldn't do it."

I'm not sure about Gwen. She seems pretty capable. But Daniel is right. He and Gizmo would be trapped in here without help. I put my shoulder into the door and shove. There's a slight give, but the door isn't budging for me. "Going to need help."

The moment the words leave my mouth, Daniel and Gizmo throw their feeble weight into the door. After turning her back to the door, even Gwen adds her body to the effort. The hatch moves, but it's like there's someone on the other side, pushing back. When the door budges a little and water surges in, I understand why. We might not be adrift at sea, but we're not totally out of the water yet, either.

"We need to get it above the water line!" I shout, before grinding my teeth and shoving harder. Daniel shouts beside me, putting every ounce of muscle his little body has into the effort.

Water surges past my ankles as the hatch lifts higher. The warm liquid rushes to the back of the cabin, sloshing against the far end and the door leading to the cockpit.

The pilots.

The hatch is freed from the water, and it rises up. The sudden rush of water sweeps the go-packs at my feet away, and Gizmo along with them. Hand striking out like a snake, I catch Gizmo's flight suit before he's pulled back inside the cabin. With one hand supporting the hatch, I toss Gizmo outside, into two feet of water. It's going to fill the cabin until it's even with the water outside. The pilots will be trapped. I crack my last glowstick and toss it outside, just beyond the water. A sandy beach is revealed.

"Can you hold this up?" I ask Daniel and Gwen.

"What? Why?" Daniel's indignant. Afraid.

"The pilots," I say. "They're—"

"There *are* no pilots," Daniel says. "It's a drone."

A drone?

A drone! A litany of three-, four- and five-letter words flows through my mind as a series of phrases that I think are something like poetry, an ode to obscenities. I keep it all inside, though. But I'm seriously going to punch someone in the face when I find out whose idea it was to send a bunch of kids across the ocean aboard drones.

"Go," I say to Gwen. When she ducks her shoulders down to leave with Mandi, the weight of the hatch becomes almost unbearable. Daniel grunts from the sudden strain.

When my arms start to shake, I glance down at Daniel. "Get ready, Danny-boy."

"Dan...iel," he says through gritted teeth. Then he pulls his hands away and dives into the water. The dive is graceful, but he's forgotten about the go-packs around his arms and on his back. He slaps into the water, but quickly shoves up out of it, sputtering and gasping. It would be funny if I wasn't now losing the battle with the hatch.

"C'mon!" Gwen shouts. "Jump!"

And I do. My feet push off, but there's no traction. The foam-gel beneath my feet, mixed with the oncoming rush of water, has become something like soap. Instead of diving forward, I belly-flop out, my legs from the knees down landing inside the transport. I flip over and shove up from the water in time to see the hatch fall down like some kind of medieval execution device. I yank my legs back, but it's not enough.

My eyes scrunch shut as I wait for the explosive pain. Instead there's a loud clang, and then pressure on my shoulders. As I'm dragged back, I see a piece of metal debris shoved into the door. Daniel is backing away from it. Kid saved my life. But he had help. I look up and see Gizmo straining to pull me. If not for the water taking some of my weight, I doubt he could move me an inch, though the look in his eyes says he would try.

There's a loud shriek as the shard of metal slips sideways and falls. The hatch slams shut, the gong of its impact sounding like the start of some ancient challenge. I half expect a video game announcer to shout, 'Fight!'

Instead, I hear more crushing silence.

It's followed by the gentle lapping of waves.

And then Gizmo's small voice for the first time. "What the *hell* is going on?"

Before anyone can answer Gizmo's question, a new 'sunset' fills the sky in the East. It blooms orange, rising up and drowning out the night sky. Then it fades back down to a flicker before disappearing entirely. With the light extinguished, the world plunges back into a sickly green-lit night. The sun has fallen in the West, or perhaps has been fully consumed by the storm still headed toward us.

"Whatever we saw fall from the sky must have crashed over there," Daniel says, his face lit by the glowstick in his hand, eyes turned toward the east. "Must have been huge."

A hiss rises from behind me, and for a moment I think that Gwen is shushing Daniel. But then the sound rushes past me, dousing me with a curtain of cold water. It lashes against my face, stealing the warmth from the air. The green light from the glowstick Daniel's holding makes the dime-sized rain drops look like Mountain Dew. Soda was outlawed for kids under eighteen, five years ago, but I'm old enough to remember it.

I hear a voice shouting at me, but I can't make out the words. I turn to find a waterlogged Gwen staring at me, the limp form of Mandi still in her arms.

"What?" I can barely hear my own voice over the watery, windblown bedlam.

"We need shelter!" Gwen shouts.

I look inland, but the ring of green light that lets us see each other fades after ten feet. This patch of land we've crashed on could end twenty feet away, for all we know. The subtle scent of vegetation slowly being drowned out by the smell of ozone says otherwise, but until I actually see it...

I look for the second glowstick and find it submerged under two feet of water, illuminating the rear hatch of the crashed transport. Partially buoyant, it wobbles with each crashing wave.

Lightning cracks through the sky overhead, the volume of its sudden arrival making us all duck. It also gives me a brief view of our surroundings. Thirty feet ahead, at the end of a gently sloping white-sand beach, is a wall of tropical vegetation that looks impenetrable. The brilliant light disappears as quickly as it arrived, but a luminous green afterimage remains in my vision, the colors reversed like an old film negative. The island isn't small, and it rises up at the center. *Of course it does,* I think. We're in the Pacific, where pretty much all islands were formed by volcanic activity.

"Let's head inland," I shout.

Gwen nods and replies, "My go-pack should have a tent in it. If we can find a spot where the wind—"

Her voice is cut short by Daniel, who is yanking hard on my arm. "Effie!"

"What?" I shout, feeling overwhelmed and angry.

When I see the mortified look on his face, I feel bad for snapping at him. But he's not looking at me, he's looking back at the ocean. "The glowstick!"

I turn toward the crashed transport, expecting to see the cylinder of green light tossed by angry waves, but it's gone. I scan left and right, finding the chemical light as a green pinpoint, quickly sliding away. *Did a fish take it?*

"It's headed east!" Daniel shouts.

"Toward the crash!" the higher pitched Gizmo chimes in. The small boy is now clinging to Daniel's arm. Apparently, both of them have already figured out why the glowstick is making a beeline for the horizon.

And then I do, too.

A violent spear of light stabs the sky, illuminating the scene, confirming our fears.

The ocean is gone. Well, not gone, but surging away from the island, rushing east like a drain has opened up in the Earth. But that's not what's happening. Even non-genius kids have seen enough disaster movies to know what this means.

Tsunami.

"Run!" I shout. "Inland!" I scoop up little Gizmo and throw him over my shoulder.

Despite being a little pudgy, in the way all computer-focused kids are, Daniel moves like a sprinter leaping off the line. He takes the lead, kicking up divots of sand, the green glowstick clutched in his hand giving the rest of us a direction to follow.

Gwen follows in his tracks, Mandi now over her shoulder. The run is going to be rough for the unconscious girl, but the alternative is to die horribly in a wall of water.

It's rough for Gizmo, too, but he's able to hold himself up, hands clinging to my go-pack, arms supporting his torso like flying buttresses. Lightning flashes. For me, it lights up the jungle, now ten feet ahead. And it reveals Gwen charging through a hole in the foliage. For Gizmo, it must reveal something horrible. I feel the boy's slender muscles snap tight, and he's suddenly harder to hold.

I think he's screaming, too, but as I punch through the large leafy plants lining the beach, the hiss of rain on the leaves drowns out everything. The darkness beneath the windblown canopy becomes absolute.

I charge ahead, despite my blindness, one arm around Gizmo's legs, one outstretched to keep me from running into a tree. A blinking green light guides me forward, my own personal Tinker Bell. But it's growing more distant, flickering as Daniel passes behind trees. Within ten seconds of entering the jungle, I'm lost. I could be running back toward the ocean and I wouldn't even know it.

Gizmo's small fist beating my shoulder like a jockey's whip prods me onward. And that's when I feel it. The slope beneath my feet. Uphill is good. Using the energy it takes to make each upward step my guide, I follow the grade, hoping it doesn't end at a cliff.

I didn't think it was possible, but the volume of the jungle-lashing rain grows louder, drowning out my thoughts. My mind is a blank slate, instinct guiding my feet.

And then Gizmo's voice breaks through. He's wrapped himself around my back and is shouting directly in my ear. "It's here!"

An elastic band of clarity snaps in my mind. The rush of water I'm hearing isn't from above, it's from behind. The ocean has returned like President Washington crossing the Delaware, turning retreat into world-changing victory. I would never admit it, but I know my history. I devour history books with the voracious appetite other kids save for pizza. Not that General Washington's victory over the British provides any useful information at the moment. That comes from above.

A point of green light waves back and forth, but it's so high up, I think Daniel must have scaled a cliff. The truth is revealed underfoot, as a tangle of roots trips me up. I stumble forward, careening into the broad trunk of a moss-covered tree.

The hint of a shouting voice pricks my ears. A slice of lightning makes it through the canopy, revealing Gwen on a branch above us, reaching down. She's shouting, but I can't hear the words. High above her, I see Daniel straddling a branch, hugging Mandi to the tree's core.

As the roar of oncoming death grows louder, I hoist Gizmo up. Gwen takes his small wrist in one hand and lifts him onto the branch. His spindly frame makes short work of the branch network above her.

Gwen's hand returns, and in another flash of light, I read her lips. "Jump!"

My legs bend and spring, but I don't move upward. I move sideways, knocked off my feet by an onrush of three-foot-deep water. I cling to the tangle of roots on the ground, but the rising torrent is too powerful. As my fingernails bend back, something solid strikes my leg, knocking me free and sweeping me away.

I tumble through darkness, the gurgling rush of ocean filling my mouth before being coughed out.

My feet strike something solid, and I shove. When the world grows loud again, I know I've broken the surface. I gasp in a deep breath before my gut wraps around the trunk of a palm. I cling to the rough surface, shivering from fear and cold, and then I climb higher.

But the water rises along with me, and the rubbery tree is bending from the force. With a shudder, the tree's shallow root system gives way. As I drop back into the water, I cling to the trunk. The buoyant spear keeps me above the fray, but its broad, leafy top catches the water like a sail. I'm catapulted through the jungle.

For what feels like several minutes, the tree slams its way uphill, a water-propelled battering ram, intent on striking down everything in its path. A jarring impact nearly dislodges me, but I hold fast at the expense of the sinews in my arms, which I can feel stretching and popping. Water rushes past and surges over me. It' s trying to peel me away from the tree, which wedges against something strong enough to stand against the battering ram.

And then the current shifts. The flow of water cuts into my face, tries to work its way into my lungs. Still, I fight it. If I can survive falling out of the sky, I'm not going to die just after reaching the ground. The palm tree, clinging to whatever stopped it, slowly lowers back to the jungle floor. The rush of water dwindles to salty streams trickling downhill.

My fingers uncoil. My arms fall slack. I can't do anything to stop gravity's pull. I flop onto my back, landing on a bed of tangled vegetation. It's oddly comfortable.

Lightning flashes again. The canopy above my head is less dense. The trees that blocked the sky now lie beside me, or further uphill, or maybe they've been swept back out to sea. Rain lashes against my face. The storm rages in the sky above, radiant with blossoms of electric blue and fiery orange light. Despite the raging world, I close my eyes, place my hand over the waterproof pouch inside my chest pocket, and dream of a world where I'm not perpetually alone.

A seagull alarm clock pulls me from the oblivion of sleep, and for a moment, I understand the appeal of atheism. Could there be any better rest than non-existence? Then I remember my dream. Hooked fingers dragging lines in the sand, as a horde of faceless zombies pulls me away from the nameless parents I never knew.

The photo I have of them came into my possession through subterfuge and a box of matches. The woman at the child welfare office made no effort to hide the folder labeled with my name. She knew who I was. Could read the names of my real parents. Could have given me their address.

But she didn't.

Instead, she said, "Well, you have his eyes. But you're not eighteen."

I nearly reached through the window and slapped the woman.

She must have seen the look of abject horror in my eyes, because she added, "The record is sealed until then. Nothing I can do about that."

"You don't understand," I pleaded. "I don't have an adopted family. No foster-parents want me."

And then she set my fiery plan in action while simultaneously adding herself to my mental list of arch-nemeses. "Well, hon, it would appear that your parents didn't, either."

Restraint has never been my thing, but I managed it that day. When I want something—really want something—there isn't much that can stand in my way. Even my own foibles. I stared at her for a quiet moment and gave her the squinty-eyed glare of doom. Before she could add some sass sauce to the bitter disappointment she'd served up, I walked away.

Then I lit a match.

I turned the small flare of light and smoke around on the book of matches, which lit up with a hiss. I dropped the conflagration into an empty trash can. There was no danger of a real fire, but a book of matches puts off enough smoke to trigger a fire alarm. And in a public building like that one, when one alarm goes off, they all go off.

The child welfare woman bounded to her feet and stuck her head out the locked door to the lobby. One breath and she lost all of the cold veneer that could turn down a fifteen-year-old looking for her parents.

"I smell smoke!" She shouted it back into the office and bolted, never seeing me behind the waiting room's silk Ficus tree. As my newest nemesis's heels clacked out a steady fading beat, I made for the slowly closing door and slipped inside the office. The main room was empty, but there were two smaller offices at the back. I couldn't see inside them. The allure of the manila folder sitting atop the desk overrode my sense of caution. I didn't even need to take it. With my memory, all I really had to do was read the information and scoot.

But when I flung the folder open and saw the two faces staring back at me, each with recognizable parts of me, I froze. The image of my parents blurred, as tears filled my eyes. I tried looking at the documents below the photo, but the wet lenses of my eyes hid the information.

"Hey!" a man shouted. "You can't be back here!" And then, like safety was an afterthought, "There's a fire!"

I pinched the corner of the folder and ran, intending on taking everything. They would know it was me. Might even try to find me. Arrest me. It didn't matter. If I could find my parents...

Everything would be different.

But all I managed to do was spread the details of my real life across the floor. There was no time to stop for them. The only reason I escaped was because the man with the chubby beet-red face was already winded from running across half the office. He couldn't chase me beyond the door, but he would have caught me if I stopped. I exited through the side emergency door and walked away, staring at the photo of the man and woman on the beach, oblivious to the sound of approaching emergency vehicles.

When my eyes cleared, I turned the photo over and found three words written in blue ballpoint pen that had dented the image. The penmanship was rigid. Masculine. It said, *Mom, Dad and Euphemia.*

Mom.

Dad.

At some point in the past, when this photo was taken, and later, when it was developed and admired, my parents took ownership of me. 'Mom' and 'Dad' are personal. Had the child welfare Nazi written this, or anyone else who wasn't my real father, it would have said 'Mother and Father,' or even more likely, there wouldn't be any writing on it at all.

So why had they given me up?

No clue.

And as I open my eyes to a blue sky full of impossibly bright cumulus clouds, in the middle of the Pacific Ocean, I'm beginning to think I might never find out.

I sit up with a groan, every part of me aching. My abdomen shakes as the battered muscles strain against the added weight of my go-pack, which according to the ache in my spine, I slept on all night. A flash of pain snaps to life between my eyes, spinning my vision. A high-pitched ringing fills my ears. I breathe through it, focusing on the seagull's calls.

I once read a novel featuring genetically altered man-eating seagulls with piranha mouths. As the bird overhead makes lazy circles, gives me a casual glance and then rides a breeze toward the ocean, I'm grateful I haven't washed up on that horrible place. Jungle debris surrounds me like a nest, piled high enough that I need to stand to see beyond it. The pain in my head returns as I stand, my vision cutting to the right over and over. The ringing in my ears becomes a rumble. After a minute of waiting, I can see the world again, but the rumble has become a strange warbling sound.

I'm a few hundred feet from the shore, which I can see, because I'm also at least fifty feet above sea level. But even if I weren't, enough trees have been mowed down, along with all the undergrowth, that I'm pretty sure I'd have a clear view of the water, even if the land was level. The ocean beyond the island is a swirl of dark and light blue water; it's light where the bottom is sand, dark where the bottom is earth scoured off the island. I can see some of it streaked over the beach as well.

Halfway between me and the ocean is a tall tree with a tangle of branches. It's taller than the surrounding pines, but it has been stripped bare of at least half its leaves. I didn't get a clear view of the tree the others escaped into during the storm, but since this one is the only one that fits the bill, I decide to check it out. The trouble is, I can see most of the branches, and I don't see any people.

Could the water have reached that high?

Maybe the wind blew them out during the night?

Maybe it's the wrong tree?

Burning with unanswerable questions, I take one step and groan. Everything feels swollen and tight. I steady myself with a hand on the palm tree that plowed a path to safety for me, and I try to touch my toes. My extended fingers only make it to my knees. The blood rushing toward my head kicks off a fresh wave of pain, and I stand back up, steadying myself until it fades.

I'll loosen up if I move, I decide, but I know that's not really true. If anything, I'll make my injuries worse. But for the first time in my life, I'd rather not be alone. There's something about nearly being killed multiple times that gives you an appreciation for the living, whether you know them or not.

The jungle floor is even harder to walk on than it was the night before. Each step is uneven. The network of branches, brush and dead fish underfoot is as impossible to walk on as it sounds. My ankles would turn and twist with each step, if not for the thick Unity boots. I fall constantly, the impacts reminding me that I'm alive, but that death is one bad step away.

The sun, while it warms my skin, makes things even worse. It's rising in the corner of my eye, making me squint on one side. I fall to my right more than I do to the left, as a result. It takes me fifteen minutes to make it halfway to the tree, which now looms high above me. Whatever species it is, it doesn't look native. I glance around the half-cleared hillside and see other odd species, their twisting branches and fluttering leaves providing an interesting contrast to the broad palms bending in the morning's breeze.

Still sopping wet, I pause to catch my breath. I attempt to assess my wounds, but the pain is so overarching that I'm not sure where to look. I'm not even sure I want to. What if I lift my shirt to find a broad purple patch that reveals internal bleeding? And if I survive that, what if it clots and shoots into my brain? I could have a stroke, and there would be no one around to help.

Get a grip.

This isn't you.

I have felt despair before. It's crippling. And it's not my friend.

Compartmentalize the fear, I tell myself. *The pain, too. Make those Unity psychologists proud. And if you see them again, commence face-punching retribution.* Not just for my pain. Or for the fact that I nearly lost my life. But for the five kids I know for certain did. I don't know their names, but I will never forget their upside-down, lifeless faces. It's an offense someone needs to answer for.

Thinking of the dead reminds me of Sig.

I search the beach for signs of a second transport crash, but even our transport has been swept away by the retreating tsunami. The island behind me looks the same as it did the night before, except permanently lit by the sun. *Where are you, Sig?* I wonder, and I say a prayer, hoping that someone beyond oblivion is listening. I throw in Hutch for good measure, but hold out little hope for the passengers in Transport 38. It would have fallen short of the island. Even if the foam safety system saved fifty percent of them, they would have been bobbing in the ocean to be scooped up and thrashed by the tsunami.

A nearby squawking makes me think that the gathering seagulls have finally realized that the island is now covered in dead fish, but then I understand the sound. And I recognize the voice. Gizmo. Sounds like he's losing his mind. Or in danger. It's hard to tell with the warbling rumble and the ringing still plaguing my hearing. But there are definitely voices within the chaos.

With renewed effort, I scrabble through the debris, heading for the big tree. Piles of palm trunks and brush block my view and muffle the sound from the far side, but it's clear he's upset.

Gwen's voice comes next. Angry. Defiant. And then pleading.

What I hear next locks my legs in place. I had nearly shouted to them, but now I hold my breath. There's a new voice. A man. And while I don't recognize the voice, I know the tone.

Threatening.

Sinister.

I search for a weapon, but all I find are leaves and branches either too big to wield or too fresh to break. Gwen seemed to think our go-packs were full of survival gear. Maybe there's a knife in mine? I put the pack on the ground and gently undo the magnetic strip holding it shut. The perfect, tight seal has kept the contents dry, but I'm confused by what I find. Gray, chemical-scented foam. The kind electronics are packaged in.

I pull up, and the top layer comes off, revealing a single item. It's a Unity Point symbol, black around the base and edges, red on top. I pull it out of the foam, feeling its weight, the hardness of its tip. I think I can use it as a weapon. It's thin, but it feels solid enough to stab with, if need be. Then I notice it's the same size as the badge on my chest. I place the symbol against its twin on my chest, and it snaps tight. *The badge is magnetic,* I think, and I leave it so I can inspect the rest of my go-pack's contents.

The next layer contains a twisted coil of rope. I lift it out and loop it over my head and shoulder.

As the voices beyond the wall of vegetation get louder, I toss the foam layer aside and remove the next one. Inside is a pack of matches and a knife. Seven inch blade. It's sheathed on a belt, which I remove and strap on. On the right side of the belt, opposite the sheathed blade, is an empty holster.

I glance at it for a moment, wondering why they would give me a holster.

When I remove the last layer of foam, I understand why.

There's a gun inside the go-pack.

Gripping my head against a sudden stabbing pain, I stare down at the weapon. It's black and ominous. A knife can take a life, but it's also a tool, used more for practical, everyday living. But a gun? There is no other use for it than taking a life, deserving or not.

Why did they give me a gun? Outside of video games, I've never fired one. Never handled one. I have been on the receiving end of one, though. So I understand the fear that small black barrel can generate. I also remember how powerful the person holding it can appear.

I don't want to shoot anyone. But maybe I don't have to.

I lift the weapon out of the foam and find the reason why my go-pack weighed so much more than the others; guns are heavy. There are two magazines in the foam. I pluck out one and pocket it. I fumble with the second, but figure out how to slide it into the gun's handle.

The voices on the far side of the debris wall reach a crescendo, everyone speaking at once, the comingling sounds more like a howling wind. Something horrible is about to happen.

I holster the gun and scramble over the piled trees, reaching the top in five strides. The sun stabs my eyes, setting off a flare of pain. The voices explode, reacting to my arrival. With a hand raised to block the sun, I look down to find Daniel, Gizmo and Mandi cowering behind Gwen. She's wielding a branch like a long sword, holding off a man I can't clearly see.

"Hey!" I shout at the man.

His fuzzy image resolves a little. He's wearing a red, plaid, flannel shirt and blue jeans. There's a shotgun in his hands, now leveled at me. His face is still a blur.

"They letting just anyone become Points now?" he says.

"Leave," I tell him. "Now." I've got my right hip turned away from the man. He can see the sheathed knife, but not the gun. This knowledge bolsters my resolve, though I'm still not sure I can kill a man.

He chuckles like a man who gets his kicks from torturing animals.

I know him.

The memory is old. But clear. It's the man with the gun. A foster-father's brother. My 'uncle' for a year.

His face resolves, hairy from not caring and red from alcohol.

"Howard?"

He grins. "Never were the sharpest tool in the drawer."

"How did you... What..."

My head throbs with pain. Waves of sound crash through me. Howard's rough smoker's voice grates on me.

He breaks into song, adding a fake Southern twang to his voice. "Somebody's darling, so young and so brave. Wearing still on his sweet yet pale face. Soon to be hid in the dust of the grave. The lingering light of his boyhood's grace."

He cracks a chipped-tooth grin at me and raises the shotgun at Daniel.

"Stop!" I shout, and I draw the handgun, pointing it at his head, trying to keep it steady. I'm trying to keep my eyes open against the pain in my skull.

"Somebody's darling, somebody's pride. Who'll tell his mother where her boy died?" Howard does a little jig and looks over the barrel of his shotgun. In a moment, he'll say, 'Pow!' like he used to do to me, or he'll really pull the trigger—like he did to his girlfriend. I have no memory of those events, but I heard about it and a mysterious lone witness, on the news before I was sent to another home, where TV was forbidden and psychologist visits were frequent.

I pull my trigger before Uncle Howard can.

The loud crack cuts through the roar in my ears and hits the spot between my eyes like a bullet. I drop to my knees atop the awkward pile of debris.

Then I hear screaming, and I know the danger isn't over. I shove myself up and aim toward Howard again.

Only Howard isn't there.

Did he run away?

I search the area, but see nothing.

"Effie," Gwen says, but I ignore her.

Howard is nowhere to be seen. How did he get away? I can see for at least a mile, and the ground is so torn up that running anywhere fast should be impossible.

He's behind the tree, I think.

"Effie!" Gwen shouts, annoyed.

"What?" I yell back, looking down at her.

Looking down at nothing.

Gwen is gone.

Daniel, Gizmo and Mandi, too.

How...

"Effie," Gwen says again, her voice like a ghost's, coming from nowhere. "Ease down."

"Where are you?" I ask, looking up at the tree, thinking they must have returned to their high hiding spot.

"You're hallucinating," she says, calm now.

The pain in my head spikes. I hear screaming voices. I raise the weapon toward them. Howard's laugh mocks me.

"*Effie.*" It's Gwen again. "What you're seeing and hearing isn't real. But the gun in your hand is. And I would prefer you not shoot me."

"I wouldn't shoot you," I say.

"You might, if I looked like Howard."

"He's not really here?"

With a serene calmness that sounds practiced, Gwen says, "It's just you and me."

"The others—"

"Are safe," she says, "though to be honest, they're feeling a little afraid right now. Of you."

The gun grows impossibly heavy in my hands. My arms go slack, my fingers just barely holding on to the weapon's handle.

"I'm going to take it from your hand now," she says. I feel her fingers, rough and gritty, slide over mine. Then the weight of the weapon leaves my hands. To my surprise, I feel its weight move to my hip. She holstered the gun.

"You didn't take it," I say.

"It's your burden to bear." I feel Gwen's hands on my shoulders, reassuring and redirecting my body, turning me around. "It's your job. I can add my strength to yours, but the actions you take—right or wrong—can be determined only by you."

Gwen's face comes into view as I'm turned around. Her blonde hair is caked with mud. Her face is covered in flecks of blood. She holds up her hand, showing me her brand. "I can only offer support."

In that moment, the roles of Base, Support and Point become a littler clearer. Since things went bad, I have been the one directing our action, naturally leading, while Gwen has been helping me. Supporting me. And Daniel, a Base, has been using his intellect to help guide my actions. Part of me loathes the idea that Unity was able to accurately separate us into these natural roles, but I also see how it worked. And it's not that Gwen and Daniel are incapable of taking action, but they follow my lead. Unless I'm shooting at imaginary people.

Gwen's face goes in and out of focus. Her strong hands keep me steady and upright. "Point... Is that like in the military? Being on point? Leading the way?"

"That's one way to look at it," she says, trying to guide me back down the debris pile. "Careful. Big step on your right."

She buffers me as I nearly topple over and then straightens me back up. "But I think the intended analogy was that of a spear. The point."

The red color at the top of the triangle takes on a different meaning.

"I'm...a weapon?"

"Not quite," she says to my relief. But then she adds, "Not yet."

Before I can reply, my vision narrows. I feel gravity's pull, and a fresh wave of pain pummels me from the inside. Oblivion returns, and I plunge headlong into its merciful grasp.

7

My life hasn't contained a lot of what I would call 'traditional beauty.' No manicured gardens. No stylish décor. No pristine landscapes. I've never been in a forest. Never climbed a mountain. Never been to an art museum. I've seen the inside of a lot of haggard homes and a few mediocre ones. In fact, the nicest place I've probably ever been was Brook Meadow. The building was new and they seemed to have state funding up the wazoo. Everything was clean. The lines were smooth. The architecture interesting. But I never really appreciated it.

By the time I reached Brook Meadow, I saw the world through resentment-skewed lenses. The flashy building and the new tech made available to every student simply reminded me that life, as I knew it, was malignant. On the surface, I was prodded to join

Unity, but on the inside, I wanted to join. Time and distance would be the scalpel that finally separated me from my life.

And now, three weeks later, despite the tumorous sixteen-year-old growth still fresh in my mind, I find myself appreciating beauty.

Blue water stretches to the horizon, where lines of white clouds slip through the sky. Gentle waves roll against the reshaped beach, commingling with lines of soil pulled out by the retreating waves. The contrast of white, blue, tan and brown is captivating. Even the salty scent of the water contains a kind of beauty. The concept of a beautiful smell had never once occurred to me before. It draws a laugh from me.

And then a frown.

I'm drugged, I realize, trying to sit up and failing. The pain that wracked my body has faded, but it's been replaced by numbness.

I'm not feeling *anything.*

My head lolls to the side as I take a look around. To my right is all beach, bending away. It's littered with bits of jungle. So is the water. I'm supported by a lounge chair of go-packs. Above me is a fluttering stretch of plastic, held up by two branches. It's blocking the sun.

I turn left and flinch backward when I come face-to-face with Daniel.

"I think you gave her too much," he says.

Gwen sits up behind him, looking me over. "She needed to rest."

Gizmo approaches; each step through the sand is labored. He drops to his knees beside me and holds up a water bottle. "Your body and mind can't recover if you're not hydrated."

I understand now that this is a Base's way of saying, 'You'll feel better if you have a drink.'

I take the offered bottle, unscrew the cap and chug the contents in four gulps, squeezing the water out the way Howard used to do beer from cans. When I'm done, I find three shocked faces staring back at me.

My voice sounds like a frog's croak. "What?"

"There were four bottles of water in the go-packs we recovered," Daniel says. "Now there are three."

"We need to ration what we have," Gwen says.

"Or," I say, "We find more." I try to push myself up again, but only make it a few inches. "What did you give me?"

"Morphine," Gwen says. "Immune boosters. Electrolytes. The works. The painkillers will wear off in an hour. I wouldn't move until then or you risk injuring yourself further. You're okay, by the way. No broken bones. No internal injuries. There are five stitches in your forehead."

I touch my head and feel the prickly ends of the wire sticking out of my skin. "Thanks."

"Wasn't me," Gwen says.

I'm surprised to see Gizmo smiling, his teeth brilliant white. "I like to fix things."

"But...your nickname. I assumed electronics were your thing."

"People and machines aren't that different," he says. "Moving parts. Electrical impulses. Wires. Cables."

Daniel moves away, looking paler. "Ugh. If you can handle the blood. Computers don't bleed."

"You play violent video games," Gizmo says to Daniel, a smile on his face. Of all of us, he seems to be the most resilient, like this is...fun.

Isn't it fun? I ask myself, horrified by the idea.

Aren't you enjoying this?

Don't you feel alive?

It's the morphine, I decide, and I push the offensive questions from my mind. People died last night. Kids. *I* almost died last night.

But you didn't.

You survived.

You found friends.

"The blood in video games doesn't smell like dirty pennies," Daniel says. "If it did, I wouldn't play them."

Looking past Daniel and Gwen, I see a pair of small booted feet. "Is that Mandi?"

The joking boys lose their smiles. Gwen looks over her left shoulder, and then back to me. She gives a straight-faced nod.

"Is she..."

"In a coma," Gwen says. "I think. She's breathing, but that's about it. Without a way to get fluids or nutrients in her, she's not going to last more than a couple of days."

"We won't be here a couple of days," I say.

The three stony faces staring back at me sour my stomach.

"They'll know we crashed."

"We can't assume that," Gwen says. "We need to prepare for the worst."

I don't want to ask, but I do. "Which is?"

"The size of the wave that struck the island last night, the time it took to arrive after the impact and the fact that we could see the impact's glow over the horizon, all suggest that it originated perhaps six miles away. This island is volcanic. We're basically sitting on top of a mountain. So when the wave approached, it didn't rise up the slope of a continental plate, it crashed against a wall of stone. But when that wave reached a true coastline, it would have grown. Maybe a hundred feet tall and moving five hundred miles per hour." Daniel sags under the weight of his own knowledge. "The point is, the Unity carrier was off the coast of San Diego, where the wave has certainly already struck. Even if they were alerted when our transports lost power, which is possible, and even if they discovered that we'd survived the crash—

unlikely—there might not be anyone left alive who even knows where we are."

Gwen brushes sand from her hands. She's not looking at me, but she's definitely speaking to me. "Unity taught us to react to every situation like it was a worst case scenario, because it's the best way of preventing them. But in this case, we can't prevent what has already occurred. We can only react. But we need to do it smart. And that means we need *you* to think before you act."

"I was only there three weeks," I say.

"I'm not reminding you of something you already learned," Gwen says. "I'm *teaching* you something you haven't."

My impulse is to argue. To defend my intellect against a girl who is younger than I am. But I long ago accepted that Sig knows more than me. Why not Gwen? I've been subjected to more than a few IQ tests over the years, and the 'superior intelligence' results have been waggled in my face in response to low grades. But now my 137 IQ is probably the lowest on this island.

"Okay then, teach me," I say. "Tell me what to do."

Gwen rolls her eyes and groans. "Teaching you and telling you what to do are different things. If I could confidently decide on a course of action, and take it, I'd be a Point. But I'm not, I'm a *Support*. Did you even finish testing?"

"I don't know."

"Did you receive any hand-to-hand combat training?" Gizmo asks. The words 'hand-to-hand combat' sound funny coming from him, but the implications aren't funny at all.

"No."

"Flight simulator?" Gwen asks.

"What? Are you serious?"

"What about psy-controls?" Daniel looks from me to Gwen. "That comes before flight sims, right?"

"I don't even know what psy-controls are," I say, feeling suddenly inadequate.

Gwen squints at me. "Three weeks, you said... Why would they group you with us?"

"If they had no other choice," Daniel guesses and raises his hands to me, placating. "No offense."

I give my head a slow shake. "I'm as confused as you."

Silence returns to the beach. I close my eyes. My mind feels dulled by the morphine. *Maybe this will all make more sense when it wears off?* I doubt it. So I let my thoughts drift. I hear the waves, gentle and soothing. The stiff shaking of plastic in the ocean breeze. And nothing else. No hum of civilization. No signs of life beyond this beach.

Sig.

My eyes snap open. "How long was I out?"

"Six hours," Gwen says.

"What time is it? How long until nightfall?"

Gwen turns her head toward me, eyebrows furrowed. She's confused by the sudden determin-ation in my voice. "Four in the afternoon."

Daniel has a slight grin on his face. "This time of year, sunset will come in roughly five hours."

I push myself up and am consumed by dizziness. I hold still, wait for it to pass and then move again. Getting to my feet feels like it takes the same effort as clinging to that water-propelled palm trunk last night, but I manage it with just a single stumble. Once I'm up, I stretch, take a deep breath and say, "Pick up your gear and Mandi."

"What?" Gwen says. "Why?"

"We don't know what caused that wave," I say. "We don't know if it will happen again. If we're treating this like a worst case scenario, the beach isn't a safe place to be. We need to find shelter in the next five hours." I point up past the ruined hillside, where the trees were untouched by the wave. "Up there. Tomorrow, we'll find food and water." *And Sig.*

"There isn't time to sit around waiting for me to feel good." I pick up one of the go-packs that I had been leaning against, put it around my shoulders and strike out inland, focusing all 137 points of my IQ on not face-planting in front of everyone.

As the others gather their gear, and Mandi, I hear Daniel whisper, "See, that's why she's here," and I'm glad at least one of us has faith in me.

"Why did you dip your hair in orange?" It's about the tenth question from Gizmo since we struck out from the beach, but it's the first I bother to answer.

"I like orange." Probably not the insightful answer he was hoping for.

"I like green," he says. "But I wouldn't put it in my hair."

I step over a fallen palm that's leaning on a large rock, blocking our path like a security gate. I pause to help Gizmo climb over, lifting his light frame under the armpits. He smiles as I put him down, like we're out for a casual nature hike. Daniel handles the obstacle on his own, leaping it with his hands on the trunk, whispering a 'Wha-cha' sound effect in time with the jump. While I haven't felt like a kid in a very long time, it's clear that Daniel and Gizmo are not only young in age, but also at heart. Gwen accepts my hand and moves carefully over the tree. While my balance, and full-body pain, have returned with the morphine's fading effects, Mandi's limp form has Gwen in a permanent state of instability. And she refuses to let me take the girl. They were either good friends, or Gwen is over-committed to the Support dogma.

Daniel, in the lead now, says, "People modify their bodies for a variety of reasons. The first was likely spiritual. Circumcision, for instance."

Gizmo pauses to shake his body and say, "Ugh."

"Gross," Gwen says. It's one of the few things she's said since we left the beach.

"It's not like people don't still do it," Daniel says. "And there are other reasons. Social. Aesthetic." He lifts his right hand, showing his Base brand. "Identification. The most recent and soon-to-be prevalent body modification is technological upgrading. And I'm not talking just the 3D-printed replacement organs. Full-on cyborgs. Enhanced physical capabilities."

"Like ExoFrames inside the body," Gizmo says.

Daniel thrusts a finger in the air, head down, watching his step. "Exactly."

"Sign me up," Gizmo says. "I don't want to be weak forev—"

"You're a Base," Gwen says. "Strength is not a requirement."

"Maybe I don't want to be a Base," Gizmo says, waiting for me to lift him over another fallen trunk. This one is low to the ground, and I think he could easily make it over, but he pauses, lifts his arms slightly and waits for me to hoist him over.

Are we bonding? Is this what bonding feels like? Is he doing it on purpose or is this a natural thing? Survival bonding?

"Body piercing," Daniel says, unfurling a finger with each word. "Tattoos. Scarification. Subdermal implants. Tongue splitting."

"Okay," Gwen says. "Enough. Seriously."

"That's not even the grossest stuff," Daniel says. His voice has become higher, almost bird like. He's getting a kick out of this. I think he meant to razz me, but he's satisfied with grossing out Gwen. To his credit, he doesn't push the subject any further into the obscene. "The point is, people change their bodies for a variety of reasons, but not simply because they like a color. It's an outward expression of the psyche, or psychosis, depending on the person. Which brings us back to Gizmo's question, why color your hair orange?"

I sigh. In addition to being smart, another Base trait seems to be persistence. "This is the most I've had to talk in years."

"You're doing great," Daniel says with fake exuberance and a smile, turning around and giving his fist a chipper thrust. The move nearly spills him on his butt and gets a laugh from everyone, including me.

"Fine," I say. "My foster-mother hates it."

"Is she nice?" Gizmo asks.

"This one is. Most of them weren't."

"Oh." His forehead furrows, but he continues onward and upward. "Why not?"

"I was a way for them to get money." I take a few steps and realize there's more to it than that. "And I wasn't an easy kid."

"None of us are," Gwen says and then clarifies, "Unity recruits. Daniel, Sig, even me. We're different. Most people don't understand the way we think."

"But we do," Daniel says. "It's why you and Sig became friends. It's why you like us."

The argument against this statement comes and goes like a breeze. I *do* like them. Having friends feels alien, and while I can admit it to myself, I don't really want to talk about it, or rehash the ping-pong match between foster homes that was my childhood.

So I deflect like a pro. "The orange streak is a warning."

Daniel looks at me with wide eyes and a half grin. He likes the sound of that.

"It says I'm different. I'm unpredictable. It says I'd rather not knock your lights out, but I will if you mess with me."

"Like a poison dart frog," Daniel says. "Other frogs hide. Try to blend in. But the poison dart frogs are brightly colored. They're easy to spot, but no one messes with them because the color says, 'Eat me and die.' So it's the frogs who try to hide that get eaten."

I smile. Always an example with this one. "Doesn't always work out that way, but yeah. That's the idea."

Gizmo stops at a log I know for sure he can make it over and lifts his arms. "Cool."

I lift him up, but stop short of putting him back down. The jungle ahead has caught my attention. We're nearly at the crest of one of many hills, all rising toward the barren volcanic cone several miles inland. Fifteen feet ahead is a line of destruction, where the flood waters deposited their passengers and slid away. Beyond the piles of debris is the untouched jungle.

I put Gizmo down, looking at the trees.

Gwen stops beside me, sweaty and out of breath. "What is it?"

"Look at the trees," I say. "The water line ends here, but the trees ahead are thin. You can see the sky through them."

Daniel hops on top of a large rock, scanning the treeline. "You're right, but maybe the jungle is thinning because of the elevation?"

"We're not *that* high," Gwen says.

"I still don't see the problem," Daniel says.

"It means there's a clearing," I say. "And in a jungle like this, that doesn't happen naturally."

"Oh," Daniel says, and then his face brightens up. "Oh!" He leaps down from the rock and charges up the hillside, scrambling over the last few feet of torn up terrain. Then he's in the trees, bolting into the shadows.

"Daniel! Wait for us." Gwen shouts after him, but then Gizmo breaks for the trees, too.

"I'll get him!" the small boy says.

Gwen isn't as worried as she is annoyed. "Can you stay with them?"

"You sure?" I ask, thinking more about how much it's going to hurt to chase after them than I am about not leaving Gwen behind.

"I'll catch up," she says.

The pain in my legs flares hotter as I double-time my walk. But my pace isn't nearly fast enough to catch the spritely boys. So I shift into a jog, and the invisible cleavers slicing through my muscles nearly make me cry out. But by the time I leave the awkward footing of the debris field behind and step on the more cushiony earth of the jungle, my legs have already begun to limber up. As my eyes adjust to the jungle's shade, I find relief from the hot sun. Moisture trapped beneath the canopy collects on my face.

"Guys," I say, keeping my voice hushed for some reason.

No reply.

I look ahead to where the sky once again cuts through the green ceiling. The trees have definitely been cleared. The question is why. As I near the jungle's edge, I crouch walk, moving with caution. Again, I'm not sure why. Something about this doesn't feel right. Of course, *nothing* has felt right since I was roused from a sound sleep and tossed on a transport. So this is just one more thing in a growing list of wrongness.

The jungle ends at the crest of a downward slope. I drop to my hands and knees, crawling up to the edge. Still in the shadows, I lie on my belly and take in the scene below.

A bowl of vegetation in the center of a valley has been cleared. Every plant and tree has been mowed down and dragged away, leaving patches of tall, windblown grasses and lumps of embedded stone. At the center of the clearing is a flat rectangle of concrete, bleached by the sun, but still dark enough to see the white lines painted on the surface. The paint divides the concrete into three equal-sized squares. Each segment contains a large Unity triangle with a T in its core. It doesn't take a Base to figure out that this is where the transports were supposed to land. Three transports. Three landing pads.

We nearly made it.

Whispering to my right pulls my attention away from the landing site. I put my hand atop a large fern and slowly lower it. Daniel and Gizmo are lying on the ground, just a few feet away, staring into the clearing and having some kind of argument.

"Hey," I whisper, and both boys go into some kind of spasm, like they've just been on the receiving end of a taser, trembling arms, rolling away and very nearly screaming.

"It's me!" I say, still trying to whisper, but also trying to be heard over their thrashing. I sit up, my outstretched palms urging calm. "Keep it down!"

Both boys end up on their backs, breathing hard, smiling up at me.

"That was awesome," Daniel says. "How'd you sneak up on us?"

"Sneak? Did you not hear me calling you?"

The boys look at each other. Geniuses both, but in the wild, it wouldn't be long before they went the way of the dodo bird. In their world of laboratories and computer labs, there's no reason to be on guard. But out here, and even more so among the darker bits of human civilization, their good natured naiveté could get them in trouble.

"Why are you worried?" Daniel asks.

"We crash landed on an island that none of us knows anything about."

"It would be rare to find large predators on an uninhabited Pacific island," Daniel points out. "If that's what you're worried about?"

"First, you don't know how large this island is. Second, you also don't know if it's uninhabited. There could be roving bands of cannibals, for all you know."

"Roving bands of cannibals?" Gizmo looks amused. "This island seems normal enough to me."

I sweep my arm out to the empty landing site. "Does this look normal to you?"

"Looks like a traditional Unity landing pad to me," Daniel says.

"Then why were you whispering?" I ask.

They have no answer, and honestly, neither do I.

"Let's check it out," Gwen says from behind us, making all three of us flinch and spin around.

This place has me spooked. Given the fact that I've nearly been killed several times, I've hallucinated and I'm lost in the middle of nowhere, a little paranoia is understandable. But something about this place is making me squirrelly. Like I can feel danger and I should be in a tree, twitching my tail.

The others don't seem to feel it, though, and they start down the cleared hill without a second thought. After a moment of scanning the jungle on the far side of the valley and finding nothing to cause alarm, I follow them. I keep my hand on my holstered gun, like I've done this before. Like I know how to fight. I'm pretty sure the only thing I'd be able to shoot is a vision of Howard.

"You guys aren't hallucinations, are you?" I ask.

Daniel just chuckles and continues on with Gizmo.

Gwen pauses and looks back at me. She notes my hand on the gun. "Feeling okay?"

"Just making sure," I say.

I'm about to joke it off. Gwen is starting to feel like a younger-than-me mother. Always concerned for my wellbeing. Always ready to help. She probably would have been a great mother, but she wasn't any of mine. And I don't want her to be now. But before I can speak, an inhuman shriek echoes through the valley.

The gun is heavy, but I still manage to lift it into a two-handed grip, the kind they use in movies. I assume that's something actors are taught from people who know. I can picture the scene. The camera moves around me to the left, shooting in slow motion. I spin to the right, looking over the site, eyes squinted, scanning for danger. Cue the sweeping music. Turn on the fans to blow my hair. And that's how it plays out for about a second. Then my weary arms start to tremble, and long before I'm sure Gizmo's scream was unjustified, my arms drop.

At least no one saw my dramatic-turned-feeble display. Unless we *are* being watched. I look at the jungle perimeter surrounding the valley.

Gizmo and Daniel look down at a stand of tall grass, faces screwed up in fear, but bodies rooted in place. Gun back on my hip, I follow Gwen to the scene, expecting to see a snake. In fact, if it's anything less than a snake, Gizmo's going to need some kind of 'man up' pep talk. But who's going to give him that? Daniel? Maybe. He didn't scream.

The boys step aside, and as I once again think of them as 'boys,' I decide to cut Gizmo some slack and not mention the scream. While my childhood was cut short by about a decade, I understand the importance of playing—and innocence. Judging by the look on Gizmo's face, he's losing his right now.

Tall grass bends as I approach, keeping the secret a moment longer, the reeds shushing in the breeze. Is the thing in the reeds warning us away, or luring us into a trap?

Gwen steps to the side, letting me closer. She can't see past the grass yet, either, but with Mandi over her shoulder, she can't do much about it. I raise a foot next to the grass, and Gizmo takes a step back like whatever is in there might leap out and attach itself to my face. "Am I safe doing this?"

"Yeah," Daniel says, leaning forward for a second look, despite his obvious fear.

I move my boot through the grass, bending it over.

A face stares up at me, bleached white with hollow eyes. A human skull is half-buried in the earth, grass growing from its void sockets, as though it were a plant pot. Gwen fails to contain a gasp, and Daniel flinches, despite knowing what was coming. Gizmo is penguin-stepping away, eyes wandering everywhere but down. But he looks, and nearly screams again, when I bend down, take hold of the grass growing from the skull's eyes, nose and mouth, and pull. The green tendrils come up with balls of dirt held in place by tangles of roots. I toss the vegetation aside, revealing an unobstructed view of the unfortunate deceased.

Earth holds the jaw open in a permanent scream, but it's not the only thing that suggests a horrid ending to this person's life. There's a neat hole in one side of the head, leading to a jagged, baseball-sized opening on the other.

"He was shot," Daniel says.

Gwen shuffles on her feet. "You don't know that."

"Pretty sure he's right." The bullet hole is impossible to miss, and the jaw structure is pretty masculine. I put my hands beneath his chin and drag the soil away. A chunky band of dirty bone is revealed. This isn't just a skull. There's a whole body here. I look up at Daniel. "Help me."

He doesn't say a word, but he starts pulling up grass when I do. We work downward from the skull, clearing a three-foot-long, two-foot-wide rectangle. *Far enough,* I decide, and I shift to dragging dirt away. Daniel stops helping me. Touching something like grass is probably a foreign experience to the boy, never mind dragging dirt away from a rib cage. Not that *I've* ever done it before. The question of why

I'm doing it now rattles through my head, and before I can answer the question for myself, Gwen asks it aloud.

My response is a grunt and a doubling of effort. The soil working its way under my fingernails feels familiar, reminding me of a half dozen backyards, where I spent a good portion of my childhood. But that dirt probably wasn't full of a dead person's lingering bits. When the thought of having someone's DNA trapped under my nails starts to make me shiver, I lean back.

The rib cage is exposed, and like a shaman divining with bones, the white arches rising from the ground tell me a story—but this one reveals the past, not the future.

"Holy crap," Gizmo says, working up the nerve to look again.

Something heavy and sharp cleaved a path downward through the right side of this man's rib cage. The bones are bent downward, a jagged gap separating the two sides. It would have been a mortal blow. Whoever killed him either shot him in the head and then savaged his body, or swept a blade through his chest and then finished the job with a gun. Either way, the man I'm now thinking of as a victim wasn't just killed, he was overkilled.

The gun in my go-pack makes a little more sense now. This island, in the recent past, has been a violent place.

But is it now?

I'd rather not find out.

"Any of you have forensic training?" I ask.

Daniel takes a step back. "Eww."

"I think what killed him is clear enough," Gwen says. A scowl now resides on her face.

"But we don't know who he is," I argue, and then correct myself. "Was."

"He's been out here for a while," Daniel says. "There isn't any clothing left."

It occurs to me that the man might not have been wearing clothes. This could have been an execution. We're also in a jungle that's buzzing with insects. Given the humidity and temperature of the place, the body could have decomposed and been consumed within a few weeks. The only real passage-of-time indication is the grass growing from his orifices. But grass spreads and grows quickly. Best guess, he's been out here between six months and two years. Tops. I keep these thoughts to myself.

"We're losing daylight," Gwen says. Her words have an immediate effect on the boys. Their shoulders lower and they look away from the body. Her words have given them permission to move on. When she meets my eyes with the most serious gaze I've seen from her mostly-serious face thus far, I know that her disinterest is a charade.

"We need to search the area before leaving," I say.

"What?" Gizmo's voice has raised an octave. He wants to get as far away from the dead man as possible. "Why?"

"If this landing pad was built by Unity, there might be a way to contact them nearby. A callbox. Emergency beacon. Supply drop." I'm fishing for reasons, but Gizmo and Daniel look sold already, until I point further inland and say, "You two check that end. Gwen and I will search down here."

"Why are we splitting up?" Daniel asks, trying and failing to mask his fear.

"Faster we search the area, the sooner we can leave," Gwen says.

We're on the same page.

"Just walk the perimeter," I say. "We'll meet on the far side. If you see anything weird—"

"Like another dead dude?" Daniel asks.

"Or a way to call home—" *I'm trying to keep things positive, Daniel.* "—just call us over. We won't be far, and we won't lose sight of each other."

A dejected looking Gizmo tugs on Daniel's arm. "Let's just go, so we can leave."

Daniel squints at me, letting Gizmo pull him. He knows something is up, but he doesn't say anything. "Make it quick," he says, and then turns to follow Gizmo.

When they're out of earshot, Gwen steps atop the concrete pad and heads in the opposite direction. Walking on the smooth, flat landing pad is both harder on the legs, and easier. While my ankles get a reprieve from the constant twisting of uneven ground, each step sends a jarring impact through my bones. What I wouldn't give for an island-sized trampoline.

"He hasn't been dead very long," Gwen says, supporting my conclusion. "Maybe a year."

"Yup," I say. "But it doesn't change much for us."

Gwen's reply isn't emotional, despite the content. "How could a brutally murdered man not change much for us?"

"One body doesn't mean we've been dumped on an island with a tribe of head hunters, cannibals or even a serial killer. For all we know, the person who killed him was acting in self-defense." The grass along the length of the landing pad grows even and lush, so I stop looking at it and focus on the end of the concrete slab, still fifty feet ahead, where the grass is uneven. "Besides, what could we do differently? We still need to find food, shelter and water." *And Sig.* "If there's a reason to be afraid for our lives on this island, we're not going to spot it if we're running around like frightened turkeys."

Gwen lets out a little chuckle, and it catches me off guard. When she sees me looking, she explains. "I grew up on a farm. We had a lot of turkeys. Dumbest animals on the planet, I swear. Get them worked up and they'd practically throw themselves on the chopping block."

I can picture rugged Gwen on a farm. Working the land. Bored out of her skull. She's been lugging Mandi around all day like she's accustomed to carrying sacks of potatoes.

"I've seen what kind of force is needed to cut through bone, Effie." She gives me a sidelong glance, her smile retreating. "Whoever did that back there... We *don't* want to meet him."

"'Him?'"

"Call me a sexist if you want, but I've never met a woman capable of doing that to a man. Not even my mom, and she was a big woman."

I'm not sure if she means physically capable or emotionally capable, but I don't argue the point. While I haven't met any women physically or emotionally capable of such a thing, I *have* met men who are both. Are there brutally savage women in the world? Without a doubt. But I've never met them, which leads me to believe that the male variety are far more pervasive. History and its wars agree. Even now, women generally aren't on the front line or part of any special forces. What kind of women would want to be?

Feet scuff over concrete as Gwen and I slow to a stop in unison. We're just five feet from the far end of the landing pad strip, and the flecks of white hidden among the uneven grass are easy to see.

Now *this*...

This changes things.

SUPPORT

"How many are there?" Gwen hovers at the edge of the landing pad, while I wade through the tall grass, counting.

"Too many," I mumble, still counting. "Way too many."

In some places it's hard to tell one skeleton from the next. These people were either dumped here, or they were killed in a very small area, landing atop each other as they fell. Both scenarios seem possible, as the cause of death is pretty clear.

Bullets.

And a lot of them.

Parts of bones have been chipped away. Holes in skulls. Ribs fractured. Someone held the trigger down on these people and didn't let go until they were pulp. I half expect to find the ground still stained red, but nature's cleanup crew has done an efficient job. There's no way to know if these people died at the same time as the first man we found or not. Could have been weeks or months earlier, or later.

But the savagery of both attacks seems consistent. They could have been killed by the same person, or by a group of people.

The gun on my hip suddenly seems very inadequate. They should have sent me with a bazooka.

"Seven," I say, but I'm not sure. "Give or take one or two."

"Give or take?"

"Some of these skulls are in more than one piece." With every new bone uncovered from the grass, my anxiety grows. But I'm not worried about me; I'm worried about Sig. If she's alive on this hellish island, she might not be for long. I rip through the grass, looking for any signs of what happened here, aside from the obvious.

"Move slower," Gwen says. "They'll know something is wrong."

By 'they', she means Daniel and Gizmo. "We can't let them see," was the first thing she said after we recognized the flecks of white for what they were. While I agree that panicking the boys won't help us at all, my conscience is struggling with not giving them information that could make them more alert, and more likely to spot danger.

I glance back at Daniel and Gizmo, searching the far end of the landing site. Every few steps, one of them flinches and the other follows suit. Their imaginations must be running wild with visions of killers, monsters and the dead. To be honest, mine is, too.

Gwen is right. They don't need to know.

I wish *I* didn't know.

My eyes catch sight of something that isn't brilliant green, dark, earthy brown or sun-bleached white. It's a sliver of gleaming yellow.

"Found something." Crouching in the grass, I brush away the dirt. With each sweep of my fingers, my stomach clenches. By the time the object is clear enough to see, I think I might puke.

"What is it?" Gwen asks.

When I look up to tell her, I see motion in the background. The boys are walking toward us, leaning to the side, trying to see me around Gwen.

Daniel sees me looking. "What did you find?" His shout echoes in the valley, making me cringe.

I shout back. "A little privacy! I'm peeing!"

Daniel frowns and turns around. Gizmo spins away so fast that his legs get tangled and he tumbles over. He recovers quickly, scrambling to his feet, embarrassment muting any pain he might be feeling from the fall.

When I'm positive the boys aren't going to look again, I lift the triangular object from the ground and show Gwen. When she reels back as though electrocuted, she nearly drops Mandi, and I think it's too much for her, too. But then she snaps her fingers at me and extends her open hand. "Let me see it."

She holds the pendant close to her mouth and blows away the remaining grit. Then she polishes it and rubs it on her thigh. When she lifts it up again, the black and orange pendant looks almost new. It's just like the one I found in my go-pack, except that it's a Support symbol.

"Could you have known them?" I ask.

She shakes her head, in a daze. "I think they're older than three months. I don't remember any kids I knew leaving."

While I hear all fifteen words she's just spoken, only one of them sticks with me.

I return to the ground, furiously tearing away grass and brushing dirt. It's sloppy, rushed work, but the image starts to emerge, and it's exactly as I feared. The man we found was clearly a full grown specimen. At least eighteen, anyway. But these small-boned bodies, some no more than four feet tall...

These were kids.

Like us.

While I've found only one badge, I think it's safe to assume that these kids were dropped off on this island, like we were supposed to be, and someone slaughtered them. The question is, who? And why?

The where and how seem pretty obvious. The when is close enough to now to make me nervous.

Really nervous.

"They were Unity," I tell Gwen. "Like us. A bunch of kids."

She looks a little pale. "What do we do?"

"This might change our outlook, but our...mission is the same." I stand up, looking at the boys. They're still at the far end, backs turned to us and no longer searching. Probably waiting for permission to turn in any other direction but back at the peeing girl. "We need food, water and shelter. We just need to find those things more quietly than we might have done before. Keep our eyes open for signs of recent human activity. Find a way to contact home, or get off this island."

"And if we can't?" she asks. "If they find us?"

"Then our Point will protect us." The voice is small and slightly muffled, coming from Gwen's back.

Gwen shifts Mandi's small frame up over her shoulder and into her arms. "You're awake." Her surprise gives way to suspicion. "How *long* have you been awake?"

Long enough to have heard what we're up against, I think, but my guess turns out to be an under-estimation.

"An hour," Mandi says.

Gwen moves to put her down, but the young girl winces, and she's not acting.

"Are your legs hurt?" Gwen asks, frozen in place.

"I don't think so," Mandi says. "But my head—"

Gwen puts the girl on her feet. She looks unsteady for a moment, but that's not surprising. She spent a good portion of the day hanging upside down over Gwen's shoulder. And for an hour of that time, she was conscious. And listening. Observing.

What kind of kid does that? I wonder, and then I decide, *a sneaky one.* More than that, she remained still and silent even when Gizmo screamed, even when we uncovered the skeletal man, and the mass grave of murdered Unity kids.

"Can you stand?" Gwen asks.

"I'm okay," Mandi says.

Gwen's voice shifts from concerned to irate. "Don't do that again. Honesty is key to all successful unification pairings." She speaks the line like she's reciting it from a manual I never got.

"None of us have been paired," Mandi says.

Sneaky and snippy.

Gwen leans over the shorter girl, hands on her hips. "The five of us were paired the moment we crashed on this island."

"We crashed?" Mandi says, looking confused, rubbing her head like she can smooth out the wrinkles, find her lost memory. But it's not there. "I remember losing power. We survived, so it couldn't have been too bad."

Someone got too many gold stars on their charts growing up.

"Listen, Mandi," I say, standing up and moving away from the field of dead, "the first time I laid eyes on you, she—" I point to Gwen, "—was carrying your butt out of a crashed transport, and then up a hillside away from a tsunami. And then up a tree. She saved your life more than once, and she's been carrying you ever since, so I think you should drop the attitude and show her a little respect and thanks."

She reacts like I've just whipped out a butcher knife and stabbed her Teddy bear to death. And I nearly apologize, but then I remember she's already seen and heard horrible things without reacting at all. My little scolding isn't going to breach her defenses so easily.

"Nice try, kid," I say. "Not buying it."

She smiles at me and shrugs.

I put a hand on my holstered gun and say, "There's room in this field for one more."

It's clear that she doesn't take the threat seriously, but she groans, looks up at Gwen and says, "Thanks." Before I can urge her to be a little more detailed, she looks at me and says, "And I don't do apologies, so don't bother."

"Mandi!" Daniel's voice echoes again, and it makes me cringe. "You're awake!" The boys are heading in our direction again.

Mandi takes a step toward them, but I catch her arm. It's tiny in my hand. Big attitude for such a small kid. "Not a word," I say.

She nods. "I won't tell them. The boys are fragile. I'll keep this a secret as long as you do your job." She looks from my eyes, to the holstered gun and back again. Then she taps the Point symbol on my chest and yanks her arm away. She heads toward the boys again, on course to meet them half way, rubbing her head as she goes.

"You know her well?" I ask.

Gwen leans to the side, stretching the shoulder that has been bearing the brunt of the girl's weight and boney hips. "Well enough. She says she never apologizes because she's never wrong. She might even be right about that, but she's got a pretty severe chip on her shoulder. Like you. But she's okay—when she's not on defense."

I grin at Gwen's dig. "And what about me? Am I okay?"

She gives me a half-smirk. "Still trying to figure that out." She reaches out a hand to help me back up onto the concrete. It's not a big step, but my fatigue must be showing. "C'mon, I got you."

I take her hand and am once again surprised by her resilient strength. But as she pulls me back up onto the landing pad, I slip into the past.

“**I got you,**” he said.

I’d never been a fan of obstacle courses. Life had enough hurdles. I didn’t want to jump, duck and dodge them for fun. Or exercise. And I certainly didn’t want to maneuver my way through one while being watched by adults with clipboards. *Get it over with,* I told myself, and I threw myself into it, trying to show the observers how inadequate their gauntlet was. When I reached the end, I was spent. I had wasted too much energy on the first 90% of the course, and I didn’t have much left to get me up the knotted rope hanging down from a twenty-foot-high, wooden wall.

But I wasn’t about to show weakness now. Not ever. Adults can spot it. Take advantage of it. Feeling weak is normal. Showing it is a problem. So I heaved myself up the dry, oil-scented cable and grunted with each muscle pop. It would hurt for a week, but I didn’t care.

The problem was, when I reached the end, I had nothing left. Absolutely nothing. Like a spaceship trying to fly through the center of a black hole, I was lost. I was nothing. And everyone watching was about to see it.

Then a hand locked onto my wrist and a voice said, “I got you.”

I didn’t look up. Couldn’t. I put all of my energy into locking my hand around my rescuer’s wrist and held on while the last few feet were completed by someone else. In my eyes, I had failed. So when I saw that it was

Hutch who had pulled me up, this boy who followed me everywhere and whose apparent affection felt like a foreign invader, I reacted like Mandi. I didn't thank him. Instead, I shouted, "Just stay away from me!" and stormed off. I never did apologize.

"You all right?"

The question pulls me back to the present. Mandi is leaning in front of me, looking concerned.

"Not really," I say. "There's nothing right about this."

"Guys!" It's Daniel again. I start toward him, fully intent on chewing him out for swallowing a megaphone. But then he says, grinning, "We found something!" and I find myself jogging toward him, foolish enough to get my hopes up.

My hopes aren't exactly dashed when I see what has Daniel worked up, but it kind of feels like an elephant took a big steaming dump on them.

"It's a path," he says, like we can't see that for ourselves.

The winding line of hard-packed earth leads through the grass, where it's partially concealed by shifting reeds. It leads into the jungle at the valley's end. It's not a call box, homing beacon or other modern device portending rescue, but it *is* a sign of civilization.

The question is, who made it? Unity? Or the people who killed Unity kids? It might lead us right to them. Pigs in a slaughter house, walking naively to the bolt gun, putting it against our own foreheads. Suicidal lemming pigs.

Gwen's sour expression means she's thinking the same thing. Or something similar. Some other non-swine analogy. Of course, she's the farm girl, so her vision of slaughtered pigs is probably more graphic and better informed.

Daniel is surprised by our lack of excitement, or maybe he expects us to be clucking proud. That's how I picture his mother, gasping at all his accomplishments, pinching his cheeks. That's what good mothers do, isn't it?

Daniel hops down from the landing pad and crouches beside the path. He scratches at its surface, which flakes but remains mostly intact. "It's been packed down hard. The rain didn't turn it to mush. Not all of it, anyway. And look..." He digs a blade of still-green grass out of the surface. "This grass is still alive. The path is new. It was made by a machine. Probably within the last few days."

"We don't know who made it, or where it goes," I point out.

"It's a newly made path leading away from a Unity landing pad, where we were most likely meant to land." Daniel stands, looking frustrated with me. He's not used to having his opinions questioned, and he's clinging to hope.

Like me.

Like all of us.

"So we follow the path," I say. "And then what?"

He shrugs. "Beats me."

"That's *your* job," Mandi says. There's a snippy attitude in her voice I'd like to slap out of her, but when no one comes to my defense, I realize that's how they all feel. It doesn't matter that I've been with the Unity program for just three weeks, or that I'm uninitiated and uncomfortable with the roles of Base, Support and Point. When they look at me, all they see is a black triangle with a red tip.

A Point.

The tip of a spear.

A weapon.

A leader.

All I see is a tattoo I never asked for, and had I known the implications, I would have turned them down.

But I'm not sure that's entirely true, either. The alternative to this would have been Brook Meadow. Without Sig to keep me grounded, I would have most likely been kicked out of school by now. And that would have been it for me. No high school diploma. No college degree. I would have been on course for a life of mediocrity and hardship. It was a course I'd been on since the day my mother popped me out of her womb and decided, 'I don't love this child, take her away.'

Had I known about all this, about the crash, the tsunami, the death, the island, the murders and the responsibility thrust upon me by four total strangers who think I'm something I'm not, would I still be here?

Yes, I decide, considering the alternative.

Better to die young, fighting for something. Better than going to the grave an old woman with nothing to show for eighty years of sucking oxygen from the atmosphere. That's what animals do. Biologists say that people are just animals, too, whose primary functions are to eat, sleep and procreate, but it just sounds like an excuse to not live fully. To not dream of something bigger and better. I know what that feels like—to be dreamless. To lack hope from something beyond existing.

And right now, for the first time in my life, I feel like I exist. Like I'm more than alive. Like I'm living.

Before I decide I'm actually enjoying myself here and start worrying about my psyche, I say, "Okay."

"Okay what?" Daniel asks.

"We'll follow the path. See where it leads. Whatever happens after that will depend on what we find at the end. But our priority is still food, water and shelter. If we find any of those things, the mystery of this path's terminus will have to wait a few days."

"A few *days?*" Gizmo exclaims. He lacks Mandi's edge, but still sounds surprisingly aghast.

This path is providing our Base members with hope, but far too much of it. Even if we find a way to contact the outside world, if Daniel was right about the size and force of the wave, it might be a very long time before rescue comes. I don't want to be the one to crush their hope, though, so I redirect it.

"Transport 37 went down not far from us. If the five of us survived the crash, it's possible some of them did, too. First thing in the morning, we're going to find them."

"If they landed in the water," Daniel says. "Like 38..."

Mandi sits on the side of the concrete landing pad, head lowered into her hands, elbows on knees. "All three transports crashed?"

She's only been awake for an hour, I remember. She doesn't know everything.

"38 landed in the ocean?" she asks. "*Before* the tsunami?"

Gizmo sits next to her, hand on her shoulder. "I'm sorry." His small voice carries weight, and I'm surprised when a sob hiccups from the tough little girl.

"Damn," Daniel says. "Mand, I didn't think before I said—"

Mandi sniffs, wipes her nose and sits up straight. "Not your fault."

I give Gwen a confused look. She leans in close, whispering, "Hutch is her brother."

The news is like a sucker punch. A short gasp escapes my lips, but long enough to be heard. Mandi's red-rimmed, wet eyes snap toward me. "That's right." She stands and steps toward me. "He was my brother. And *you*... You humiliated him. Made him useless. He was one of the best Supports. Top scores. And they paired him with *you*. *You!* The girl whose pity party never ends. The girl whose only friend was the girl who couldn't talk."

"Hey," Daniel says, placing a calm hand on Mandi's shoulder. But she shrugs away and steps closer to me, well inside my comfort zone. "We all know who you are, Eff. And we all know that Sig's potential was the only reason they brought you along."

"That's not true," I say, but it sounds true, even to me.

"But she *didn't* need you. Just people who understood her." Mandi puts her hand on my chest, between my breasts, breaching all kinds of personal boundaries, and shoves. I stumble back a step, but hold my ground, my face turning hot.

"So what to do with you?" she says, closing the fresh gap between us. She raises a finger in the air, like she's just had a great idea. She performs the most sarcastic impression of an adult I've ever witnessed, all intercut with her own cutting remarks. "Oh, I know, let's put the worst of them—*that's you*—with the best of them—*Hutch*—and see if he can't elevate her. She's not good at much besides unrestrained violence... *Yeah, we hacked your records, boo hoo for you.* So let's make her a Point." The impression ends there. "But the problem with that is that as a Point, your actions and decisions affect everyone else who is trained to follow your lead. They might as well have put that insignia on a gorilla's hand, since that's clearly who raised you."

My fists clench, tightening with each beat of my heart. My arms churn with energy looking for a release. I've done it before. Let the power explode from my chest, flow down my arm, to my fist. Step into it. Put my soul into it. I see her on the ground, knocked out cold. It would take just one punch to knock her mouth shut, probably for months if her small jaw broke.

I resist for the simple fact that she's recently woken up after being unconscious for a day. A punch like the one I can deliver could kill her. That and the fact that she's berating me out of grief for a lost brother, who I did, in fact, treat like garbage. Had I understood Supports then, the way I do now...

Then I see something else in the ferocity of her glare.

Intent.

Her emotions are real, but she's pushing me on purpose. Challenging me to do what? Strike her? Kill her?

No, I decide, those are the things she's hoping I won't do. But not because getting knocked out would hurt. She's hoping I'll rise above the action. Show them that Hutch wasn't assigned to the dregs of the program, that his death could be redeemed—by me.

Fighting my nature, which she has succinctly pointed out is violent, I rise to the challenge.

She continues to vent. And push. But I calm myself. Lower my heart rate. My fingers open up and my hands rise to my hips. Classic Wonder Woman pose. Boosting confidence.

She pauses her verbal and physical assault.

"Are you done?" I ask her.

She blinks. It's not exactly an expression of shock, but I've caught her off guard.

"Because if you really want to honor your brother's death, you will *shut your loud mouth,* and fall in line." Geez, I sound like an adult. But it works. Her lips clamp shut, though I'm not sure if it's because I told her to or that she's just remembered we have a very good reason to be stealthy. "I didn't know your brother well, and that *is* my fault, but from what little I did know of him, he'd want us to work together, to survive, and to find your friends, his and mine."

True to form, she doesn't apologize for what she's said or for endangering us by yelling. In her mind, it was all justified, and maybe it was. At the very least, I can't blame her for it. She did just lose her brother, and through her words and actions, she's forced me to step headlong into the role assigned to me by Unity. She steps back, motions to the path, and says, "After you, Point."

We spend the night under the stars, doing our best to sleep, but it's not easy. Every time I close my eyes, I see the crash. I think of the kids who didn't make it. The people on the other transports. So I spend most of the night staring at the stars, trying to imagine what life far away from this planet would be like. I nod off close to dawn, and then wake up with the sun. We need to move.

Five minutes into the new day's hike, my legs are reminding me that I should have spent the night in an infirmary eating fistfuls of pain medication. But I'm sure the others are hurting, too. Mandi must be. But none of them are complaining, so I push past it. The winding trail moves steadily upward. Most of the time, it winds around trees, following the steady grade, but occasionally, we hit a series of switchbacks. They zigzag their way up the hill, turning a hundred vertical feet into a half-mile walk.

We can't see the sun's passage through the sky as the canopy once again blocks it out. But we can feel it in shifts of temperature and humidity. By midday we're soaked, partly from our own sweat, partly from the jungle's. I haven't seen many birds, but I can hear them. Insects, too. And the smell? It's like something out of a dream. Earthy, but sweet in a way that's making me salivate.

I try not to think about eating though. We've got limited food supplies and have agreed to hold off on eating until we're sure we don't need to ration what we have over days, or weeks.

After thirty minutes of walking in a silent, single-file line, the others following me with quiet confidence that makes me question every step, Gwen double-times her pace and walks next to me. She looks much more comfortable without Mandi slung over her shoulder.

"Can you smell it?" she asks, keeping her voice low.

"I can smell a lot," I say, "but I'm not sure what it is."

"Close your eyes," she says. "Try to picture what you're smelling."

"Please don't tell me Unity trained you how to smell."

She grins. It's weary, but not defeated. "I spent a fair amount of time in the woods. Most of this—" She looks around us at the lush greenery. "—is foreign to me, but some things smell the same no matter where you go."

We're heading up a perfectly straight incline of a switchback, so I indulge her, closing my eyes as I walk. I breathe deeply, taking in the world through my nose, trying to separate and identify each individual scent. The first is dirt. Decomposing things. Then flowers. Maybe fruit, but we haven't seen any. What else is there? A hint of ocean. Salt water. Nothing that stands out as important. "I have no idea."

My eyes are still closed when she says, "It's coming from above us, rolling downhill on the cool air."

I haven't felt any cool air all day, so I'm not sure what she's talking about, but I turn my face uphill and breathe again. I'm typically not one for guessing games, but this is getting my mind off grim subjects, like Sig's potential fate and Hutch's certain fate. Then I get a nose full of it. My eyes open wide.

"Water."

"Uh-huh," she says. "Running water. We'll hear it at the top of the hill."

I'm not sure how she could know that, but as we round the final switchback and approach the hill's crest, it's like someone has turned up the volume on a rushing water track, the kind people fall asleep to. There's a deep roaring that suggests a waterfall. And a gurgling of rocks over stones. I might not be able to visualize scents, but I have no trouble with sounds.

And neither do the others.

Daniel is the first to react. "Water!" He rushes past me, but I manage to snag his go-pack and yank him to a stop. Neither Gizmo nor Mandi share his exuberance or energy. They remain twenty feet back, trudging upward at the same slug's pace.

"Water is a good thing, but we can't..." How can I say this without revealing the bodies Gwen and I found?

Thankfully, Daniel keeps me from having to lie. "We might not be alone. I get it. But one body isn't—" He eyes me, suspicious. "One body isn't enough to be this cautious, is it?"

I glance at Gwen. She shrugs. Apparently, these kinds of decisions are mine to make on my own.

"No," I say to Daniel, meeting his eyes with a serious gaze of my own. "It's not."

He leans forward, whispering. "There were more, right? I knew it. You weren't peeing. Girls don't just pee out in the open. I'm not stupid."

"First, if you ever see me crouched down in a field of tall grass, there's a good chance I might *actually* be peeing, so don't sneak up on me. Second, there were more, but..." I glance back at Mandi and Gizmo. He's a little older than they are, but not much more emotionally mature than Gizmo, and far less than Mandi. Still, he thinks I'm letting him in on something that's just for the big kids, which gives him a sense of responsibility and keeps him from freaking out over the news.

"Right," he says.

After cresting the switchback, it's hard to keep from breaking into a run. The sound and smell of water calls to me like the mythological Sirens singing to Odysseus. But unlike those beautifully dangerous creatures, the water source ahead promises life.

But that doesn't mean it's safe. When the loud rush of water grows so loud that I have no doubt its source is just ahead, I stop the group. "You guys wait here. If I'm not back in fifteen minutes, or you hear gunshots, bolt."

"And then what?" Gizmo asks.

"We'll wait on the far side of the landing pad valley," Gwen offers.

I nod. "And if you see anyone other than me..." I don't finish the sentence, because I have nothing to offer. If I'm subdued while armed with a pistol, there is little hope for this lot. I know it and so do they.

"Great," Mandi grumbles, but she sits herself down on a rock, rubbing her head.

"Stay quiet." I draw my handgun, trying to look confident, trying to fill the enormous shoes these kids expect me to. "And stay here."

Only Gwen nods, but she tends to speak for them all. I return her nod and leave. The path goes further than I would have thought, and I shift from walking to jogging, so I don't miss my self-imposed fifteen-minute deadline.

Earth gives way to rocky terrain, the soil long ago eroded by flooding. Then the trees thin, and all I can hear is the roar of water.

And then, all at once, I see it. It's a river, flowing downhill from high up on the volcanic mountain. It's at least fifteen feet across, but only a foot deep, the glass-clear fluid slipping smoothly over large slabs of stone. To the right is a lagoon, fed by a waterfall. Even from here, I can see to the bottom of the crystal clear waters, and I can see the fish that reside in them. Food *and* water.

But all of this natural beauty and the promise of survival only holds my attention for a moment. The wooden bridge, crude but solid, crosses the river to a continuing path on the far side. It looks like something out of a summer camp catalog, the wooden boards thick and moss covered. The path leads up a short hill on the far side, atop of which I can once again see that the trees have been cleared. There's something over there. Something put there by the builders of this path, and the landing pad. By Unity.

With time to spare, I cross the bridge, trying to pay equal attention to my surroundings and the slick mossy wood, still holding water from the previous night's deluge. Gun raised, I sweep back and forth, while I follow the path. Ahead, the trees give way to open sky.

The man-made clearing stops me in my tracks. This is what we were meant to find on the first night. The jungle floor has been cleared of debris and the trees thinned, but not fully removed. Hanging between many of the trees are a network of hammocks, spread out in bunches. I don't count, but if I had to guess, I'd say there are thirty.

At the center of it all is a hut made of branches and roofed with palm fronds. I can see what it was supposed to look like, but it's in shambles, torn apart by the storm. My perspective begins to shift. Had we arrived on a clear day, without crashing, and we hadn't found the skeletons apparently overlooked by Unity, this might have all felt like a grand adventure. It would have been like one of those old TV shows, leaving a bunch of strangers in a remote location, watching them come together or tear each other down.

Is that what Unity wanted? Bonding through extreme circumstances? Harsh life lessons experienced as a group? If so, I have news for them. Even with everything that's gone wrong and the potential for far worse, this still feels like a positive turn for me.

As I move through the campsite, I'm struck by a warm, much drier breeze. My weapon lowers as I approach the far end of camp. An unused fire pit lies in wait at the precipice of a cliff.

I shuffle up toward the edge, stopping when dirt turns to stone. We're a good thousand feet up, looking over the west end of the island. A ring of pale sand is surrounded by endless ocean. At ground level, a person's view is three miles to the horizon. From up here, it's closer to forty miles. The vast emptiness of it makes me dizzy, and

I lower my eyes to the island below. The jungle, while far smaller than the endless ocean, feels just as vast. It's a roof of green, protecting who knows how many secrets.

Or killers.

But the canopy isn't perfectly solid. It's pocked by clearings, which could be ponds, campsites or any number of things. There's no way to know from here. We're going to have to explore this island. There's no way around that.

My eyes follow a winding line that I think must be the river's course. It leads out to the coast, smearing a stretch of beach and darkening a patch of ocean with dark soil and stones. But there is no damage from the tsunami on this part of the island. All of that is behind us. There is, however, a straight line extending out from the river below.

Or is the line heading toward the river?

I trace the line with my finger, extending it back and turning around, pointing toward the East, where the transports came from. Lost in thought, I nearly scream when my extended finger stops between a pair of eyes.

"Are you *trying* to get killed?" I shout at Mandi, whose foot-shorter-than-mine head is directly in the path of my pointed finger.

"I don't think you're capable," she says, raising an eyebrow.

This kid...

I turn my pointed finger down to the gun in my hand, the one that's aimed at her chest. "I nearly shot you."

She glances down, unimpressed. "Your finger isn't even on the—"

"Because I took it off when I saw your dumb face staring up at me." If I make it off this island without punching her, it's going to be some kind of miracle. I lean around Mandi, drawn by the sound of running feet on hard-packed earth. For a moment, my pulse races again, as I imagine a horde of serial killers bearing down on us.

Gwen leads the charge, followed by Daniel and Gizmo, who stop short, breathing hard and taking in the web of hammocks with wide eyes. Gwen doesn't seem to notice the campsite. Her eyes are on Mandi and Mandi alone.

And she's not happy.

Not at all.

"What the hell do you think you're doing?" Gwen looks huge. Frightening even. She puts her hand on Mandi's small shoulder and shoves. The girl stumbles back, past me, toward the cliff. "Are you trying to get yourself killed?"

Shove.

Gwen glances up past Mandi, double-taking at the view, but her anger doesn't waver. "You know how this works. How we work. We're not on the carrier. We're not in a computer lab. We are in the wild, and that means our Point is in command. Right now, that's Effie and only Effie. And if she's not around, Support is in charge. And when she came up here, that was me. Do you understand what that means?"

Mandi's lip twitches, but she doesn't reply.

"It means that if you had run off this cliff, or if Effie shot you, or a hundred other possible outcomes that end with you dead, it would have been *my* fault."

Shove.

"So if you're going to continue being insubordinate, putting your life at risk, and *ours*, I might as well push you off this cliff right now. Then I could at least start dealing with the guilt now. Maybe be a functional part of the team again by morning."

Holy... Gwen is hardcore. I thought I'd seen her angry, but this... This is drill instructor material. She's just leaving out words like, 'maggot,' and 'pissant'.

Mandi looks back over her shoulder. The dizzying drop is just a few feet away. A hard hit from Gwen really could send her over the edge. The girl's hard edge wavers.

"Maybe Effie can shoot you," Gwen says, "and we can share the guilt. That might wo—"

"Okay." The word is mumbled. Barely audible.

"Louder," Gwen says.

Mandi purses her lips, crushing them white for a moment. "Okay."

"Okay, what?"

"I'll listen to you." Mandi looks from Gwen to me. Her nose crinkles. "And Effie."

A good portion of Gwen's mania slips away, like rain from a waxed surface. If it was an act, Gwen missed her calling as an actress. But I think she's just satisfied. While Mandi's acquiescence isn't anything close to an apology, I suspect it's the closest she's ever gotten to one.

Gwen takes Mandi's right hand, lifting it up to reveal the brand. "You're a Base, Mandi. You might get a chance to tell both of us—" She glances over at me. "—what to do. But only if you survive long enough." She pulls the girl away from the cliff. "Stay away from the edge."

The scolded Mandi storms off. For a moment it looks like she's going to leave the campsite, breaking protocol once again, but she stops at a hammock, climbs inside and lies back with her arms crossed.

"You're still holding your gun," Gwen says.

I look down at the weapon that very nearly took Mandi's life. I holster it on my hip. "I nearly shot her."

"She's lucky you didn't. Most Points wouldn't have hesitated." Gwen puts her hand on my shoulder, turning me to face her. "Next time, pull the trigger."

"What?"

"You didn't know it was Mandi. Next time it might not be."

"I would have killed her."

She nods slowly. "But if someone kills you, the rest of us won't last long."

I'm not sure that's true. Gwen has shown herself to be equally tough, if not tougher and more resourceful than I am. The only reason I'm leading this bunch is because they're insisting I do so.

"I don't think I could recover if I—"

"We both know you could," she says. "It's part of what makes you a Point. You get the hard calls because you can *live* with them. Your job is sometimes heart-breaking, but...that's nothing new to you, is it?"

And there it is. Why I'm a Point.

The fact that my life has been so miserable makes me the right person for a position that sometimes requires pulling a trigger without hesitation. And she's right. I would have felt bad about shooting Mandi, but I wouldn't have blamed myself. I'd have compressed the pain, locked it up in a box and filed it away to get lost in the mental warehouse of other bad memories.

But I'm not as cold as they think, or as cold as I would like to be. Hutch's death, despite the fact that I had nothing to do with it, is still nibbling at my psyche, like a rabbit with a lettuce leaf. Ceaseless munching.

"Whoa!" Daniel's exuberance seems undaunted by the drama that just played out on the cliff's edge. When I see him and Gizmo standing at the ruined hut, pushing through fallen palm fronds, I wonder if they even noticed. The boys have an excited air about them, like they've just stumbled upon a magical land. And maybe that's how they see it. All these hammocks. Signs of civilization. Of what should have been our welcome. There might even be an acoustic guitar hidden around here, with sticks and marshmallows and the lyrics for Kumbaya.

As Gwen and I walk toward the pair, Daniel and Gizmo become a flurry of motion and words, totally focused on whatever it is they've found. I can't understand a word they're saying, but it sounds like sped up techno-babble. Daniel grabs several large palm leaves and lays them down on the ground, flattening them out into an even surface.

"Here," I hear him say as I approach. "Put it here."

Standing above them, I immediately recognize the device they're pulling out of a thin, black bag. It's a Featherlight.

"Is it working?" Gwen asks.

"We're about to find out," Gizmo says, laying the touch-screen device on the palm fronds like he's handling an ancient relic that might crumble from his touch.

"What about the EMP?" I ask. "We weren't that far from here when it hit."

Daniel taps the now empty black bag. "It's a standard Featherlight bag."

"Is that supposed to mean something?" I ask. Outside of school, I've never handled a Featherlight, and I've certainly never seen the packaging one comes in.

"They're waterproof, and their packaging, thanks to a thin layer of flexible metal foam—copper and nickel mostly—makes them safe from an EMP's E1 energy." He pushes and holds down the power button. A Unity logo appears, the color shifting from blue at the bottom, to orange on the sides and red at the top, momentarily displaying each insignia as the device boots.

"Sounds like they should have coated the transports in the stuff," I say.

"It's prohibitively expensive," Daniel says. "To effectively coat all vehicles would require an astronomical amount of money. EMP protection is generally limited to high-end, small electronics and military vehicles and systems. But our go-packs are similar to the Featherlight bag." His excitement dwindles. "If I hadn't taken my Featherlight out on the transport..."

I place my hand over my chest where the photo of my parents still safely resides in its pocket. It's just one old photo of people I've never actually met, but it's more than he has now. Of course, he has years of happy memories locked away in his brain. I still just have the one photo.

The seven-inch screen blinks and then shows the standard operating system, which has very few icons displayed. This thing is bare-bones. Daniel tries to open a folder, but nothing happens. He taps it several more times with no luck.

"It's fried," Gizmo declares.

Daniel shakes his head. "It's working fine. It's just—"

The screen turns black for a moment, and then the frozen first frame of a video appears. It's a generic backdrop. White wall and a Unity logo featuring all three colors mixed together. But it's the woman that holds my attention. She's older. Her brown hair is cut short. Her smile is gone. But it's her.

And I'm not the only one who sees it.

Daniel whips around toward me, eyes wide. "Eff?"

My guts churn in time with my spinning head.

I stagger back a step.

Mom, Dad and Euphemia.

My shock morphs into anger.

This is the woman who gave me up.

The woman who set me on a dark path.

And she's not downtrodden, or frail or suffering from any of the dozen conditions—including death—that I would have found acceptable reasons for giving me up. She's healthy and physically strong. The look in her bright blue eyes suggests she's mentally competent, too. As does the Unity uniform she's wearing—a tight, black, leather, Unity flight suit.

"Play it," I say through grinding teeth. "I want to hear what my mother has to say."

"I'm sure you're wondering why you've been dragged out of bed, flown to the middle of the Pacific Ocean and dropped off on a deserted island. You're probably tired and confused."

My mother speaks with a calm assurance. Her smile says that everything is okay. Her tone is so cool and relaxed and poised that anyone already freaking out would be placated by her cooing. She's so good at it that I wonder if she's had practice.

Did she have other kids?

Was she someone else's mother?

"I would be, too," she says. "In fact, I was. Like you, I once found myself in a remote location with just my fellow Unity crews."

"Pause it," I say, and Daniel does. I pull the photo out of my pocket and stare at the man and woman. They're wrapped up in each other. Happy. And both of their right hands are covered. There was no way I could have known. But did they know about me? Have they been watching me? I shake my head. The idea that the parents who gave me up have been watching me struggle from a distance is hard to accept. It would make them monsters, and me the daughter of monsters.

But it can't be a coincidence that I'm here now, after just three weeks of testing, listening to a message from my mother. Or could it? Maybe this message has been played for hundreds of Unity crews? She could be an actress, the whole thing staged, and she's really down and out, taking on talking-head jobs for a living, giving the weather on some local channel. That would be better than this being real.

"Go ahead," I say, and the video resumes.

"The experience forged bonds that remain unbroken to this day. Life and death are the glue that bind Base, Support and Point. Together we're strong."

"Divided we fall," Gwen says at the same time as my mother. It must be an unofficial Unity motto I haven't heard yet.

"Since you're watching this message," my mother continues, "you already know the island has sources of food and water. How and if you retrieve them is up to you, but all the resources you need are standing around you in the bodies and minds of your confederates. Work together. Survive. We will return for you—for all of you—in one month."

Daniel pauses the video again. "A month. We're going to be here for *a month*."

"At least," Gwen says.

Daniel's frown deepens. "Right. The wave."

"She's your mother?" Mandi asks. She's standing behind us, arms crossed, but she's as interested in the video as the rest of us.

"Do you know her?" I ask, sounding something close to pitiful. I shouldn't want to know this woman who gave me up. Who didn't care enough to keep me. Who named me and let me go like some wild animal born in captivity, sent out into the jungle—in this case, literally. I shouldn't care about her. But I do.

"I've seen her," Mandi says. "On the carrier."

"When?" I ask.

"With the Admiral."

"The who?" I've never heard of this person, but the way she says 'The Admiral' indicates a capital T and capital A, like the man doesn't need a first name.

"No kidding?" Gizmo says.

Judging by the looks of surprise on everyone's faces but mine, I'm once again out of the loop.

"He founded Unity," Daniel explains. "He was bonkers rich. Put his whole fortune into creating the Unity program, which is worldwide and not dependent on any government. Judging by the age of your mother, she must have gotten in on the ground floor."

"What does the Admiral look like?" I ask.

Daniel understands the real question. "It's not him." *Him* being my father. "The Admiral must be seventy by now."

"And the name?" I ask.

"He was an actual admiral once," Gwen says. "That's what they say. His real name is a secret. Pretty much everything we know about him is rumor, including his wealth."

"Only someone with endless funding could create something like Unity," Daniel says.

"Let's just finish the video," Mandi says, and for once, we're on the same page. Compared to my mother and our current situation, The Admiral is about as interesting as a crack in the ceiling.

"Do it," I say, and Daniel once again complies.

My mother leans forward, shifting her hands. Her finger taps the desktop. She's either nervous or impatient. Either way, her comfortable visage is fading a little. "Some of you have been with the program for a while. Some of you just a short time."

I hold my breath.

Is she speaking about me?

To me?

"Some of you have been partially integrated into the Unity program, understanding our organization and methodology, while others are still just getting their feet wet. I assure you, this was not a mistake. You are here for a reason. You're here because we believe you are ready. Even if you do not."

Pause.

Daniel taps the screen. "Look!"

We all lean forward, looking at my mother's hand. She's had her left hand covering her right the whole time, but between shifting around and tapping the desktop, she's revealed a small part of the back of her hand and the brand it holds. The black bottom and orange side are impossible to mistake.

"She's a Support," Gwen says, a trace of admiration in her voice.

"She's not a good person," I snap. "Not someone you should look up to. Or trust. All of you. No matter how good she looks or sounds."

A hush falls over the group. I think they're all holding their breaths.

"She gave me away," I say. "And now she's sent me, and all of you, here."

"They didn't mean for us to crash," Gizmo says, sounding hopeful.

"Crash or not, they sent some of us here to die." I meet Gwen's eyes. She opens her mouth to argue, but I cut her short. "They might not have known about the bodies, but they knew those people died. They knew they never made it off this island. And they sent us here anyway. This is a trial by fire."

"*Bodies?*" Gizmo says.

Hell. I reach over Daniel's shoulder, dodging the question and hitting play.

My mother gives the desk a few more nervous taps and finishes with, "One month. Just one month and this will make sense. Everything will make sense."

The video goes black. The plain background returns. Daniel starts tapping the screen again and this time it responds. He accesses the settings panel, but finds it mostly empty. "This is a bare-bones model. No apps. No connectivity. Cell, Wi-Fi, satellite, nothing. I mean, the parts might be in here, but none of it is enabled, and there's no way to turn them on."

"Because they didn't want us to," Gwen says.

Daniel nods. "Would appear so, and the message suggests the same. The only thing on here is the video of—" He looks at me.

"You can say it."

"Of Effie's mother."

"There's more," Mandi says.

"*What?*" Daniel scoffs and rolls his eyes. "Trust me, there is nothing on here besides the stripped-down operating system, and that's just there to enable the video playback."

"*In* the video, you plebeian." Mandi snags the Featherlight, and after a few taps, starts the video again. She places it back on the palm leaves.

My mother's soothing voice grates on me. She runs through her uplifting spiel and then gets nervous, her fingers tapping.

"Be safe," Mandi says, staring at the video.

We're looking at the same screen, but she's seeing or hearing something I'm not.

"Be strong."

"It's Morse code," Daniel whispers. "She's tapping it on the desk."

I try to follow the taps, but can't make sense of them. I understand the mechanics of Morse code, but I've never bothered to learn it.

"Speak well," Mandi says, just before my mother signs off.

The words pummel me.

I stagger back. The back of my legs catch on a low hanging hammock. I fall.

My butt lands in the hammock's basin and I start to roll backward, unwilling and unable to stop myself from falling. I'm already plummeting, descending into a pit of confusion so deep I'm not sure I will even climb back out.

The hammock is caught, its spin stopped short, my bruised body spared another jarring impact.

"Hey," Gwen says, her voice distant, masked by a rumbling. "Hey!"

My cheek stings, the poignant sharpness of it returning my senses. Gwen is winding up to slap me again.

"Are you back?" she asks. "Or are you checking out?"

"Please, let me."

She lowers her hand and uses it to help steady the hammock. "Not a chance."

The others gather behind her, their faces glowing orange in the light of our second sunset in this beautiful hell.

"'Be safe,'" Gwen says. "'Be strong. Speak well.' You know what it means, don't you?"

I nod. "My name. Euphemia. The Greek translation is 'to speak well.'"

My four companions, these people my mother tells me are confederates, people with whom I am in league or am allied with against something or someone else, lean in, the mystery hanging between us like a darkness waiting to be illuminated.

"It means she was speaking to me."

I push up off the hammock and stand.

"It means she never did forget about me."

Gwen moves aside as I step toward her, allowing me to pass. I pause for a moment, looking back over my shoulder. "It means she is a monster, after all."

Growing up primarily on the not-so-nice streets of smaller cities, where all the stereotypes about drugs, violence and thievery aren't stereotypes, I rarely went outside at night. The one house I lived in that did have a postcard-sized backyard, which smelled like the neighbor's ash tray, provided a view of the nighttime sky with very few stars. The light reaching Earth from billions of light years away just couldn't compete with the ambient glow from the surrounding homes, street lights and the city beyond. Civilization had cut me off from the lights that inspired, guided and fueled the imaginations of nearly every generation of homo sapiens from their meager beginnings. I had heard that there were places still on Earth where the night sky could still be seen without light pollution, but I couldn't picture it.

Lying in a hammock, staring up at what I'd previously experienced as a black sky with a few dozen pinpoints of light, I now see more light than darkness. The vastness of it makes my head spin, like looking to the horizon from the cliff. The number of stars overhead is like a fog, so thick and alive that I think I should be able to taste it. I read once that outer space smells like seared steak.

My stomach growls as I picture a constellation-sized hunk of beef.

I had my protein bar ration, but it barely touched my gnawing hunger. *Tomorrow,* I think, picturing fish from the river sizzling over an open flame.

Stop thinking about food!

I push visions of cooking meat from my mind and remember why I had started thinking about the stars in the first place: to forget about her.

My mother, still nameless, is alive. And well. And she sent me a message via Morse code, which leads me to believe that making contact wasn't sanctioned for some reason. *Unity doesn't know I'm her daughter,* I decide. But she knows. And I don't think she just figured it out.

And that creates a cascade of overlapping questions to which I will likely never have answers. If she was on the Unity carrier, she might be dead. And even if she's not, there's a good chance none of us will make it off this island alive. Because it's not just an island with limited food and water that a bunch of kids can survive on if they work together. It's a killing ground.

A month would have been bad enough, but unless we can make contact with the outside world, there's a good chance we'll be out here a lot longer than that.

I roll my head to the side. The campsite is mostly dark. We could have started a fire—one outdoorsy thing I am good at, though not for any genuine outdoorsy reason. But that would be asking for trouble. A fire atop the cliff would be easy to see. Nothing like inviting the island's cannibal residents over for a meal.

They're not cannibals, I tell myself. Just murderers. The bodies were shot and left for dead, not disassembled, slaughtered or cooked. I might be the most street smart of our group, but even my imagination is getting out of control. Probably because the best case scenario is that all those people were killed by a lone crazy person. And while one person feels better than a tribe, it doesn't change the fact that whoever else is on this island, one or a dozen, they managed to kill eight Unity members, who probably weren't that different from us.

I focus on the lone source of light coming from the far side of the camp. It's inside the hut that Gwen and I repaired to the best of our abilities, while the others watched the sun slide into the horizon. Gizmo's go-pack was mostly filled with small sets of tools, the kind you'd use on...well, gizmos, and a box of spare parts that were protected from the EMP. After a quick glance at the parts, Gizmo declared they were for building an old fashioned radio. Suggested that if he built it, we might get a second message from Unity, which could contain information about the island, resources or even challenges to complete. But since our goal is communication with—and rescue from—the outside world, Gizmo is using the parts, along with the pillaged Unity Featherlight, to repair Daniel's EMP-fried Featherlight, instead.

The delicate operation is taking place under the dull blue glow of a single LED light, held by Mandi. Daniel offers verbal support and occasional ideas. Somehow, despite being surrounded by jungle and an endless ocean, they're suddenly in their element. And if they're successful, we'll have satellite communication with the outside world via the Internet. Help will be a chat window away.

A shuffle of feet announces a visitor. I see the silhouette slip through the star fog and realize I have no idea who it is. With my hand on the holstered gun, and my heart pounding, I ask, "Gwen?"

"Yeah," she says. "Who else did you think—never mind. That was dumb."

I hear a creak of stretching hammock strands as she lies down a few feet beside me. We lie there in silence, listening to the three high-pitched voices trying to whisper in the hut. A cool breeze rolls down from the volcanic mountain high above us, sweeping through the camp and spilling over the cliff. An invisible river of air and jungle smells.

"I could get used to this," Gwen says.

"Used to this?" I lean up and look at Gwen, but see only darkness.

"It's peaceful."

I look back up at the stars and take a deep breath. She's right about that. "If not for the dead people, killer waves and being stranded."

"A toilet would be nice, too," she says. "And a steak."

"I know, right?"

In a moment of clarity, I realize I'm smiling. I wouldn't have thought it was possible, but Gwen has become a friend. Daniel, too. I still don't know Gizmo very well, but his adorability is unquestionable. Mandi is another matter. We're not friends, but I do have a kind of respect for her. For her toughness. We're like a lion and a hyena on the African savannah, when such things still existed. We're at odds, but respectful of each other.

Gwen and I fall silent again, and I close my eyes, listening to the scrape of windblown palm leaves.

I jump when Gwen speaks again, this time in a gentle, almost inaudible, voice. "What is that?" She's talking to herself, but a question like that, on this island, can't be ignored.

With my head still turned in her direction, I open my eyes. "What?"

I see the shadow of her arm rise up through the stars on the horizon. "Up there."

The night sky looks like it did several minutes ago, except shifted a few degrees to the west. "What did you—"

And then I see it, too. Flecks of orange light, flaring to life and then fading away. A moment later, streaks of light trace lines across the sky, objects burning up in the atmosphere. Whatever they are, they're not as big as the object that crash landed, but there's still some kind of chaos taking place in orbit.

More flashes of orange.

More streaks of light.

The show is stunning, but disturbing. It doesn't take a vivid imagination to see the broad strokes of this mystery. The flares of light are explosions, big enough to see from the ground. The streaks of light are debris from the explosions, burning up in the atmosphere. None of it is big enough to crash into the ocean and bury us beneath a killer wave, but it's still disturbing.

"It's like a war," Gwen says.

"Between what?"

"Satellites," she says, sounding confident. "They're a strategic target. The enemy can't organize if they can't communicate."

"But there are just as many land-based modes of communication. Cell towers. Cables. The Internet.

Not to mention things no one can stop, like HAM radio."

"Maybe there are satellites with weapons?" she asks.

"Maybe," I say, thinking Daniel would know.

A series of orange orbs sparkle across the sky.

"Geez," Gwen says.

A quilt of orange lines follows, as the Earth spins its way through the ruins of whatever was just destroyed.

Three voices rise up from the hut, squealing. I move to stand up too fast, fearing the worst. The hammock spins me around like a luchador wrestler and slams me onto the ground. I cough and wince, but waste no time feeling embarrassed. Gwen couldn't see me anyway, and I hear her feet behind me.

My tension slides away as I make out words among the squeals, which now sound happy.

"We did it," Daniel says. "We're connected."

The three kids flinch when Gwen and I suddenly appear in the doorway, but their surprise is quickly replaced by excitement. A dissected Featherlight, the one containing my mother's message, lies on the hut floor. Beside it is a newly assembled device, made from parts of both. A Franken-Featherlight.

"It's looking for a connection," Gizmo says, pointing out the spinning icon at the top of the screen. The spinning stops, and then starts again.

"No Wi-Fi," Daniel says. "No surprise there."

The spinning icon stops once more and starts right back up.

"That was the cell signal search," Gizmo says.

"Again, no surprise." Daniel rubs his hands together like he's warming them over a fire. "C'mon, baby."

The spinning stops.

Daniel's blurred hands snap back into focus. "What happened?"

A message is displayed on the screen. 'No connection detected.'

"What?" Daniel says. "No! That's not even possible. There are satellites everywhere now. You could get a connection on the South Pole! We must have done something wrong."

"I don't screw up electronics," Gizmo says, on full defense.

Daniel thrusts his hands out at the unconnected device. "Well, you did this time, because—"

"Daniel," Gwen says, and then again, louder. "Daniel!'

The boy's building tirade comes to an abrupt stop. "What?"

"Gizmo didn't do anything wrong."

The three kids stare up at her. The world of tech is their domain. How could she, a deep woods-loving farm girl-turned-Support know that Gizmo had done his job right, when she hadn't even been in the room? Even Gizmo looks confused.

"How could you possibly know that?" Daniel asks. "He's good, but he's still human. Still fallible." He looks at Gizmo. "You're not incapable of making—"

"It's because the satellites are being destroyed," I say.

Daniel fake laughs. "Real funny, Eff, but I don't think this is the right—"

I raise a single eyebrow at him, my frown unflinching.

"You...you're not joking?"

"Come see for yourself," I say.

We spend the next half hour watching a fiery drama play out in Earth's orbit. Theories abound, but only one thing is certain: we won't be calling for help.

Help won't be coming any time soon.

And if the chaos in the sky above is indicative of things around the world, help might not ever come.

Even when life is glum, there is something about a sunrise that promises a better future. Like a Biblical rainbow over Noah's Ark. I'm not sure if it's the warmth, the innate knowledge that all life on Earth depends on it, or if it's simply because most everyone is still asleep. Sunrise used to be safe. Even in bad neighborhoods.

But not here.

The assumption hasn't been entirely confirmed, if you don't include the crash or the tsunami. Still, believing the sun's promise could prove fatal, I'm up before the others, stretching out the kinks and trying not to dwell on the light show we saw last night. Worrying about something to which answers cannot be found is a waste of brain power. We have more pressing problems.

The first of which, in my mind, is finding Sig.

Or what's left of her.

Shut up!

My inner voice is loud and has a split personality this morning.

I'm drawn to the cliff's edge. The jungle below is still in shadow. The sky above is a lightening purple. In the distant West, purple fades to black, the night sky being chased away.

Looking back to the straight line extending out from the river, a yawn becomes something like a wounded vulture call. I choke on the sound, but barely notice.

"What is it?" Gwen says behind me. I hear a twist of fabric and an, "oof." Then footsteps. Gwen is by my side, hands on knees, breathing hard. "What? What happened?"

"Follow the river," I say.

I don't look to see if she's listening. I know she is.

"Smoke." She stands up straight. "That's from a campfire."

"See the line cut through the jungle?" I point to it. "I think that might be where Transport 37 came down."

"If that's them, they don't know about the bodies." She meets my eyes. "They don't know this place is dangerous."

"I'm going down there," I say.

"I know."

"You're not going to stop me?"

She shrugs. "We both know I couldn't."

"But she's not going alone," Mandi says, turning us around. "I'm going, too."

The girl looks wide awake and determined, despite having spent the first day and a half on this island unconscious. And despite being a Base. She's a little bit of a square peg in a round hole. She's got the know-how and skills of a Base, but a personality better suited to a Point. But she's small, and not at all physically imposing or athletic. The Unity 'Powers That Be' probably made her a Base with the hopes she could overcome her headstrong personality. Part of her is really good at that, but I can tell she's not thrilled by the role.

"You need to rest," Gwen says.

"The boys," she says, motioning to Daniel and Gizmo, who are still dead to the world in their hammocks, "need to keep working on reaching the outside world. They don't need my help." She points at Gwen. "And you need to keep them safe."

"If anyone is going with her," Gwen says, "it's me. I'm Support."

"And in this case, the best thing you can do is make sure Daniel and Gizmo stay alive long enough to make contact. Your immediate job might be the support of Point, but we need to think long-term now. We need to be strategic. And that's my job. Plus, I have medical training. If someone is hurt, I can help."

"You'll be defenseless," I tell her, not about to give up my knife or gun.

Gwen crosses her arms. "Hey."

"I'll have you," Mandi says to me. "I don't need a weapon."

"You can't complain," I tell her. "About anything."

"Including—"

"Including me."

"Fine."

"Guys," Gwen says. "You can't just decide this without me."

"I think we just did." I pat her on the shoulder and manage to get a hint of a smile out of Mandi. I'm not sure why I care whether or not Mandi likes me, or that she smiles, but I do. Probably guilt over being a jerk to Hutch. Part of me needs forgiveness for that.

"Get one protein bar for us to share," I say to Mandi, "and the two empty water bottles. We'll refill them on the way."

When she hurries off, I do my best to reassure Gwen. "We're going to follow the river. If we find the transport, we'll check out the campfire. If we don't, we'll leave it alone. Come straight back here. Maybe two hours out, an hour to look around and two hours back. We'll be back in time for dinner. Speaking of which..."

She nods. "I'll catch some fish."

"And keep your guard up." I look at Daniel and Gizmo. "Don't let them out of your sight. If you see anyone that isn't us, hide."

Mandi returns with a go-pack over her shoulders. "Set."

"Be safe," Gwen says, surprising me with a hug.

"Be strong," I tell her. I flinch when I realize we've just repeated my mother's secret message to me.

"Ugh," Mandi says, and with that, we head into the jungle, following the path to the river, and then the river down the side of the mountain.

Walking along the river's edge makes for quick and easy travel. Moving downhill helps, too. But compared to trudging through the layers of green growing along the jungle floor, this is simple. And air conditioned. Compared to the sticky wet air trapped under the foliage, the air along the river is at least ten degrees cooler, and thanks to the lack of trees allowing the sun through, much drier.

The only downside is the river's noise. When it's not rushing, it's gurgling. There could be a marching band sneaking up on us, and we wouldn't know it. But the opposite is true, too. No one is going to hear us coming.

And after an hour of silent hiking, even I feel comfortable enough to talk. "You don't have medical training, do you?"

Mandi hops from one water-smoothed rock to another. "I brought Band-Aids."

"Why did you really come?"

She hops again, perching atop a stone after landing on it. "I don't trust you."

The grit beneath my feet grinds to a stop. "You don't trust... What do you think I would do?"

"You mean besides ditch us?" she asks.

"Why would I do that?"

She rolls her eyes like the answer is obvious. "In a situation like this, the easiest way for a Point to survive is to go solo. Support and Base are like pack animals. Safety in numbers. The odds of one of us surviving goes up if we're in a group. But you...you have no reason to stay, and we all know how you treated Hutch."

"I didn't know how things worked. No one told me about Support. Or Base. Nothing. They were just labels without meaning to me."

"Uh-huh."

Mandi's jabs get under my skin with the ease of a mosquito's proboscis. If she'd been clinging to my arm, I might have actually slapped her just the same. But she's keeping a safe distance.

"Listen," I say, "If I wanted to leave, I could have. I could right now, and there would be nothing you could do to stop me."

She leaps off the stone with surprising speed, gets right up close and stares up into my eyes. "You want to put that to the test?"

I'm not remotely impressed or intimidated. The staring contest lasts for five seconds. I end it with, "This is great, I'm stuck on an island with a girl who has short man syndrome."

Her smile comes and goes in a blink, but I saw it.

"Look, as much as you might want to be, you're not a Point. Or Support. That wasn't my call. And if the people who gave us these jobs are any good at theirs, maybe you should just embrace it and see what you can do." I sigh and turn away. "Now let's—"

My hip suddenly feels lighter.

The gun.

When I turn back around I find the weapon pointed at my chest. Mandi has tears in her eyes. She's serious. But I've been here before.

"I'll give you three seconds to kill me," I tell her. "And then I'm taking it back."

I countdown in my head, reach out and put my hand on the top of the handgun. She's still holding it. Still has her finger around the trigger. If I tried to yank it away, it would fire for sure.

"I understand now why you're not a Point," I say. "You don't want to kill anyone. Even if you think they deserve it." I pull the gun and her finger squeezes the trigger. But not far enough. She gasps and yanks her hands away from the weapon.

"Are you nuts?" she says.

I holster the weapon. "Aren't all Points?"

"No," she says. "Not at all!"

"Then it must just be me." I turn my back to her again and climb atop a large, angled stone, like a sacrificial table that's lost its supports on one side. The moment I reach my full height, I drop down onto my hands like I'm about to start doing jump-burpee pushups.

As I crawl back up to the edge of the angled stone, Mandi lies down beside me. "What is it?"

I don't answer. I just slide myself upward and peek over the top of the stone. The jungle ahead of us has a long, straight line carved through it. Rows of trees have been knocked over, all lying down facing away from us. The cleared path leads downhill several hundred feet, angling away from the river. At the far end is a long gray cylinder that looks even more like a school bus when it's on the ground.

"We found it," Mandi whispers, sounding amazed. "You really weren't leaving."

"You really thought I was?"

She has no reply, which is confirmation enough.

"Look at me," I say, and I wait until she does. "That is *not* who I am. I don't leave people I care about. Not ever. Got it?"

"Okay," she says.

I watch her eyes for a moment, until I'm satisfied she believes me, and I believe her. Then I get up and head for the wide path carved through the jungle by a crashing transport labeled with the number 37.

I'm coming, Sig.

We run through the ravaged trail, leaping over fallen trees, climbing over exposed boulders and ducking under suspended piles of debris. I'm surprised when Mandi keeps up with me, but then I remember she's been running the obstacle course at the Unity carrier far longer than I have. And with that thought comes the realization that all that testing and training might have had real world applications. But how could they know we'd find ourselves in a situation like this? Three weeks ago, I couldn't have imagined it.

Fifty feet from the transport, I slow down. "Mandi."

The girl continues past me.

"Mandi!" My shout comes out more as a loud hiss, urgent, but not loud enough to be heard very far past the walls of vegetation surrounding us.

She looks back at me, an argument in her eyes, but then she sees the gun in my hands, and stops. The weapon is currently aimed at the ground. It's not meant as a threat to Mandi. But it's an obvious reminder that we might not be alone here. If there are other people still on this island, this crash site and the campfire this morning, might have attracted the attention of less savory people. We need to be careful.

Mandi waits for me to catch up, and I do something I wouldn't have considered earlier this morning. I unsheathe my knife and hand it to her. It looks big and awkward in her small hands, but she accepts the weapon and holds it out in front of her.

"Just keep the blade pointed away from you," I tell her. "In case you trip."

An eye roll confirms that she's heard me.

The breeze sweeping in from the river behind us shifts, reversing direction for just a moment, but it's enough.

Mandi and I both stop, wincing at the foul, meaty odor.

"What is that?" she asks.

I've never smelled dead people before, but I'm pretty sure that's what is assaulting my nose. Whoever is inside the transport is not only very dead, but they've been baking inside a metal oven warmed by a tropical sun for two days.

"Wait here," I say, and I step forward. We need to do this quickly. I'm focusing equal parts of my attention on the surrounding jungle, on the festering transport and on not barfing from the smell of it. We're vulnerable and distracted.

The transport is right side up, its rear hatch lying open. *Someone got out,* I think. I hope. It could have just as easily been knocked open during the crash. I glance back through the debris field, most of which is ruined jungle, but there are parts of the transport's hull lying about as well. While Transport 36 crashed into shallow water and sand, Transport 37 tumbled through the jungle. Instead of surviving one jarring impact, trapped inside solid foam, the passengers of 37 would have been thrashed about, trapped in an out-of-control centrifuge.

I step around the open hatch, watching the jungle, but not because I'm afraid of attack. I'm afraid to look. I'm going to see dead bodies, that's a given. But unlike the skeletons in the field, these are going to be fresh. Recognizable. And maybe—probably—one of them will be my best friend.

Buzzing flies from inside the open transport confirm the smell's origin. The island is already working hard to reduce the dead to bones. The sound sends a quiver through my body. My teeth vibrate. My stomach lurches. I can *taste* the dead now.

Get it over with, I tell myself. *Just look and get the hell out.*

I hold my breath and turn.

The inside of the long transport is in shadow, but sunlight reflecting off the treeline behind me illuminates the interior with a light green tinge.

I can see everything.

Every detail.

And it's far worse than I imagined.

There are four dead bodies, bloated and still seated, two on either side of the transport. Gaps between them suggest that some people are missing. It could also be that these people were spread out. They could all still be here.

My confusion comes from the dark red mash covering the walls, floor and ceiling of the transport's front half. If not for the bits of things that are recognizably human—bones, clothing, a face—I'm not sure I would have realized they were bodies. The rapid expanding foam system must have failed in the front, revealing what happens to the human body without it. This wasn't a centrifuge, it was a blender.

I stagger back, hand over my mouth, scanning the four visible faces one last time. Sig isn't one of them, but that doesn't mean she isn't in there. The amount of...material...suggests that the human slurry holds more than one body.

"Allo, love."

The loud voice freezes me in place. It's a man. British accent. Something about the tone tells me he is not a kind person.

"Turn 'round. Nice an' slow. Twitch, and she's dead."

She?

Mandi!

I turn slowly, shifting my gun around my leg and behind my back. My heart pounds, its thud muted by the buzzing of gorging flies. Mandi quivers in the man's grasp, his dirty hand wrapped around her mouth, crushing her cheeks. The knife I gave her lies on the ground by her feet. For a blink, my mind descends into blind rage, but the man sees it and says, "Ah, ah, ah. Wouldn't want to put a hole in sweetie's chest."

That's when I see his gun, the barrel pressed against the side of Mandi's ribcage. The weapon looks a lot like mine, but all handguns that aren't revolvers look the same to me. He hasn't told me to drop my weapon. He hasn't seen it. But it's essentially useless anyway. I'd either miss entirely or shoot Mandi myself.

The man gives me a once over, grinning while biting his lower lip. His head is shaved on the sides and a dirty mop on top. The hair might be blond, but it's hard to tell, because it's also full of mud. His shirtless body is also caked in dirt, but I can see tattoos beneath the grime. Tattered red pants that have been torn short are his only real clothing. Even his feet are bare. The man looks savage. Primal.

He gives two quick whistles and calls, "Biscuit!"

A dog emerges from the jungle, though to describe it as a dog doesn't really do it justice. The Irish wolfhound is like a horse with canine teeth. On all fours, it's taller than Mandi. On its hind legs, it would be much taller than me. Its shaggy gray fur looks like the man's hair, and I realize that if it laid down, it would blend in perfectly with the forest floor.

Biscuit doesn't do anything outwardly aggressive. No snarling, growling or lowered ears. But it also doesn't take its pale gray eyes off of me. Not for a second. It is locked on target.

"You're a fit bird for a Point," he says. I'm not sure what that means, but the way he's looking at me when he says it makes me uncomfortable. "Fancy the hair. Not quite regulation, so you must be fresh meat, eh?"

He squints at me, waggling the gun in my direction for a moment. "Why'd they send kids like you to a place like this, I wonder." He shrugs. "S'pose all that matters is that you're here. Thanks to Unity for the early Christmas gifts, right?"

A network of tattoos on the man's arm, the colors dulled by grime, leads to a triangle that started as a symbol for hope, but has become a harbinger of death, violence and betrayal. At some point in the past, this man, who I suspect is no older than twenty, was part of Unity. The orange sides of the Unity brand identify him as a Support.

His head twitches. "Say, what *is* the date, love?"

"December twenty-fifth." I lie, but the man is clearly insane, and the date might distract him. To what end, I have no idea. Anything to keep him talking, maybe let his guard down.

The man freezes in place, his bit lower lip smiling like a Halloween mask. Then he bursts out laughing. The dog doesn't even flinch.

Mandi is crying now, her tears rolling over the man's hand, leaving clean streaks.

"We'll be okay," I tell her, and the man's laughing stops.

"Okay?" He swishes his mouth around like he's sucking on a lollipop. "Nothing is okay anymore. Did you *see* the sky last night? They've come early. Like Christmas! Oh, Christmas tree. Oh, Christmas tree."

The gun against Mandi's ribs points downward while the man sings.

"How lovely are your—" The man's eyes snap toward me before I can lift my gun up and around my back. But he sees the violent intention in my eyes.

"No," he says. "No, no, no. You're no good. Spoiled meat." He sniffs the air. "I can smell you from here. You and your spoiled friends. Not like the others though. They're still fresh. Tasty." His voice shifts, sounding almost childlike. "But those are for Quinlan. He gets them first." He squeezes Mandi's cheeks harder, making her cry out. "Always first!"

He cranes his head from side to side, looking me over again, this time in disgust. "You're trouble, love. I can see it in your eyes. A real Point. No breaking you, is there? You're already broken."

He giggles.

"Don't look so surprised. You're all the same. Bad meat. Tough and bad."

"Please," I say, and I'm ashamed of the quiver in my voice. "We'll come with you. We'll be *your* friends. Not Quinlan's."

I'm desperate. Trying to stall what's coming. The man's intellect is questionable. Probably malleable. Broken by whoever Quinlan is. Turned into this strange creature of a man.

He bites his lip again, laughing a hiss through his teeth. "*My* friends." The leer in his eyes returns. "*My* meat. Ohh, that sounds..." He looks behind him. "The others will know. Bugger. They..." Back to me. "*You...* You see? Cor, blimey, you nearly had me, you did. But I ain't daft, despite appearances to the contrary. And Quinlan, he's *my* Point."

The gun returns to Mandi's ribs. He looks at her with hungry eyes, then to me, and then to the dog, Biscuit. The beast is stoic and silent, waiting. "Points are bad meat. Spoiled, like I said. But Biscuit isn't choosy, are you, mate? And it's a small island. Grub can be tough to come by."

The man whistles three times and shouts, "Din, din."

The dog is suddenly alert. It's ears perk up. Mouth open. Tongue unfurled. Drool dangling.

"Go get 'er!" the man says, and the dog barks so loud and deep that I can feel it in my chest.

What happens next is all instinct. There isn't time for thought. I just act.

I spin with the gun, lifting it.

The man sees it and shouts, "No!"

But it's too late to stop the wolfhound's assault, and my defense.

The dog lunges.

My finger squeezes the trigger.

A loud bang is punctuated by a yelp that seems impossibly high-pitched for an animal this big.

The dog lands in a heap at my feet, its head a bloody mess.

"Biscuit!" the man shrieks, and a second gunshot punches my ears.

And it's my turn to scream. "Mandi!"

A puff of pink bursts from Mandi's chest. The bullet snuck between her ribs, slipped through her body and emerged from the other side. And then she falls, discarded, like meat, by the man now turning his gun toward me.

Instinct propels me sideways.

Had I thought about what I was doing, I probably would have stopped.

I'd also be dead.

The bullet buzzes through the air, slicing the arm of my flight suit and the skin beneath. It stings, but it's nowhere near as unpleasant as where I've landed. I slide across a slick floor, bumping into the foot of a dead boy. Jostled flies burst into the cabin, frantically looking for a new place to land. And eat. And spawn.

My hand slips through clammy sludge, like pudding with lumps, as I push myself up. When I see the congealed blood ooze up between my fingers, my stomach lurches. But a shadow draws my attention. The man is coming.

His voice warbles as he screams. "Biscuit! God, no!"

Two rounds ping off the transport's interior, fired wild. They ricochet and then nestle inside the bodies of two corpses who no longer feel pain. The man walks in front of the open hatch. He's looking at the dog while holding the gun in my direction, firing off shots without looking.

"Biscuit!"

I return fire, squeezing off two shots, and I prove that hitting the dog with one shot was a fluke. Both bullets miss and neither frightens the man away from his mourning.

"Open your eyes, mate!" Six more shots into the cabin and six more misses. Not that he'd even know. He's focused solely on the dog. But he's eventually going to realize that Biscuit can't open his eyes. Then he's going to turn toward me. Going to aim.

Leaning back in the muck, I make myself as small a target as possible, hold the gun in both hands and aim between my feet. If I miss this time, I might punch a hole through my foot.

Don't miss, I think. *Please, don't miss.*

I pull the trigger.

The round finds a target of flesh and blood, but it's not the man. I've shot Biscuit. *Again.*

The man lets out a heart-wrenching wail that manages to make me feel bad for him. He might be a psychotic murderer, maybe even the person responsible for all those dead kids in the field, but he definitely loved that dog. His pain is real, and deep.

My hesitation nearly gets me killed.

"You *bloody trollop!*" The man thrusts his weapon at me and pulls the trigger. The bullet sparks off the metal wall beside my head. He pulls the trigger again, but all it does is click. He's emptied the magazine.

I blink at the sound of the gun clicking empty, fully expecting to be dead. Then I fire again. And again. Pull, pull, pull. A bullet connects with the man's left shoulder and sends him into a clumsy pirouette. I get off one more shot, but miss, as the man falls atop his dog.

My feet slip through gore, scrambling as I try to stand. I run from the transport on unsteady legs, planning to circumvent the wounded, insane man and make for the jungle. But he's not about to let that happen.

Tendrils of drool stretch from his snarling mouth as he heaves air in and out, sounding more ape-like than human. Blood covers the mud and tattoos on his left arm. When he leaps to his feet, pounds his bare chest and screams, "C'mon, then!" I realize he's mistaken my retreat as attack.

And now I have no choice.

Blood and stench chase me out of the transport, fueling my own mania. But I don't lose control. I don't get tunnel vision. While being on the receiving end of a gun unnerves me, I've been looking down the barrels of my own fists for years. The only difference now is that I'll be fighting for my life.

I'm not sure what kind of attack the man is expecting, but it's not what he gets. He's totally caught off-guard when I tackle him around the waist, lift his hundred and sixty-ish pounds and then slam him down on his back. His chest compresses beneath my weight. Air expels as a voiceless wheeze. And then there's a moment of resistance followed by a sudden give, as one of his ribs breaks.

But I've only just begun.

While he sucks in a breath, I get to my knees and launch a fist into his face.

Then another.

I aim for his temple, knowing I possess the strength to end this fight with my next punch.

But my fist sails past his head, as I'm yanked back. The man's feet, wrapped around my neck, slam me to my back. My head lands atop Biscuit's torso, sparing it from an impact with the ground.

Then he's on top of me, straddling my waist and delivering the hardest punch I've ever felt—the kind I normally dole out. And that one hit nearly ends the fight. Through a cloud of spinning lights, I see the wound in his shoulder like a target, and I launch my finger toward it like an arrow. The tip of my finger slips over his bloody skin and pokes the wound. For a moment, I think I've yanked my hand back in revulsion—because:

gross—but the man has sprawl-ed away like he's been struck by lightning.

We stand in unison. Both wounded. Both feeling the anguish of loss and the thirst for vengeance.

"You're a scrapper. I like that." He wipes blood from his eyebrow where one of my punches opened up a gash.

I've got blood on my face, too, but I leave it alone. It will make me slippery.

"I think maybe I'll keep you, after all. Make you my new pet." He cuts the fingers of his right hand in the air like scissors. "Snip off them toes and fingers. Then train you how to be a good pup. Eh?"

His left arm hangs low, not quite useless, but he's definitely avoiding moving it.

"You can try," I say. "But we both know there's a reason I'm Point and you're Support." I don't believe a word of what I say next, but the way he spoke about his Point—Quinlan—makes me think *he* believes it. "It's because you're weak."

He hisses at me, spraying bloody spit. "The military doesn't make people weak."

The military?

"It makes us killers." He lunges, and I'm surprised by his form. He kicks for my head, and when that misses, his other foot comes up in a spin kick. The sole of his bare foot makes a breeze across my face, as I lean back away from it. Before I can fully recover from the dodge, he's spun forward again. A punch follows, striking my shoulder hard enough to shift the bone out of its socket. When it pops back in, a numbing tingling rockets through the limb and into my chest.

He throws a second punch with the same hand. Instead of blocking or dodging the blow, I move inside it. His forearm strikes the side of my head, but I use the energy, adding it to the thrust of my head-butt, which lands on his left shoulder, bludgeoning the bullet wound with a wet slap.

His body arches with pain, leaving him exposed. I kick him hard, between the legs, drawing a howl of pain from his mouth. But the strike also seems to focus him. Adopting my fighting style, he charges forward, absorbing a punch to his head without flinching. He catches me under the ribs and lifts me up. But instead of dropping himself down on top of me, he pumps his arms and tosses me.

I see him wince as I topple away, and I know he didn't jump atop me because he's hurting. Then I land, this time with no dog to cushion my fall. My hip strikes a fallen tree stump, spinning me backwards. I hit the ground with enough force to black out.

Blazing pain brings me back a moment later.

He's stalking toward me, a manic smile sliding onto his face.

Nausea sweeps through me, lolling my head to the side.

Mandi is there, soaked in her own blood. Her little chest rises. And then falls. I look up. Her eyes lock with mine. Then she glances down.

To her feet.

To the knife.

The blade is partially covered by a palm frond, but I can see the handle.

I turn back to face my attacker. His stalking has morphed into a confident strut. He sings, "Fingers and toes. Fingers and toes."

I reach.

He dives, arms outstretched, my throat the target.

I've never killed a person and have negative desire to do so. Maybe that's why I missed with the gun? Even though this guy shot Mandi and is trying to kill me, I still feel bad about trying to kill him. When my fingers wrap around the knife's handle, I find that I lack the will to plunge it into him.

Knowing that I'm going to die if he isn't stopped, I settle on a middle ground.

I pull the knife in over my chest and turn the blade upward.

He sees the weapon too late. He's already airborne, and though he tries to arrest his fall with his arms, his wounded arm provides no support. With a cut-short cry, the man impales himself on the knife and falls still. His dead body weight pushes the knife handle into my chest. With a grunt, I roll him off.

The sky above looks impossibly blue, and for a moment, it's just me and the sky and the fresh memory of killing a man.

Then I hear the raspy breath of Mandi and roll toward her.

The parts of her that aren't red with blood are pale.

Each small breath sounds wet and ragged. A punctured lung. Along with other things.

Her lips move, lifting me past my pain, drawing my closer.

By the time my hand reaches the back of her small head, I'm a mess, barely holding back sobs. I have never known anguish quite like this. It is sharp and deep. All the way to my soul.

I try to speak, to offer some comfort, but the sounds that come from my quivering lips aren't recognizable as any language.

She whispers, but the faint breeze of her words are inaudible against the buzzing backdrop of flies, some of which are already settling in on the man's blood-soaked wounds. I lean in closer, my ears nearly pushed against her lips.

"They're...coming," she says.

I pull my head back and hear them. Footsteps crashing through the jungle. Urgent voices. Men. Not kids.

Her hand tightens around mine, and I see her lips moving again. I lean down and hear two words that break my heart. "I'm...sorry."

"No," I say, pulling back. "Don't say it. Don't ever—"

Mandi's eyes are staring past me, toward the sun, unblinking in its brightness.

"Hey!" someone shouts.

I've been spotted, but the voice is distant. Still in the trees.

I take the time to kiss Mandi's forehead and whisper, "I'm sorry, too," and then I'm up and on my feet, pushing past the worst pain I've felt in my entire wretched life. I crouch over my fallen enemy and pull the knife from his chest. Then I recover my gun, and I'm chased into the jungle by angry voices and the men—*the killers*—to whom they belong.

Tear-blurred eyes obscure my view of the world around me. I'm like a boulder, rolling downhill, crashing through every unseen obstacle, letting gravity guide me. Despite hitting every low branch on the way down, and stumbling over rocks and brush, I stay ahead of the men behind me. Maybe I'm out-pacing them, or maybe they're just being cautious after seeing their dead friend.

I think the most likely scenario is that this slope will eventually end at the ocean. I could swim for it, but we're in the South Pacific. How long would it take for a shark to spot me? They can smell a drop of blood from what, a mile away? And I'm covered in the stuff. Might as well ring the dinner bell.

I crush my eyes tight for a moment, squeezing the tears away. I can't escape if I can't see. But I also can't stop thinking about Mandi's face. About how her eyes shifted from life to death. I've seen violence in my life. And I've known death. But I've never witnessed it before.

Mandi had an edge about her that made me want to smack her, but mostly because she reminded me of...well, me. A better me, who is now dead, because of me.

I shouldn't have shot the dog.

If I were dead, she would still be alive.

As a prisoner.

A slave.

Maybe worse.

The man *did* threaten to cut off my fingers and toes and turn me into a replacement dog.

My mind is a whirl of contradictions, none of which will help me survive. And I owe Mandi at least that much. To live. To help her friends survive.

The men behind me fall silent. I don't think they've given up. They're just no longer talking. They're focused. Moving in for the kill.

I need to change things up.

With my eyes clear, I reach out and catch a palm trunk, using it to shift my course ninety degrees to the right, moving parallel to the beach, which isn't far off now. I can hear the crashing waves filtering through the trees.

And then I hear a crunch behind me. One of the men has just turned after me, the sudden movement giving his position away. But how far back? I don't dare look.

Where is the second man? I wonder, and then I get my answer in a blur of motion. He's coming in from the right, barreling down the hill so fast that he looks almost out of control. In that fraction of a glimpse, as the man flickers between trees, I take stock of him.

He's short. Maybe my height. Maybe even my age. And skinny. Malnourished. And I wonder if by 'meat,' Mandi's killer was being literal. Maybe these men really are cannibals? He's dressed in torn pants, but he looks clean. Unlike the first man, this one has a sense of hygiene. He's also tattoo-less, except for the triangle on his hand—a triangle with a blue bottom.

A Base.

And that tells me everything I really need to know. He might have been out here for years. Hunting, killing, eating people. He's become a savage but he's pretending. Like Daniel and Gizmo and Mandi—who was caught completely unaware by the man with the dog—this guy lacks the instincts that make a Point dangerous. He lacks all the qualities that have been instilled in me throughout my life. He's a prop sword facing off with a blade hardened and tempered in a fiery forge. When I turn toward him, instead of away, and meet his eyes, I see that I'm right.

He doesn't back down. He's motivated by something he fears more than a beaten and bleeding girl. But he's gone tunnel vision. He's no longer thinking.

His friend on the other hand... "Duff! Use your gun!" The voice is at least fifty feet back, too far to use his own gun effectively while both of us are running.

Rather than helping, the command just confuses Duff. What would have been a tackle, turns into a stumbling grasp for his weapon. When he reaches me, all he has to do is dive and we would both roll down the hill. It would have been over. But he's still several feet higher up the grade and fumbling for his weapon when we collide. And it's not him hitting me; it's me hitting him. His legs sweep out from under him as my shoulder collides with his thigh. The impact jars my wounded shoulder, drawing a cry of pain, but it doesn't help Duff. Newton's First Law of Motion is on full display. An object in motion tends to remain in motion until acted on by an external force.

Duff is the object.

I'm the external force.

He somersaults onto his back with a cough.

The impact and pain slow me, but don't stop me. Nor does it slow the second man, who is now gaining on me.

"Get up, idiot!" the man shouts, revealing his position. *Much* closer. I think he would eventually catch me, even if I wasn't injured, even if I hadn't collided with Duff.

They're going to catch me.

I'm nearing the edge of exhaustion. I was almost there when this chase began. But stopping to fight is a bad idea. If Duff has a gun, I'm sure his pal does, too, and my only weapons are an empty handgun and a knife. If I stop and turn around, it will be to stare down my killer for a moment before he puts a bullet between my eyes.

Mix things up, I think. Rabbits evading wolves don't run in a straight line. They confuse the wolf.

But I'm *the wolf,* I think, feeling angry at having to run at all. *A wolf pretending to be a rabbit,* I decide, and I turn left, dropping down over a four-foot ledge. The move sends jolts of pain through my core, but I manage it without slowing.

Feet slap the ground behind me a moment later, but the sound is followed by a grunt. If my pursuer is a former Unity member, like the others, I don't think he's a Point. If he was, I'd probably already be dead.

In my mind, I'm running the obstacle course again, safe on the Unity cruiser, being watched by a cadre of adults with clipboards and stopwatches. Leap the tree. Climb the rocks. The jungle is a slalom. Back and forth, up and down. Behind me, I hear grunts of pain, whispered curses and clumsy progress. There is nothing stealthy about the man now, as he just tries to keep up.

And then he gives up running and sends his bullets to chase me instead.

The first four shots make me flinch. I duck while I run, putting my hands behind my head, like that will help. I'll just end up with a hole in my hand *and* my head.

The fifth shot makes me scream.

A hot iron has been thrust through my side. It spins me around, crossing my legs and tripping me. The ground beneath me is thick with soil, but the cushion is a ruse. I land on a tangle of roots, the hard limbs grinding into me. For a moment, I'm blinded by agony, and then, somehow, I'm up and running again.

"Oh, c'mon," the man behind me grumbles, sounding exhausted. Definitely not a Point. I've been beat up, shot twice and watched a new friend die, and I've *still* got more drive than this guy. I'm also leaving a trail of blood that will be easy to follow. It oozes between my fingers, which are covering the hole in my front, and flows freely out the back. He must see that, too, because when I look back, he's just watching me, hands on his knees, a smile on his face. And a Support brand on his right hand.

"You can stop," he says. "And I won't kill you."

I watch him as I back away.

"You're going to die from that," he says. Before this guy, who looks too young to drink, turned into a savage, he would have been handsome. His accent is slightly Portuguese, which is spoken in several countries from Portugal to Mozambique, but his skin tone, which is similar to mine, says Brazil. "We're not like Mack. Probably good that you killed him."

When I just eye him and continue backing away, catching my breath, he says, "Fine," and raises the gun.

I dodge to the side, running behind a tree, which takes the bullet for me.

Then I'm off and running again, spurting blood like a fountain.

How far can I get like this?

Not far, I decide when my vision blurs.

I'm going to die.

The hillside ahead becomes a cliff, stretching a hundred feet up. With a wall of stone to the right, and the ocean just a hundred feet to the left, the only direction I can go is straight. And that's not going to save me. Because nothing can save me.

I stumble along the cliff's base, sliding one hand along the cool gray stone, propping myself up. Gulping air doesn't help. So I stop. I draw the knife from its sheath, the handle still tacky with Mack's blood, and I turn to face my pursuers. If they run around the bend, maybe I can get one of them. It's more likely that I'll be shot again, but that might be better than being caught. I doubt Mack was the only one of them with a questionable moral compass. The hole in my side agrees.

But the voice that makes me flinch doesn't come from in front of me. Or from behind.

It comes from above.

"Hey."

I flinch and swing the knife in an upward arc, narrowly missing the hand that had been reaching down for me.

"Effie! It's me!" The voice sounds familiar, but it's muffled by my fading consciousness. *How much blood have I lost?*

Too much.

And then I hear it. Those words. They break through my chest, grab my heart and squeeze. "Take my hand. I got you."

I. Got. You.

Feeling something between relief and horror, I turn my head up and look at the bruised face of Hutch. The boy whose life I made miserable for the last three weeks, because I misunderstood his constant presence. The boy whose sister I just watched die. Whose life might have ended because of my impulsive instincts.

"Hutch," I shake my head like he's just asked me something. "You're safer without me."

He looks in the direction from which I came. I don't know if he can see the men chasing me, but he seems to know they're there.

Gunshots, stupid. Of course he knows.

"I won't leave you," he says and lowers his hand again. The hand is stamped with an orange-sided triangle. He won't leave me. Of this there is no doubt.

Voices wash over me. Duff is being chastised. They don't seem to be in a hurry. They're following my blood, expecting to find a corpse at the end of its trail.

"Hold on," I say, and I hobble further along the cliff.

Hutch hisses something at me, but I ignore him. A pool of blood at the cliff's edge will reveal our hiding spot. I take a few steps into the jungle and flick the congealing blood from my hand deeper into the foliage, creating a false path. Then I work my way back.

Hutch's hand waits for me. "Good thinking."

We lock hands, and I'm surprised by his strength, which dwarfs Gwen's. When I'm half way up, he says, "Put your feet against the stone and walk up."

I'm confused for a moment, dizziness returning. Then I realize what he's telling me. My false trail won't do much good if I smear myself up the cliff's edge. My legs shake with each upward step, but Hutch does most of the work.

When I reach the top, I see a rockslide that has become overgrown and what looks like a small cave.

Behind me, the voices grow clearer.

They're going to see me.

I'm yanked hard away from the cliff. Hutch catches me, and we drop together. I nearly cry out in pain, but the hand clasped over my mouth and nose keeps the air locked in my lungs.

"You hear that?" Duff asks. His voice is just below us. "Luiz, did you—"

There's a slap of flesh on flesh. "Shut up!"

"Geez, man," Duff says, and I can picture him rubbing the slap out of his arm or cheek.

"She's going to get away. Quinlan will—"

"First of all, she's bleeding out." Luiz doesn't sound as confident as he's trying to sound. "Second, Quinlan doesn't need to know."

"But Mack is dead. He'll—"

"Mack was an animal," Luiz says. "No one will miss him. We can always say one of the three we already have killed him. But this one won't make it far. Look. Over here. Blood goes back into the jungle."

Hutch's hand slowly comes away from my face. He looks down at me, lying in his lap. His eyes look so much like Mandi's, but kinder. Hopeful, despite the situation. Loyal puppy eyes, brown, like over-milked coffee. He holds a stone in his hand. Shows it to me. I nod, and he tosses the rock straight out into the jungle. It strikes a tree trunk and thuds to the ground.

"There!" Duff says. His voice is followed by a crash of foliage. They're pursuing a ghost now, which might be accurate soon enough.

The view of Hutch above me blurs. I can feel him moving, shifting my weight off his lap. The hard cliff ledge beneath my head. His hands around my wrists. My shoulders scream out as he drags me through a curtain of green tendrils. There's a flicker of light and then nothing.

The nothing ends with an awareness that time has passed. How much, I don't know, but I'm no longer being dragged, and the darkness has turned green.

I'm leaned against the wall. The chill against my back tells me I'm shirtless before I look down. The top half of my flight suit has been peeled away. A human banana. Looking down at my exposed bra, I feel a flash of anger. Then I see the stitches in my abdomen. The skin is clean. No trace of blood remains. I gingerly feel the wound's entry point on the side of my back. It prickles with stitches. There's a bandage on my shoulder where Mack's bullet grazed me.

A face emerges from the dark, luminous green in the light of a glowstick. I lean back from it, but Hutch's soothing voice puts me at ease.

"Just me." He holds up a bandage and a roll of medical tape. "Almost done."

I stay silent as he works. He bites off pieces of tape and secures a bandage over the exit wound, then apologizes as he turns me and does the same to the entry wound. "Went straight through," he says, leaning back and looking me over. Had I not learned the nature of a Support from Gwen, I'd think he was checking me out, but I think he's just inspecting his handiwork. *Or both,* I think when our eyes meet and he gives me a sheepish grin.

"I'm not going to die?" I ask, embarrassed by how desperate I sound.

"Love handles bleed a lot when there's a hole in them, but they're not exactly a vital organ."

I raise an eyebrow at him. "'Love handles?'"

"Minimal," he says, his embarrassment eclipsing my own. "I think you have just the right amount of body fa—err, you know what I mean."

When I smile at him, he looks dubious.

"What?" I ask.

"You smiled."

"So?"

"I've never seen you smile."

The last month of memories flash back. Before landing on this island, the last time I smiled was on the transport ride to the Unity cruiser, which I made with Sig. After pondering whether or not we'd share a bunk, she said, "After all, we are besties." She even threw in a little valley girl accent. Five minutes later, we landed and were separated.

But I've smiled since crash landing and nearly dying several times. "Surviving hell can change a person."

He rifles through one of three go-packs arranged along the cave wall. "Yeah..." I barely hear him as he stares blankly at the cave wall, like he's seeing something that isn't there. Then he pulls out a black T-shirt and hands it to me. Helps me put it on when I can't lift my arms up high enough.

"What happened to you?" I ask, partially because I'm interested, partially because I'm terrified he's going to ask me.

"We went down in the ocean," he says. "Did you make it to the island?"

Don't ask! "Yeah."

He settles into a cross-legged sit, the glowstick lying on the floor between us. "Eight of us survived the crash." He stares past me. "We were a hundred feet from shore. An easy swim. Opened the hatch. Sven—a Point, like you—led us into the water as a group. Go-packs are good floatation devices, so no one had any trouble."

He doesn't need to say what happened next. I remember it. "Then the wave."

Hutch nods. "One minute we're swimming, the next we were pulled out deeper. Separated. In the dark. It was impossible to see anyone, and then..." He raises his hand like he's scooping up water. "It was like being lifted up off the planet. For a moment, I felt nearer to the stars. And then I dropped. I had the go-pack strapped to my chest. It pulled me up every time I went under. And then, there was land beneath my feet. I spent the next day on the beach, in and out of consciousness." He motions to his cheek, which is marred by a few sunburn boils. "I found two more go-packs on the beach, but no one else. No bodies. This morning I caught fish. Made a fire."

"That was *you?*"

"Why? What's wrong?"

I nearly shout at him. Nearly tell him that his fire drew those men toward the shore. That his stupid fire got Mandi killed and three others—maybe Sig—captured before we got there.

But I don't. How could he know this island is populated by killers? Why would he ever suspect Unity would send us someplace like that?

"The fire is how I found you," I explain. "And it's how *they* found you."

"Who are they?" he asks. "Why were they trying to kill you?"

"I don't know who they are," I tell him. "But I know *what* they are."

He waits.

"We found eight skeletons yesterday." He blinks at the word, 'we', but says nothing. "All murdered. Most of them shot. I'm pretty sure they were killed by the men we saw. They're Unity. Or at least used to be. The two chasing me were a Base and Support."

"They weren't *acting* like it."

No, really?

"I think their leader is a Point named Quinlan. Mean anything to you?"

He shakes his head slowly. "Why would Unity send us here? To a place like this?"

I frown.

When I do, he asks, "You know?"

So I tell him. About the campsite. About the recording. Even about my mother. While Gwen has become my right-hand woman, Hutch is technically *my* Support. And now that he's alive and with me, Gwen will let him fill that role. And I understand now that his job is to support me, physically, emotionally and psychologically. If we're going to survive this, I need to tell him everything.

Except that.

I can't tell him about his sister.

Not yet.

And it's not because I think he's not strong enough to handle it. It's because I don't think I am.

When I'm done with my story, he just watches me for a moment and then pushes himself up onto his feet. The cave is a good thirty feet tall and nearly as wide. The rough stone is angled at a slight slope, descending into darkness beyond the glowstick's illumination. He bends and picks up the chemical light. "Can you walk?"

"I'd rather not," I say.

"I think you'll want to." He reaches his hand down. "I got—"

"I know, I know. You got me." I take his hand and let him pull me up.

"Finally figured out what we're all about?" he asks.

"Gwen helped."

"Glad to hear she made it." He smiles, and I see a twinkle in his eyes. For some reason, it makes me a little jealous.

"She's one of the best," he says, and I wonder if I mistook admiration for affection.

"So..." I lean against the wall, feeling dizzy. "I'm down a few pints of blood. Show me what you want to show me and let's be on our way."

"On our way?"

"I need to be back at the campsite before nightfall, and—" I stop when his eyes widen a bit. "What time is it?"

He looks at his watch. It's an old fashioned wind-up. The kind that wouldn't be affected by an EMP. "Eight. The sun will be down soon."

I want to punch something, but my anger is muted by pain. The best I can manage is a sigh. "I told the others I would be back." I don't even mention finding the three people captured from Transport 37. Even *I* know I'm in no shape to mount some kind of rescue effort.

"First thing in the morning," he says. "Right now, you need to eat, drink and sleep, or you'll never get those missing pints back. And I doubt they'd leave the campsite tonight. Sounds like a prime setup."

"Nothing about this island is prime," I argue, and I motion toward the awaiting darkness. I don't bother mentioning that the campsite itself is a concern. What if Quinlan knows it's there? What if he's already taken the others? Voicing all this wouldn't do any good, so I contain it.

He leads me by the hand, helping me navigate the jagged floor. The dull green light is enough to see by, but the shadows are deep. Every few feet further, the temperature drops a little. It feels great. But it smells off. Faintly like oil. Something mechanical.

Hutch stops and looks back at me. "Ready?"

I flash the Point symbol on my hand. "Born ready, apparently."

He tosses the glowstick out in front of us. For a moment, I'm annoyed that he's plunged us into darkness. Why not walk right up to whatever it is he wanted to show me? Then I see it, and understand.

It's too *big* to see up close.

I don't even have to work hard to not whisper an expletive. The giant hand filling the end of the cave has robbed my lucidity. I manage an, "uhh," and then stagger into Hutch's arms, overcome by a sudden weakness.

I look at the fingers, each curled over a bit, each the size of...of a what? It's like someone built a white, double-sized Statue of Liberty, hacked off one of its hands and buried it at the end of the cave. But the joints aren't solid. It looks like it could have once been a functional robotic hand. Judging by the cables and shredded metal extending out of the severed wrist, it was clearly attached to something else at some point.

But what?

"Do you know what this is?" I ask.

Hutch shakes his head. "I've never seen anything like it."

POINT

I'm dressed in a large, shaggy dog skin, its skull resting atop my head, the canines embedded in the skin above my eyes. Rivulets of blood mask my face. Mandi lies beneath me, shouting, "I'm sorry," while I slowly lower a knife toward her chest. Her flight suit provides a moment of resistance, but then the blade slips forward, plunging into—

I wake with a scream.

The cave wall warbles in front of me, the light strange and alive.

Then Hutch is there, worried and attendant. "You're okay," he says. "It was just another dream."

I cough, and grunt and try to sit up. My butt and back are killing me. "Another?"

"You've been talking all night."

My empty stomach sours. "I was?"

What did I say?

I nearly ask, but I'm too afraid.

Hutch, on the other hand, sits down in front of me and dives right in. "Distraction can be dangerous."

"Okay..."

"If one of three fragments is discordant," he says, and I'm pretty sure he's quoting now, "Unity cannot be achieved. Base, Support and Point. Mind, Soul and Body. Three in one. A body without a mind, will die. A mind without a soul, will rot. And a soul without a body, lose its way."

As he speaks, my skepticism fades. On one hand, it feels cultish. On the other, true and poetic, which I suppose is the nature of the best lies. Or the truth. "What does it mean?"

"For you and me..." He leans forward and takes my hand. When his warm fingers wrap around my palm, I realize how cold I am. Goosebumps run up my arms, radiating from his touch. "...it means there cannot be anything between us. No filter. No lies. No words left unsaid. I cannot support you if I don't know where you need it. And if you do not...accept me..."

"You'll find a Point who will."

A slight nod. "It's the only way that Unity works."

"What does that even mean? Why is 'unity' so important? And who decided it required three people?"

He lets go of my hands and leans back, smiling. "I'm not entirely sure, but I've seen it work. When a

Base, Support and Point work together as a unit, there isn't much they can't do. But if we're talking about the end goal of all this training, I really don't know. But I believe it is good."

"Even when you're stuck with someone like me? Someone told me that they paired you, the best, with me, the worst, to buoy me. Like no one else could handle me, but you."

His chuckle fades quickly. His smile inverts. "That sounds like her."

Like *her. Like Mandi.*

We stare at each other. Too long. He knows. But what does he know? The ramblings of a nightmare-filled sleep, most of which include *me* killing Mandi. *Oh God, is that what he thinks?*

And now I understand the lecture. *No filter. No lies. No words left unsaid.* He was prepping me for this moment. It would be easier if he asked me straight out. And by 'it,' I mean lying, because the framework of his question would reveal what he already knows, or figured out, or hoped. But this... I can only assume that he believes the worst. That I sleep-confessed to the nightmare of killing Mandi.

"Mandi is dead." The words blurt out of me. I cup a hand over my mouth, ashamed by the merciless way in which I delivered the news.

His eyes are glassy, but he doesn't show any big reaction. He already knew it, or at least guessed. I notice the red rings around his eyes for the first time.

He looks exhausted. While I was dreaming about Mandi's passing, he was mourning it.

"How?"

"She survived the crash," I say, and he nods. "Gwen, Daniel and Gizmo, too. The five of us found the camp."

"And?"

"She came with me yesterday. We were looking for Transport 37. And your campfire." He doesn't need to say 'and' again. I can see the urgency in his eyes. "We found the transport. It was...most of them didn't survive the crash. That's when the man—Mack—found us."

"One of those two from yesterday?"

I shake my head. "Mack was...worse. He took Mandi hostage. Sent his dog to kill me, and when I...I..." Uncommon tears sting my eyes. My chest heaves, but it's reined in by the pain of stretching stitches. "I killed his dog, and he killed Mandi. He shot her."

After a painful silence, he asks. "How did you survive?"

I draw the knife from the sheath on my belt. The dry blood tells the story. "He's dead."

When I look back up, Hutch is crying, eyes locked on mine.

"She...she said she was sorry," I say. "But she's dead because of me."

When I sob, he leans forward, wraps an arm around my back and places his head against mine.

Aside from Sig, I have never experienced this kind of affection during my life. It unhinges me. I weep openly, letting this boy, who I worked so hard to ignore, see the pain I keep hidden from the world. "It wasn't your fault. And if she apologized to you, it means she cared about you. That's a rare gift."

"She hated me," I say.

He leans back to look me in the eyes again. "She admired you. Your strength. She was upset about being a Base, because she wanted to be like you. Strong. Independent. Immune to the words of others."

I'm not totally immune to words, because Hutch's are like a bandage on my soul. I point to my wet face. "I'm not as tough as she thought."

"Well, *I* knew that," he says, getting me to smile. He sits back. "See? We're stronger when there is nothing between us. Nothing hidden. Nothing dulled."

While I do feel better—even some pain has faded—I'm not about to admit it. My emotional walls are ancient and thick, and though he found a tunnel through, the little people that live in my head are already working hard to patch it.

He pushes himself up with a grunt. "Well, then, we should go."

Go? The concept of moving feels foreign, like climbing Mount Everest, far away and impossible without more time. To heal. To get stronger.

Seeing my reluctance, he says, "How long will the others wait before assuming the worst? How long will it be before Quinlan and his people find them? And how long will the people captured from Transport 37 survive?"

How does he seem to know me so well already?

I grunt and try to stand, and there is his hand, waiting to lift me up again. He doesn't say the words this time. Doesn't need to.

He has me.

Once I'm on my feet again, he says, "I have something for you," and he picks up one of the three go-packs. Then he opens it and pulls out a handgun identical to mine. "This one is loaded. You carry this, I'll handle the rest."

I want to argue the point, but when I slip the loaded pistol into the holster on my hip, its weight is almost too much. He shows me the metal Point badge I'd been wearing, embedded in foam next to another, probably meant for Sven, whose go-pack washed up on the beach. The last thing we do is cut off the top of my flight suit, converting it into pants. Here in the cave, the T-shirt I'm wearing feels chilly, but outside, the short sleeves and thinner material will be a relief.

Thirty minutes after climbing down from the cave with the giant robotic hand hidden in its depths, I regret leaving the flight suit top behind. Thick clouds form as though conjured by a wizard. Then they unleash a torrent. The flight suits are waterproof. The T-shirt, not so much. But the rain does quench my thirst.

Before falling asleep, I consumed most of the water and rations Hutch had. At his insistence. I fell asleep with a full belly, but I'm already feeling hungry, and with every step forward and upward, weary. But he prods me. With words. With his touch. Eventually, with his very presence, striding with determination and three go-packs, despite his own obvious pains. He reminds me of Gwen, and that memory helps me keep up.

I try to distract myself from the pain, but most everything that enters my mind is stressful. The crash. Transport 37. Mandi. My mother. So I focus on the giant hand, but that mystery is so complete, I can't think of anything beyond a litany of questions. Why is it here? Where did it come from? What was it a part of? The list goes on endlessly, once again leading me back to the angry frustration and confusion that is putting knots in my back, so the pain there matches everywhere else.

The rain stops like a fountain that's suddenly lost pressure. Twenty minutes later, the water soaking my shirt has evaporated to be replaced by my more fragrant sweat. The sun is directly overhead now, filtered by the canopy, but blazing hot where it shines through. I pause in one of the light beams, turning my face skyward, catching my breath.

"How much further?" Hutch asks.

The sun turns my closed eyelids pink. "Won't know until we find a clearing, so I can see the cliff." I can still hear the river off to my right, so I know we're heading the right way. But injured, burdened and walking uphill, we're making slow time compared to my journey with Mandi on the way down. "Few more hours, I'd guess."

He sighs, showing signs of true exhaustion for the first time.

A squeak of a voice tickles my ears.

"What?"

Hutch and I speak the word at the same time, looking at each other.

"That wasn't you?" he asks.

I search the forest around us. "No." I consider drawing my handgun, but decide not to expel that energy until I know I have to.

"Are there monkeys on this island?"

I don't think so, but I say nothing. I just listen.

And then I hear it again.

Someone is crying.

Someone small.

The sound is coming from my left, away from the river, away from the others. But a cry so gentle, so fragile, can only come from one kind of human being: a kid. Gizmo, Daniel, Sig, or someone else. There's no way to know who it is.

But I know what needs to be done.

Drawing my weapon, I head for the sound. Without a word, Hutch puts one go-pack over his shoulders, cinches it tight and places the others on the ground. Then he follows me, clutching Mack's empty handgun like it's loaded. We stalk through the woods, adrenaline working hard against my wounds, letting me focus. We reach the edge of a clearing, crouched low behind a stand of ferns.

That's when I see them. Four men—four *savages*—and three kids tied to a tree.

One of them, the girl crying, is Sig.

I recognize two of them. Duff sits atop a fallen tree, elbows on knees, eyes to the ground. Looks sad. Luiz is on his feet, animated, telling the story of my death—the girl with the bright orange-tipped hair. And that's what must have got Sig crying. She's tied up against a tree, arms and legs bound like she's about to be sacrificed to a dragon.

When I think about what little I know of Quinlan, I wonder if the analogy is very far from the truth. She looks bruised a bit. Dirty. But mostly unharmed. The way she stares at Luiz, eyes glistening, reveals she's very aware.

Seeing her like this, helpless and bound, at the mercy of brutes, fills me with a new kind of anger. I'm used to raging at the world in response to wrongs done to me, real or imagined, but this... I can watch the news and feel revolt at things happening around the world. Unjust wars. Terrorism. Geno-cide. These things make me angry, like they do any non-sociopath with a beating heart. But I'm also distant from those things. I don't take action. Don't even think about it.

This is different. Someone is going to hurt for this. Probably me, but I won't be alone.

The two Unity students tied up to trees beside Sig look familiar, but I don't know their names. The first is a freckled boy, red hair, maybe fourteen, hand branded with a Support symbol. The other is older, a very pretty girl with American Indian features and a Base brand. She's the oldest Base I've seen yet. She also looks out of it. Traumatized.

The two new men are opposites. One is short and a little chubby. Like Duff, he's a Base. The second is all muscles. Head shaved unevenly, probably by a knife, maybe by the machete sheathed on his shirtless back. His hand is branded with a Point.

Great.

"Man," Luiz says. "Mother load. Sucks that I had to pop that hot chica, but—"

"What is chica?" the chubby man asks, his accent Russian.

"A chick. A babe."

I have never, not once, ever thought of myself in these terms, nor has anyone back in the civilized world. These guys have definitely been on this island too long.

"Still have *her.*" The Russian hitches his thumb to the American Indian Base. She shows no reaction to their attention. "Even if she is vegetable."

"Exactly," Luiz says. "Quinlan is going to be—"

The Point turns his back to the others, arms crossed. For a moment, he's looking right toward us, but then he rolls his eyes. "Quinlan. He's not everything you think he is."

"Shut up, Berg," Luiz snaps. "Talking like that could get you dead."

"If he didn't have the ExoFrame, he'd..." The man named Berg lifts his head. Sniffs the air like a dog. "Someone stinks."

"We *all* stink," Duff mumbles.

"Someone else." Berg turns toward us again, looking past us, to the jungle. "Up there."

It's not until that very moment I realize there's a cool breeze on my back, rolling down the hillside, catching my stink and carrying it into the camp. That Berg can smell it isn't just impressive, it seems damn near impossible.

But then I smell it, too...and it's not me.

"Pack it up," Berg says, and I'm surprised when the four men, instead of heading off into the woods and hunting us out, start to gather their gear. They look nervous.

And it's not because of me.

I'm a ghost.

So who, or what, are they afraid of?

Doesn't matter, I decide, when they cut Sig and the others free from the trees. The kids' hands are still bound in front of them, but their legs are free.

"Hurry up," Luiz says, shoving Sig hard. She stumbles forward, trips on a root and falls over. The savage man puts a knee on her back, grabs a fist full of her straight, black hair and lifts her head. "You can do this awake and on your feet, or over my shoulder and knocked out cold."

And that's all I can take.

I look back at Hutch, and he gives a nod.

There's something in the way he backs up my resolve with his own, no questions asked, no doubts raised, that bolsters me.

Gun raised at the nameless Point, I step into the clearing, "No one move!"

And no one does. Not really. Not after turning around and seeing me and Hutch, weapons raised.

Sig's eyes go wide, and I'm afraid she'll say my name, revealing our relationship and her value to me. But she doesn't. She just watches me, eyebrows turning up in worry, but not for herself. She's afraid for me now.

The Point lets his head sag back, his mouth lolling open. He groans and looks at Luiz. "She doesn't look dead."

"Told you," Duff grumbles. "She's a Point."

"Is she now?" the Point asks, and he glares at me. "Last I heard, Points were military men, and you don't look like either." He glances from me to Hutch. "You're both kids." He motions to Sig. "Like them. Unity must be desperate. Digging through the dregs. Recruiting babies to do their killing."

Killing?

"But you don't have it in you, do you?"

Luiz raises a finger and says, "Uhh." No doubt he's about to clarify the story of Mack's fate and my part in it. But I decide to beat him to the punchline and squeeze the trigger.

The gun kicks hard in my hand, but not nearly as hard as the bullet that catches the Russian—who is standing clear of the captured Unity group—in the chest. He folds in on himself and crumples to the ground.

Holy...what did I just do? Something inside me breaks a little bit, but I file the emotions away for later.

The other three men flinch back.

Duff drops to his knees, shaking hands over his head. It happens so fast that it almost seems rehearsed. "Don't shoot! God, don't shoot!"

I now have their undivided attention.

"Let them go," I say, and I'm pleased when all three captured kids are released. Sig gives me a worried look, but walks behind me. The boy Support takes the mind-numbed Base and leads her toward me.

"You going to kill us all?" Berg asks.

That's a good question, because the Russian's body is starting to make me feel like puking. Killing

Mack was self-defense. Killing the Russian...what was it? Revenge? Anger? Do I have the heart of a murderer, like these men? Is that what makes me a Point? A willingness to pull the trigger?

"Effie." It's Hutch, whispering, trying to not be heard by the men, if that's what they are. Duff barely looks older than me. *Man enough to shoot,* I think, and then I wince. *Who am I becoming?*

"He's a Point," Hutch says, eyes leveled over the top of his unloaded gun, words directed at me. "We can't just tie him up to a tree." I don't have to ask him to clarify. That question goes without saying. He'll be free inside an hour.

And the rest of Hutch's logic doesn't need to be explained. If we let Berg go, or even subdue him, we'll never make it back to camp. He'll track us, and the next confrontation will be on his terms. All of this boils down to a simple concept: if Berg lives, we die.

But it's not that easy. Killing the first man was instinct. I did it without thought. To save Sig. But I've had time to digest that horror, and I understand the effect it will have on the rest of my life.

But is letting Berg live any different than pointing a gun at Sig's head and pulling the trigger? Just because he's not pointing a gun at me, doesn't mean killing Berg isn't self-defense.

It's pre-emptive self-defense.

And gentle Hutch supports it. But that's easy for him. He's not the one who has to pull the trigger.

But then he does, and the gun coughs a bullet. The loud report makes me duck, and that simple reaction saves my life. A black throwing knife sails over my head, its blade driving into a tree trunk at the same height as my heart.

Berg dives and rolls to the side as Hutch fires two more rounds, each missing the mark. Berg's aim is much better. He flings another knife, this one striking Hutch's hand, knocking the gun away.

I raise my weapon again. There will be no hesitation now. But I never get the chance to fire it. I'm kicked in the stomach by Luiz. The gun falls from my hand when I hit the ground. Hutch tries to punch him, but the man is too fast, ducking back, catching Hutch's overextended arm and using his momentum to throw him. The fight lasts just seconds, and it ends with Hutch and me on our backs, defeated.

Luiz, looking frenzied and angry, stalks over to the fallen Russian and takes an ax from his belt. He struts back to me. "This time, you're going to stay dead, bi—"

The insult is cut short by an arrow in his throat. He clutches the wound and falls to his knees, gagging.

I hear a crash of vegetation to my left. It's all that's left of Berg. He's bugged out, leaving just Duff, still on his knees, to face whoever fired that arrow.

Please let it be Gwen, channeling her outdoorsy past.

The man who steps out of the clearing's far side is definitely not Gwen. Like the other savages, he's dressed only in torn pants. His hair is shaved on the sides and long on top, pulled back in a tight ponytail. He's got an arrow nocked in a homemade bow, aimed at the trees where Berg fled. He glances at me, at Hutch, Sig and the others, but never points the weapon at us. He doesn't even aim it at Duff, who hasn't left his submissive position on the ground. He carries a variety of blades, but no guns. He's also ripped. Not weightlifter buff, but a healthy kind of strong. Balanced. Probably the way men looked before gluttony became normal and robots took over manual labor. But it's his face and skin that hold my attention. He looks a little like my father.

The man stops over Duff, never lowering his guard. "Duff."

The frail Base looks up, relief flooding his face. "Vegas. Thank, God."

"You going to leave him now?" the newcomer named Vegas asks, his Spanish accent thickening as he gets upset.

"He'll find me," Duff says. "He'll *kill* me."

"Probably will anyway," Vegas says. "The question is, how do you want to die? As Los Diablos? Or Los Perseverantes?"

As one of 'The Devils.' Or 'The Persevering.'

"I just want to live, man," Duff says.

"Then go," Vegas says. "And when you're ready to come home...you'll be welcome."

Duff nods, climbs to his shaky legs and runs away. Vegas lets him leave.

I turn around to Sig and envelope her in a hug. She's stiff for a moment, but then leans into me. I feel a sob building in my chest. Tears threaten to reveal my weakness. This small person is the most important force for good that has ever been a part of my life. I kiss the top of her head and lean back.

"I knew you'd come," she says, and when she sees my quizzical expression, she adds, "Because you were alive."

"How did you know that?"

"I would have felt it," she says, "if you had died."

I'm not sure what to say. I've heard stories about people feeling that a loved one has died before actually being told, but I always wrote them off as superstition. But at the same time, I have believed, against all odds, that Sig still lived. And here she is. Maybe she's right? Maybe we're connected on some kind of spiritual level? I'd like to think so. It would be a hint of something more, of some life beyond the physical.

Of hope.

I bend to pick up my gun, but I'm stopped by a command. "Wait."

My fingers are on the handle. It would take just a second to pick it up, turn it toward him and pull the trigger, but I'm pretty sure he'd put an arrow in me before I got my fingers around it.

"Who are you?" he asks.

Our group responds with silence.

"Why are you here?"

If there were crickets on this island, this is the point when you'd hear them, comically filling the void.

"Why did you shoot Bear?"

Bear? Ahh, the Russian. Kind of a stereotypical nickname, but none of the natives strike me as creative types. There are no paintings happening on this island. No limericks. No Kumbaya, after all. Just killing and surviving. And now we're part of that cycle.

My response is simple. I turn my hand, the one reaching for the gun, so he can see the brand.

I'm a Point, I think, *same as you.* I have no doubt that in the same situation, he would have done the same. Only he didn't. He let Duff live. They're on opposing sides, but still friends. Maybe Bear was his friend, too?

Before my concern can register on my face, there's a pop and a fizzle of sound that retreats skyward. It's Luiz, not quite dead yet, hand lifted to the sky, holding an orange gun. The flare's red glow, arching up over the jungle, is easy to see.

An arrow pierces Luiz's chest, ending his life.

When I look back up to Vegas, he's sliding the bow over his shoulder. "Get your gear. We need to leave. Now."

"We're not—"

He backs away, holding out his hands in a way that says, 'my hands are clean if you stay.' "If he finds you, there's nothing you or I can do to stop him."

I'm about to argue that we have two guns—two loaded guns, thanks for telling me Hutch—but then I remember they didn't help against Berg, and I doubt they'd help against Vegas.

"Him, who?" I ask. "Quinlan?"

He turns around, heading for the jungle. "You can hang around and find out for yourself." He glances back. "But I think Gwen would prefer it if you came with me."

The first thirty minutes of our hike pass in hurried silence, each person following this Vegas guy through the jungle toward a glimmer of hope. But for all I know, he's got Gwen rotating over a spit and is going to lock us up in whatever cannibals use for a pantry. That's not the vibe I get from him, though. If it was, I'd shoot him—or try to. Still, I'm not about to let my guard down.

Problem is, my body is not complying with the wishes of my mind. The wound in my left side has stayed together. Hutch did a good job sewing it up. But the meat and muscle inside is still shredded and swollen. Hutch has tried to support my weight a few times, but I've shrugged him off. At first I'm not sure why, because I could really use the help. When Vegas looks back at us, waiting for us to catch up, and I stiffen and put on a brave face, then move a little faster, I realize I'm trying to impress him.

Maybe because he's a bona fide alpha male stud.

Maybe because he's a seasoned Point and I'm a newbie.

Either way, the realization makes me a little disgusted.

I don't need to impress you, I think at Vegas's back, but I also don't ask Hutch for help. I'm starting to hobble like an old crone. The kind that lives in a gingerbread house, or gives poisoned apples to pretty people.

Sig stops and waits for me, falling in line beside me when I catch up. Hutch brings up the rear of our little parade. The few times I've looked back at him, I've expected him to be watching me. Maybe even checking me out. But his eyes are on the jungle. Watching. Protecting. Always thinking of others. And here I am, dwelling on the woes of my physical pain, and the stranger who might eat us.

Sig looks me up and down and says, "You've changed."

"Getting shot does that."

"You killed that man," she says, not talking about my physical appearance.

The image of Bear collapsing, his life stolen by my hand, flashes through my thoughts. I squeeze my eyes, like it will help, and I focus on Sig, alive, well and judgmental. "I've killed two men."

We walk in silence for a moment, and then, "Why?"

"The first man..." I look back at Hutch. He's a good fifteen feet back, gun in hand, walking backward as he watches the jungle for danger. I lower my voice. "The first man killed Mandi and tried to kill me." I don't mention the dog. For some reason, I think she'd think even less of me for killing a dog, even if it was a hellhound intent on gnawing my bones to dust.

"Oh..." The news strikes a chord.

She doesn't ask about Bear, but I feel like I owe her an explanation. "The second man, I needed them to believe I would do it. That I would kill them if they didn't let you go."

"You would, right?" She looks up at me with her big green eyes. Sig was born in the United States, but her parents are Armenian immigrants. She has the slightest of accents, olive skin and a delicate face, but it's those innocent eyes that really set her apart. "Kill them to save me?"

"I would," I say.

She takes my hand and squeezes. "Thanks."

Her affection nearly breaks through my emotional defenses, but then I see Vegas waiting. He motions for the American Indian girl, who has yet to speak a word, and Sean—aka: Freckles—the Support who's doing a good job keeping the American Indian girl moving, to keep going. As they pass, he snaps his fingers and points to Hutch at the back. "Take the lead. Straight up the hill."

Hutch says nothing, but looks at me. I give the slightest of nods, thinking, *you don't need my permission, dude.* If codependence is part of the Point-Support relationship, we are definitely going to make some changes to the program.

Vegas looks at Sig and motions his head toward the others. "You, too."

"There are no secrets between us," Sig argues. Her defiance surprises me. Makes me proud. I'm not the only one who has changed.

"That's good," Vegas says, and I'm pretty sure he means it, "but you still need to go."

"She's just going to tell me what you say when you're done," Sig says.

There is a trace of impatience in Vegas's voice, but he's keeping his cool for a savage. "As expected."

"It's okay," I tell her. "Go ahead."

Sig sighs, but trudges ahead. She has short legs and a shorter stride. I normally have to walk slow so she can keep up. But she has no trouble pulling ahead of my hobbling gait.

Suddenly uncomfortable at being alone with this strange man, I fill the momentary silence with a question. "So... Bear. Duff. Mack. Berg. That's a lot of four letter nicknames. Vegas is one letter too long."

"It's also not a nickname," he says, sounding conversational. I was expecting a grunt. "My parents got married in Vegas and conceived me that same night. My father was from Los Angeles, my mother was from—"

"Puerto Rico?" I guess, still seeing hints of my own father in him.

Now he grunts. "Everyone says that. My mother was *Mexican*." He eyes me. "But *you're* Puerto Rican."

"Half," I say. "I'm a mutt, like you."

"Mutt would be a good four-letter nickname."

I can't hide my hint of a smile. "I already have a nickname."

He waits for me to reveal it, but I say nothing. Then he holds his hand in front of me, unfurling his fingers to reveal two white pills. "I've been saving them. Looks like you could use them." When he sees my suspicious eyes, he adds. "Painkillers. They'll last twelve hours and won't make you loopy."

I take the pills and swallow them dry.

He smiles and holds up a canteen, sloshing it around. "You don't need to play the action hero all the time."

I take the canteen, drink until my expanding stomach flexes against the bullet wound. Had the bullet been two inches further to the side, the water would be leaking right out of my stomach.

When I hand the canteen back, he says, "Still getting used to this?"

"You mean surviving on a deserted island with cannibals?"

"No one is going to eat you," he says. "Not even Los Diablos."

The Devils. "You come up with that name?"

"And Los Perseverantes. Reminds me of home." He holds aside a low hanging branch, letting me pass. "I was talking about being a Point."

"Oh. Yeah."

"You're what, sixteen?"

Good guess. "And you're like twenty-five, right?"

He smiles and his teeth are too perfect for a caveman. "Eighteen. Was seventeen when we got here."

So they've been here for a year. Just twelve months and they've already gone *Lord of the Flies*? Seems kind of fast.

"Any military training?"

"No."

He shakes his head. "No offense, but why is a sixteen-year-old girl with no military training and hair bright enough to attract the enemy from miles away, a Point?"

"That's a question I think we'd both like answered." I glance at his muscular arm. The black tattoo on his shoulder is a winged skull over a combat knife with the words, *Death Before Dishonor*. "So you were in the military?"

"Unofficially," he says. "My father, a general, nominated me. Unity accepted me when I was fourteen. Completed Army Ranger training three months before being dropped off here. They wanted us young and elite. They made us killers and then left us." He shakes his head. "What did they think was going to happen?"

The question is clearly rhetorical, which I'm not a fan of, so I make it a legit question. "What *did* happen?"

"Quinlan," he says. "He believed we were being used. That we were brainwashed slaves. Part of a military cult. He was paranoid, but he was also charismatic and convincing. We fell in line. Erased ourselves. Lived underground. Destroyed the cameras, during storms, so it looked natural. Masked our bodies from the infra-red sensors. When Unity came back a month later, there wasn't even a footprint to reveal our presence. They searched for a week and then left. I can only assume they believed we all died, which was our intent."

"But that's not where he stopped," I guess.

"Not even close." Vegas waits for me to stumble my way through a maze of roots. He doesn't offer any help, and for a moment, I wish he was Hutch or Gwen. "Paranoia feeds on itself. Inside a month he was convinced that some of us were still working for Unity. Still in communication. When he killed a Base, my friend, the group split. Eighteen with him. Twelve with me."

"The Devils and The Persevering." *Like gang names.*

"Yeah." He pauses for a moment, cocking his head to the side, listening, sniffing the air. Then he's back to normal. "Unity left us on the island with four ExoFrames. Not the kind available to the public, or even used by the military. We'd never seen anything like them, but we figured them out pretty quick. They make the wearer stronger, faster, far more deadly and virtually impervious to harm. Before we could arm ourselves, Quinlan used an ExoFrame to destroy the others and take most of the weapons. On that first day, he killed eight of us."

"There are only four of you left?" Not much of a gang.

"Three," he says, but then he adds, "Well, now eleven. Like it or not, your people are either with us, or dead. And there's a good chance you being with us isn't going to help anyway, since you're all..." He hesitates, looking at me.

I can see him wondering if I'm going to be offended, but I already know what he's going to say, and I agree with him. "Kids."

"Exactly."

"I think," I say, forming this opinion even as I speak, "that when all of you G.I. Joes failed, Unity decided to take a different approach." I motion to the four kids trudging uphill in front of us. "They're not just kids. They're brilliant. They might not be the toughest, or brave, or even capable of violence, but their strength is up here." I tap my head. Then my chest over my heart. "And in here."

"And what about you?" he asks. "Are you like them?"

"I'm...something else."

"I noticed," he says with a smile. His attention makes my hands sweat. I wipe them on my hips. "But it still doesn't make sense..."

I stop in my tracks. "Wait, you know why they're doing this, don't you? What all of this is for? That guy, Mack, knew, too."

His eyebrows raise. "You met Mack? And you're still alive?"

"I am. He's not. Now tell me, what is all of this about? Unity. The testing. The training. Point, Support, Base."

"You really don't know?"

"I've been with the program for three weeks."

He actually flinches at this news. "Three weeks." He motions to the others. "And them?"

"Some as long. Some longer. A year at the most."

His head is shaking like a perpetual motion machine. No sign of slowing down.

He stops when I say, "But Gwen already told you most of this, didn't she?"

His facial expression flattens. Busted. "I had to make sure she was telling the truth. Again, no offense, but you all being here, and Unity thinking a bunch of smart kids can replace us—"

"The people who went native and killed each other?" I interject.

"Fair point. But it doesn't add up. They're not fighters."

They're. He left me out of the observation, and I take it as a compliment.

"So what are they training us to fight?" I ask.

He looks me in the eyes, and for a moment, I see hidden depths. Then he turns his head up, looking at the sky. "Them."

I look up, expecting to see attack helicopters, or parachuting commandos or even pterodactyls. "All I see is blue sky."

"Higher," Vegas says.

I can only see a small portion of the sky, through a wavering window of thick leaves, but there is nothing visible between me and...oh, hell. "Military training *and* a sense of humor."

When he says nothing, I turn toward him. He's not smiling.

Not joking.

I look back up at the sky. "Huh."

"Huh?" he says. "Really? That's it?"

"I've got a few choice words locked and loaded, but I'm trying to cut back." I notice that the others are getting too far ahead, and I start moving again. I don't need a view of the blue sky to imagine the impossible. And instead of getting colorful, I find myself getting scientific. "The Drake Equation, written in 1961, which estimates the number of intelligent extraterrestrial civilizations that exist in our galaxy based on known data, predicts that, at *best,* there are a hundred and fifty alien species out there as smart, or smarter, than us. At worst, there are zero. Let's meet in the middle and say there are seventy five intelligent species in our galaxy."

"Okay," he says, listening carefully while walking beside me.

"The nearest star to us is Alpha Centauri. It's four point three seven light years away. That's twenty-five point eight *trillion* miles. That's a lot of empty space. Most of them would still be trapped within the confines of their own solar system. Like us. And to achieve some kind of interstellar travel—light speed, wormholes, whatever—a species would have to be incredibly advanced. I mean thousands of years ahead of us. Probably hundreds of thousands of years. Even if they could send some kind of craft to Earth, there is no way for anything biological to survive a light-speed journey. And anything slower than that would require countless generations of travel, without accident, upheaval or evolution, all with a single-minded ambition to reach a planet whose resources are abundant in the universe."

"But not in the unique combination that makes a planet habitable."

"We've now discovered nearly two thousand Earth-like planets," I say.

"What happened to seventy five?"

"That's intelligent civilizations, and the odds of life beginning at all, even on Earth, are effectively zero. Point is, life is rare. Maybe even one-of-a-kind rare. And interstellar travel is all but impossible."

"And yet people like Stephen Hawking said that if we encountered alien life, it would likely be hostile."

I slow to look at him. "You're not as dumb as you look."

"And you're a lot more like them—" He motions to the others. "—than you'd like to admit."

Thank you, Captain Intuitive.

He smiles again—smiles too often for someone who has been living here for a year. Then he gets serious. "If life is as rare as you say, you could also argue that it is valuable."

There's no fault in his logic.

"You could say that."

"And if other natural elements are as common as you say, they would be less valuable. So life might be the most valuable thing in the universe, which makes Earth a good place to visit."

"Assuming that a civilization is advanced enough—" I hold up an index finger. "—to detect us. And don't say radio waves, because they degrade over distance and become indistinguishable from background noise after a few light years."

"So alien civilizations at Alpha Centauri aren't watching Hitler at the Olympics?"

I smile, not because of the Hitler reference, but because it's nice to meet someone who knows something about history.

"Let's put it this way," he says, "if the human race were *hypothetically* capable of interstellar travel and we discovered life on another planet, what would we do?"

I hate hypothetical questions. You might as well start with, 'This will never happen, but...'

The answer to the question is easy, though, and it has nothing to do with technology or physics. "We would go there and conquer it. Two points for Stephen Hawking."

"What do you know about the Mars colony?" he asks.

"A lot," I say, "So why don't you jump to the point." I wasn't always interested in space. I have Sig to thank for that. But I've spent the last two years dreaming of other worlds, to escape my own. The escape was always a fantasy, though. The human race will be extinct long before the solar system makes one complete revolution around the Milky Way, never mind developing the technology that would allow us to leave it.

"Give me the basics," he says.

"In 2023, the Genesis colony landed on Mars, in the basin of the Jezero crater. It was a one-way trip, so no one expected to ever see them again, but no one ever thought we'd lose contact after a month. The Genesis rover transmitted data about soil composition and water content. It looked for evidence of microbial life for a few days after the colony went silent, but then a malfunction shut it—"

"Wrong."

His sudden intrusion jolts me, and I have to fight the urge to slug him. Few things annoy me more than being interrupted. "Which part?"

"The Genesis rover is still operational." He says this with such a serious tone that I know he's not joking. And he believes what he's saying. "Always has been. They just don't want anyone to know what it found."

"And the colonists?"

"Dead. There were redundancies on top of redundancies for communication, including the rover itself. If they were alive, we'd have heard from them, just like we still are from the rover."

"And you know this how?"

"My father."

The general. Riiight.

"So what did they find?"

He shrugs. "No idea. But Unity was formed a month later."

"By a group of wealthy—"

"Governments," he says, interrupting again. "The U.S. Japan. The EU. Even Russia and China. My father signed me up. We were the first recruits. Training started normal enough. Basic. Hand-to-hand combat. Weapons. Firearms. Then it got advanced. Points trained with ExoFrames. The advanced kind, with psy-controls. They're—"

"I know what they are," I say.

"Then you also know that not even active military units use them yet." He takes hold of a dead branch in our path, snaps it, and waits for me to go through. "Supports learned how to pilot. Again, with psy-controls. And Bases... I don't understand even half of what Duff told me."

"You realize that it's hard to take someone nicknamed Duff seriously, right?"

"It's an ironic nickname," he says. "He's at least as smart as you, so maybe you have a point."

When I laugh, my humor is quickly squelched by mental self-flagellation. *This isn't high school,* I tell myself. Even in high school, I didn't react to guys the way I am to Vegas. Of course, guys in Brook Meadow weren't shirtless beefcakes, either.

"Try not to judge them all too harshly," he says. "Fear can even make strong men like Berg do things they don't want to. A handful of them, like Mack, are hardliners. They thrive off the conflict. Will probably turn on each other if they get to us. But the rest will fall in line the moment Quinlan is dead."

Was Bear one of the nice bad guys, or a hardliner? I wonder, but don't ask. I don't want to know. After clearing my mind, I remember Gwen's question about flight simulator training, and Daniel's comment about psy-controls. In my three weeks, I never saw a hint of these things, but Gwen and Daniel have already confirmed what he's telling me.

"So how does this conspiracy theory end?" I ask.

"I think you know," he says. "Unity was formed as the first stage in creating some kind of—"

"Earth Defense Force?" I say, laying on the sarcasm. *It's not nice being interrupted, is it?*

But he doesn't seem to notice. "I was going to say, Space Marine Corps, but that works, too."

"Both are horrible," I point out.

"Which is why they named it Unity," he says. "No one would suspect its true purpose was to fight aliens." Another smile. "There really is no way to say that without sounding nuts, is there?"

"Nope."

"Look," he says, "I can tell you think I'm yanking your chain, so I'll just ask one more question."

"Shoot."

"Have you not seen the sky for the past two nights?"

The words sink through me, heavy and uncomfortable. Of course I saw what happened in the sky. How could I miss it? "The EMP nearly killed us," I say. "Do you know what it was?"

"All I know is that something fell, slowly, from the sky. From *above* the sky. And what we saw last night..."

"The satellites."

"There aren't that many satellites in orbit," he says, and I realize he's right. We hadn't considered anything else, because what else could it be?

"When I joined Unity, there were thousands of recruits around the world. They would be on active duty by now. We would have been, too, if we hadn't hidden. If not for Quinlan." I hear a tinge of shame in his voice. He looks up at the sliver of sky above us. "I think that was them up there. The other recruits. I think they were fighting a war. I think they shot down whatever it was that crashed in the ocean. I think Stephen Hawking was right, and if you're right about the technological advancement required to travel to Earth from somewhere else, I think we're probably screwed." He stops and looks at me. "How's the pain?"

The sudden shift in conversation confounds me. What is he talking about? What pain? And I nearly ask the question aloud before remembering that just a few minutes ago, I was moving with all the grace and speed of someone's great grandmother. And now, I feel... "Better."

Then I get angry. "Wait, this whole conversation was just to distract me from the pain?"

His answer is cut short by a warbling bird call. His whole body goes tense. The bow is off his shoulder, and an arrow is out of the quiver hanging from his hip faster than I can sneeze. He hasn't said a word, but tension floods the jungle with enough force to stop the others, now thirty feet ahead of us. Hutch looks back, slowly drawing his pistol. I do the same.

Then Vegas cups his hand to his mouth and lets out a bird call reply.

The third call is followed by a rapid shuffling of leaves. A young man emerges, camouflaged with jungle detritus that blends in with his dark skin. He's out of breath, heaving for air as he stops in front of Vegas, who has lowered the bow.

"Slow down, Ghost," Vegas says. He sounds calm, but his body is still tense, ready to spring into action. "What's happening?"

"He's coming." Ghost takes another deep breath. "Twenty minutes, tops." His accent is subtle, but South African, I think.

"Is he alone?"

Ghost shakes his head.

"*Who* is coming?" I ask, and Ghost's eyes, which are nearly the only part of him that are identifiable as something other than jungle, whip toward me, like he's seeing me for the first time. "Los Diablos."

"Quinlan," Vegas says, and he takes my arm. He shoves me toward the others and shouts, "Move! We don't have much time to get ready."

"Ready for what?" Hutch asks.

"Odds are," Vegas says, and proves that he still follows Unity's rule of total transparency with your team, which doesn't make me feel any better about the conversation we just finished, "Ready to die."

The pain pills Vegas gave me have their limits. By the time we leave the thick jungle behind and enter a clearing, a dull throb emanates from my side with every hurried step. Despite there being fewer trees here, the sun is still mostly blocked. I glance up and see palm leaves, bound together and suspended in the gaps between the trees. From above, this would look like just another patch of endless canopy. But from below...it's an open space.

Well, not completely open. Ahead of us is a wooden wall that stretches from one side of the clearing to the other. The top of the wall is covered in wooden spikes. It ends, on both sides, at nearly vertical stone walls. They've built their fort, or whatever this is, in a bottleneck. I understand the strategy, it's how the Spartans at Thermopylae held off the Persian Empire, but as we get closer and I see the wall of stone rising up behind the camp, it also looks like a dead end. The Spartans, along with the Thespians and Thebans, who pop culture likes to forget, held off the Persians for two days. But they all still died.

Vegas sees me eyeing the thirty-foot-long structure. "It's mostly a visual deterrent."

"I hope it has a back door," I say.

"That might be up to your friends."

Before I can ask what that means, a small wooden door swings open and Gwen bounds out with a hop in her step. "Doli!" She embraces the American Indian girl first. I'm glad to see her return the hug, lifting her arms. It's the first sign of lucidity she's shown, aside from putting one foot in front of the other. Freckles is next. Gwen claps him on the shoulders in a parental way. The embrace between Hutch and Gwen is much different. It's casual. It lingers. Hutch's back sags a bit, his tension easing. Then she moves on to Sig, picking up the skinny girl off the ground, swinging her from side to side and whispering in her ear. It's nice to see Sig with other people. Then Sig is back on her feet and Gwen is smiling at me as she approaches.

Gwen gives Vegas a quick up and down glance—who wouldn't?—and then she's reaching for me, arms open for an embrace. "You look like crap."

But before Gwen can hug me, she looks at Ghost as he enters the clearing behind us, and stops. She leans to the side, looking around me, the happy reunion melting away. "Where is Mandi?"

When she looks back at me, the answer to her question is found in my quivering lip. I try to control it, but lack the strength. "I'm sorry," I say.

Her hand takes mine. Squeezes. She looks me over. "You fought back. You survived." She's trying to be strong for me. To ease my pain, by squelching her own.

"Hutch is here, now," I say. "You don't have to carry my burden."

"We're *friends,*" she tells me. "Burdens are shared."

And then I'm in her arms, feeling loved, and then extreme pain.

She lets me go when I grunt, holding my arms. "You're even worse than you look."

"Shot," I say through gritting teeth. "Twice. Once in my arm."

Her hands snap away. "Sorry." Her concern is short-lived, replaced by somber curiosity. "Does Hutch know?"

I nod, but my eyes remain locked on the ground.

"How did it happen?"

I wish I could tell her it was an accident. That it was another tsunami. Or a rockslide. Or something we could blame on a higher power. I would like to spare her the hate that I feel. But I can't. "One of them. A Diablo."

Her eyebrows rise and then pinch down, slipping quickly from surprise to anger. She turns to Vegas, who is watching the jungle leading into the valley, about to unleash her anger toward him.

"Gwen," I say, before she can vent. "The man who killed Mandi is dead."

Her mouth closes with the smooth pacing of an automatic car door. She turns back to me, looking me over, taking stock of my condition with new eyes. "You didn't..."

I nod. "I killed him."

She sucks in a tight breath and undergoes a series of rapid fire emotions that are hard to follow, but she stops with a raised chin and eyes locked on mine. "Good."

"We need to go," Ghost says. He's like living camouflage, but I can see the fear in his eyes. "We don't have much time."

Confusion overrides Gwen's pride, or whatever it is she was just feeling. "What's happening?"

"Los Diablos are on their way here," Vegas says.

"They know where this place is?" Gwen sounds astonished. She's clearly comfortable around both Ghost and Vegas, but she's still catching up. So am I.

"They helped build it." Ghost points at the faux jungle canopy. "It's how we hid from the satellites, where we would have stood our ground if Unity came for us. When we didn't need it anymore, when we...split, Quinlan left with the others. They're living on the mountain somewhere. We haven't gone looking."

A distant, but loud hooting, like a flock of agitated geese, rolls out of the jungle opposite the wooden barricade.

"We're out of time," Vegas says. He takes Gwen's arm and hurries her toward the fort.

For a moment, I'm confused. They've known each other for what, a day? And he's more concerned for her than he is for the person with a hole in her gut? Then I realize he's using the logic of a Point. Ghost has been a part of this struggle all along. He can clearly take care of himself. And me? I'm a Point. Wounded or not, my job is to stand and fight.

Of course, it's not the fighting I have a problem with, it's the standing.

Vegas snaps his fingers at our group and points at the open gate. "Inside. All of you." No one looks happy about being ordered around, but there is no denying the situation's urgency. Gwen leads them inside, but Sig lingers by the entrance, watching me, fidgeting. After being captured, tied up and who knows what else, she can't be feeling very comfortable. *I'm coming, Sig,* I think, trying to quicken my pace and ignore the pain fighting to usurp the meds.

Vegas stops me before I reach her, speaking low. "How many of your people can fight?"

"I just met most of them."

"Guess," he says.

"Hutch and Gwen will fight," I say, "but I don't know if either of them *can* fight." There's a big difference between the two, and he knows it. There are plenty of people willing to throw a punch, but most of them can't land a punch, and even fewer can take a punch. I've done all three. "Freckles, I have no idea. Doli is in la-la land. Daniel, Gizmo and Sig? Not a chance."

He nods at this. "Daniel and Gizmo are already working on the hatch."

"The hatch?"

"The back door."

I look up at him. There isn't a trace of humor in his eyes. This isn't two warriors joking around, laughing about the hopelessness of their situation and bonding before battle. "And what are they working on? Exactly?"

"There are four armored doors on the island, all of them leading into the mountain. Each has a keypad lock."

"And they're still working?"

"The keypad is still lit, so the system must be hardened against EMPs." He looks to the jungle when the hooting gets louder. The sound is still distant, but they're definitely heading this way, trying to rattle us with their noise. "We've been trying to open the hatches for eight months. Nothing has worked. Not even the ExoFrame can get through."

"Which is why you want to get it open now," I say. "If we can close that door behind us—"

"Quinlan can't touch us," he says.

I look to Sig, now just inside the gate, eyeing the trees. "Sig can help them. If it's a numbers problem, she'll figure it out."

"Ghost!" Vegas says, and the young man, now dressed in just tattered shorts, appears in the doorway. His Support brand is visible on his hand, and there are streaks of white on his cheeks, like war paint. He's armed with a long knife and a homemade spear. "Take Sig to the hatch."

Sig holds on to the side of the gate. "Effie?"

I step up to her and lean down. "It's okay, Sig. These guys are our friends. They want to keep us safe." She nods, but hardly looks convinced. "There is a door that we need to get open. Gizmo and Daniel are—"

Her eyes brighten. "Daniel?"

A small part of my brain goes, *What the heck was that? Is Sig interested in Daniel?* But the rest of me stays on task. "He needs your help getting the door open."

She thinks it over for just a moment and then nods. "'kay."

I motion to Ghost, who is already backing away. "Go with him. We'll catch up." I'm not sure that's true, but what else can I say? 'Go with him. We'll just be here being brutally murdered'?

When Sig disappears into the small camp, which looks like a collection of ramshackle huts built around tree trunks, Gwen and Hutch return. They're armed with spears. Hutch lowers a large sheet of metal that looks like part of a robot's torso, but has been turned into a kind of shield. He pulls the pistol from his waist and holds it out to Vegas. "Think you'll do better with this."

Vegas takes the weapon, pops the magazine out with one hand, checks to make sure it's loaded, slaps it back in and chambers a round. The whole process takes him about two seconds. "Thanks."

A crunch spins Vegas around, the weapon raised. He tracks a shadow slipping in and out of the trees, but lowers the weapon when the runner emerges. The scantily clad newcomer, who has gone full native, wearing something that looks like a loin cloth, is slender, wiry and unreal fast. Every subtle movement causes the muscles under his tan skin to twitch. With his blond hair and athletic abilities, he looks more like a stereotypical high school football star.

"What's the score, Twig?" Vegas asks.

"Not good," Twig says, as he gives our small band a glance. One quick breath and he's fine. Speed and endurance. I note the Support brand and wish it were a Point. We could use more people like Vegas. It's not that Twig and Ghost seem incapable, but being a Point, I know the rest of them will be looking at me to step up. To be like Vegas. I'm not sure that's possible. Not only do I lack the years of training and physical prowess, but I've also got a hole in my gut.

Vegas herds us inside the gate, but doesn't close it. "ETA?"

Twig doesn't answer.

Doesn't need to.

A war cry erupts from the jungle, growing louder and closer. I can see them winding through the trees.

Vegas and I take up positions on either side of the open gate. Hutch and Gwen are behind me. Twig lingers behind Vegas. I don't see Freckles or Doli anywhere, so I assume they're back at the door, trying to get it open.

"So," I say to Vegas. "What's the plan?"

He offers a smile that is both charming and unsettling. Part of him is looking forward to this fight, like some kind of ancient Viking, yearning for Valhalla. "What do you know about the Battle of Thermopylae?"

Ahh, crap.

"I thought you said there were eighteen?" I ask after counting the number of our enemy and coming up with ten. They're hovering at the edge of the jungle, five of them hunkered down and waiting, the other fighters still hooting. Manic and eager. Those must be the hardliners Vegas told me about, the ones loyal to Quinlan and on board with the violence. The other five, who surprisingly include the Point, Berg, look like they would rather be someplace else.

And they're not alone. I might be a Point, but that doesn't mean I'm a violence-loving sociopath. I'm comfortable slugging someone, not fighting a battle, and certainly not being killed.

"You killed Mack," he reminds me. "And Bear."

I see Gwen out of the corner of my eye, looking at me with something like shock and pride. Am

I becoming who she'd hoped I'd be? Did she *want* me to be a killer? Or is she just feeling hopeful about our dismal odds?

"You got Luiz," I say, remembering the arrow and the flare that started this newest chapter of hell. "That leaves fifteen."

"I'm not sure how doing basic math helps us," Twig complains.

Vegas and I ignore him. We're in some kind of simpatico zone.

"Quinlan isn't with them," Vegas says. "So that leaves four missing. They could be dead. Natural causes or infighting."

"And none of them are the hardliners, right? They wouldn't be the right choice for an ambush."

His nod is so subtle I nearly miss it. He's watching the jungle, trying to peer through its shadowy veil. "They're waiting for Quinlan."

Quinlan... The man with some kind of advanced military ExoFrame, who rules Los Diablos through fear and violence, bending even fellow Points to his will. But not Vegas. Not Ghost or Twig. I can't imagine how hard it was to not fall in line. To watch all those people die and still resist. It's a kind of strength and fortitude I doubt I have, but to which I can at least aspire.

"Is he normally late to the party?" I ask.

Vegas frowns. "No."

"Which means?"

"We're in tr—"

Branches crack above and behind us. It's followed by a thud that shakes the ground beneath my feet. The bound palm ceiling crumbles and falls, a halo of dried leaves fluttering around a massive body, slowly standing upright after dropping down... *From how high?* I glance up and see a cliff, a hundred feet up.

The ExoFrame is lit by a beam of sunlight stabbing down through the hole in the faux canopy. Floating dust and debris give the light a solid looking form. The perfect circle surrounding Quinlan is like a stage spotlight. Very dramatic. Almost comical.

But the ExoFrame itself is a macabre technological wonder. I've seen normal ExoFrames, the kind used by outdoor adventure junkies looking to climb Everest in an afternoon, and the ones used by the military. But you can still see the people wearing them. The frames are just that—frames. They bear weight, add strength and make humans...well, superhuman.

This...is worse.

Quinlan, if it even is Quinlan, is hidden completely from view, contained inside a mechanized suit of armor that looks more like a full-on robot than a man. The armored plates look like they were once white. Now they are covered in dirt and what looks like blood stains, all hiding a pattern of small octagons covering every inch of the thing. It has powerful looking arms and legs, spiked at the elbows and knees. The barrel chest and thick, armored shoulders look like they could deflect missiles. And the head... It's stylish and frightening, like a robot ninja, a glowing red slit where there should be eyes. I don't see any weapons, but that doesn't mean it doesn't have any—or even needs any.

"Aim for the eyes," Vegas says, and starts firing.

The eyes? I don't think our bullets will get through, nor do I think Quinlan's eyes are actually behind the red strip. But maybe if we break it, or score it, he won't be able to see. And that would be something.

I'm far from a marksman, but I look over the barrel toward Quinlan's robotic face and start squeezing the trigger.

Sparks fly from the unflinching metal head. If there is any legitimate fear that our attack could damage the ExoFrame, he's not showing it.

The slide on Vegas's gun snaps back, revealing he has spent his limited ammo. "Empty," he says, dropping the weapon and drawing a machete.

A machete...against the equivalent of a humanoid tank.

I fire off one last shot and say, "I'm out!" I lower the weapon, but don't drop it.

"The joints are the only weak points," Vegas says to the group, who are armed with simple blades at best and wooden spears at worst. I saw a movie once, where these knights attacked a fire breathing dragon with swords. They all died. This seems even more hopeless.

The hooting from the jungle grows quiet. They can sense our doom, too. They want to enjoy the show. But Quinlan doesn't attack. He looks us over, one by one, his mechanical head whirring as it rotates.

The front of his robot face pops out and lifts up, revealing the man beneath. He's got a full, shaggy beard that's so full of gunk and debris it looks like a bird has been nesting in it. His white skin is covered in dirt and flaking dried blood.

When was the last time this guy washed himself? I wonder, and then I think maybe he never even takes the suit off. With friends like his, he must have trust issues. Probably has to run to the far side of the island to take a leak.

But what stands out most about him is his light blue eyes, like a wolf's, gleaming with energy. With hunger.

"Momma hen laid some eggs," Quinlan says, and he sounds just as crazy as Mack did, but his accent is Australian.

These guys were recruited from around the world. Unity has been a global force from the start, which makes me wonder about Vegas's global defense theory. It's ludicrous, but why else would a secret military be formed, recruiting from an array of nations, some of which are historically at odds?

Twig tenses, spear in hand, ready to throw it at Quinlan's face, but even if his aim is good enough, he'll never throw *fast* enough.

Quinlan's eyes linger on me, and then turn to Gwen. "You won't mind if I collect a few, right, mate?"

Vegas doesn't take the bait, though I can't really tell if Quinlan is trying to goad Vegas into attacking or if he's being serious. And if he is, does Vegas's silence mean he's considering the offer?

"Your living conditions are bodgy, at best." Quinlan motions toward the shabby looking huts with his big arms. I assume 'bodgy' isn't a good thing. "Seriously, you live like a bunch of wombats. And you can keep living like wombats, if I leave with the sheila here." He points at me. "And this chicky babe." He points at Gwen. "And I heard you had an honest-to-goodness American Indian. Good onya, mate, but I'll be needing her, too. You can keep the rest."

When none of us move, he smiles. Then he's ogling me again, looking at my hand. At the Point brand. "Found yourself a queen, Vegas? Bet he didn't tell you about his colorful past, did he? We were tight. Like brothers, for a time. It's why he's still breathing. Why I'm trying to be polite."

Vegas is unreadable. A statue. Everything Quinlan is saying could be true, or it could be a lie. And I'm not sure it matters either way—I have my own collection of skeleton-filled closets—as long as Vegas doesn't agree.

"I'm a murderer," Quinlan confesses, catching me off guard. "I kill people. Sometimes because they get in my way. Sometimes because they deserve it.

Sometimes because I don't like the way they look at me."

I give him my best evil eye.

"But love, *you* have nothing to worry about. You'll be safe with me. Protected." He motions to Vegas with his head. "And that's more than he can offer you."

"You've been in that suit too long. I'm pretty sure you're shriveled up like a sweaty raisin," I tell him, and out of the corner of my eye, I see Vegas flinch.

I take a step toward Quinlan.

"Effie," Hutch says, his whisper sounding desperate. After all, how can he support me if I'm acting suicidal?

Quinlan grins. "Oh, *you're* going to be fun." He looks past me, to Vegas, and points at me. I notice how similar the robotic hand looks to the thirty-foot version Hutch and I found buried in the mountainside. "For now, just her. Give me the sassy one, and we'll walk. We can talk later about the others."

When Vegas doesn't tell his *mate* to screw off, I look back at him, taking stock of the man again. Did I misread his character? Did I trust the wrong person? How dark *is* his past?

"You know what," I say. "How about I answer for myself?"

This is the point where the old me would have dropped an Eff-bomb, earning my nickname, flipped him the bird and tried to slug him. The new me just raises the handgun and pulls the trigger.

The single round fires with an explosive cough.

The report is followed by a shout of pain.

A spray of pink, lit by the spotlight.

Quinlan's head jerks back, and like Goliath after receiving a stone to the head from David, the giant falls backward.

"You said you were empty." It's Hutch, sounding like a kid at a magic show.

And now for my next trick... I drop the now empty gun, draw my knife and shrug. "I lied."

Before anyone can applaud my subterfuge, a chorus of war cries turns us around. While Quinlan was bartering for me like a slab of tuna in a fish market, his men snuck up behind us. The first of them dives through the gate, his knife swiping at Vegas's gut.

The blade misses, but Vegas is forced to leap back, and the rest flood through. I count seven; the five faithful to chaos and two of the warier ones, who hold weapons at the ready, but take up defensive postures. The missing three have either fled, or stayed in the jungle, perhaps able to resist the call to arms since Quinlan bit the dust. Berg and Duff are both missing.

While two of the Diablos engage Vegas, another attacks Twig. The remaining two come for Hutch, Gwen and me. Hutch brings his shield around in front of him and Gwen, and the pair start stabbing at the air between them and the Diablo.

And that leaves me to fend for myself. Again.

A high pitched scream bellows from a toothless mouth, as the man charges me. I'm expecting a straight forward assault. A tackle. A stab from one of his two knives. But the slender man, whose pants have been cut into a skirt, sliced into four sections and rotated so that his business is covered, moves along the ground like a monkey, swaying back and forth, pounding the ground and shrieking. It's disorienting, and I think it's meant to be. This man might be crazy, but he's not stupid.

Every chaotic lunge pushes me back, on the defensive, unable to predict where he's going to move next, or when he's going to strike.

He nearly gets me with a jab when I hear Gwen shout in pain, and I look away for a moment. I leap back away from the blade, and realize I'm being herded. We all are. They're separating us. Even if some of us win these individual fights, we'll be less able to help our friends.

The man catches me off guard again when instead of swiping at me, he gives his wrist a flick and sends one of the blades sailing at my face. There's a hot sting on my cheek and then a tug on my hair. Moving in slow clarity, strands of orange slide away from my head, as I step back again, beads of blood rolling down my cheek.

He's not trying to capture me anymore. Shooting Quinlan has changed the situation. These guys are out for blood.

I shift my knife into my left hand. It's my weak hand, but he doesn't know that.

When he moves in again, I don't jump back. Our sudden proximity triggers an attack. His knife comes in from the left, and I put all my focus into parrying the strike with my own blade. Metal clangs against metal, and he never sees what's coming, because I don't broadcast it. What I'm doing with my right hand is something I can do without thinking, guided by muscle memory.

My punch connects with his cheekbone, sending a tingling pain up my arm. But the blow staggers him to one knee. He swings again, and I don't even try to block the knife this time. I let it tear through my shirt, a few layers of skin on my stomach and then continue on past. Momentum carries his arm around, the blade pointing at his own chest, and then it gets a burst of speed, as I kick his arm.

The man squeals as he stabs himself. He thrashes on the ground for a moment, a confused animal, and then lies still.

When I look up, only a few seconds have passed, and the scene hasn't changed much. Twig is on his back, holding off his attacker. Vegas is a blur of motion, fighting two men, spinning and striking with his spear, keeping his adversaries at a distance while slowly whittling them down. His arm is sliced and bleeding, but the other two have lethal looking puncture wounds in their chests, somehow sustained by their mania.

I step over Toothless, heading for Gwen and Hutch, when Hutch dives forward, leading with his shield. It looks heavy and unwieldy, but he moves fast enough to collide with the man facing off against them. The Diablo gets in a swing with his machete, but it clangs off the shield's side. Hutch goes down on top of the man, the shield between them. I expect Hutch to pin him there, but he rolls away instead, allowing the man to shove the shield away.

But that was the plan all along.

As soon as the Diablo exposes himself, Gwen thrusts her spear down. When the tip of the weapon punctures the man's chest, Gwen winces and looks ready to puke. But she holds on to the weapon, pushing until the man lies still.

"Vegas!" Twig shouts, and several things happen at once.

The man on top of Twig overpowers him, plunging a blade into his chest.

Hutch's eyes go wide, looking behind me. "Effie!"

I dodge to the left, in the opposite direction of where Hutch is looking. I feel a sharp pain in my triceps as a blade slides past.

When I hit the ground, every part of my body screams at me to stay down. If not for the painkillers, I would probably be paralyzed with agony. But inaction will lead to my death, so I roll over—and stop.

A wooden spear impales Toothless right beside the knife that he stabbed into his chest.

Hutch is frozen in place, arm outstretched, looking just as stunned as Gwen, feeling just like I did when I killed Mack. None of us are good at this, and by good I mean immune to the psychological effects of taking a life. Apparently we're all capable of the physical act.

Toothless topples over on his side and won't be getting up again.

"Twig!" Vegas shouts at the now motionless man, blood flowing from his mouth.

As Twig's killer rushes Vegas with the other two, I recover the spear from Toothless's body and turn to help.

But Vegas is incensed.

In a rage.

And the other three men, skilled and ruthless though they might be, don't stand a chance. They've pushed him over the edge, and his attack has no regard for his own safety. In the first second, he kills two of them, but takes a knife to his leg for the effort. With his spear lodged in a dead man's chest, in one side and out the other, Vegas pulls the knife from his own leg and avenges Twig's death with three quick stabs.

I'm not sure how long the fight took. It felt like years, but I think it was closer to fifteen seconds.

Vegas turns on the two men still standing at the gate. They both drop their weapons. One of them says, "We're cool, man," hands raised.

Vegas points at Twig, dead on the ground. "You could have saved him!"

With a quick jerk he pulls the spear from the dead man and throws it, killing the unarmed Diablo.

The second drops to his knees, and I see a Base brand on his hand. He's shaking. Petrified. I'm not sure a person like this could have done anything to save Twig.

Vegas recovers his knife from the dead man and stalks toward the cowering Base.

"Hey!" I shout, standing between them.

Vegas glares at me. I'm in the way of his revenge. Or is it bloodlust? If it is, I could be in trouble.

"He's done," I say. "You're better than them."

That gets through to him, and he lowers the knife. "Get up, Whitey."

Whitey is another nickname that falls into the ironic category, rather than the four letter category, because the man on his knees has dark skin. Given his reluctance to fight, I suspect the name has more to do with his quickness to surrender.

"Get the others," Vegas says to the man. "If they're not here in the next five minutes, they will never be welcome." He leans in closer, his voice a growl. "I will hunt them down."

Whitey seems to nod with every part of his body capable of moving up and down, and then he's running back out the gate, shouting for his still-hiding companions.

Motion draws my eyes back into the camp. Freckles and Doli have emerged from hiding. Doli still looks numb. Freckles is guiding her past Quinlan's limp arm. My eyes track the arm back up to Quinlan's face, but where I expect to see something bloody and horrible, I just see the robot ninja faceplate.

"Get away from him!" I shout, stepping toward Doli. "He's not—"

Before I can finish, a blade the size of my arm springs from the ExoFrame's forearm, and with the same speed, it's thrust into the redhead's back. As the boy is lifted off the ground by Quinlan, who is now getting back to his robotic feet, Doli looks on with horror.

Quinlan points the blade at me, letting Freckles slide off and fall to the ground.

The message is clear. *You're next.*

In the time it takes me to realize he's moved, Quinlan crosses the distance between us, makes a big metal fist and drives it toward my head.

"Do you think you will get married?"

The question is so out of the ordinary that despite hearing every clearly enunciated word, all I can manage in reply is, "What?"

"Isn't that what normal girls talk about?" Sig sits on a park bench, sucking on a cherry Ring Pop. I'm seated on the concrete beside her dangling legs, nursing a 7-11 mango Slurpee. From a distance, if my glowering stare could be ignored, we probably do look like two average girls, binging on sugar, talking about boys, and nail polish and cat memes.

"You *want* to be normal?" I ask.

She's quiet for a moment, and I take it as a 'yes,' but then she removes any doubt.

"It's just the two of us every day." She leans forward and makes eye contact. Says, *I'm not trying to insult you,* with her face, and then, "Don't you ever feel... I don't know...lonely?"

Sig is 100% more friends than I had a year ago, so when it's just the two of us, I feel like I'm meeting my social quota. But I also go through life with blinders on, working hard to not see or hear how much fun other people are having. Obviously, I can hear and see them, but I long ago decided girls with gaggles of friends were stupid and annoying. I sit alone, eat alone and if anyone asks me if I want to go to the bathroom with them, they're going to get a fist in the face for it. I project this attitude like plutonium does radiation. 'Come near me, you're dead.' Sig is immune to it, shielded by emotional lead. She hasn't asked to come to the bathroom with me yet, but this conversation feels like a gateway.

My hackles raise.

"No," she says, before I can grumble, "I don't want to go buy a Barbie doll—"

Not what I was going to say, but close enough.

"—but I'm not going to deny my humanity, either."

"Deny your—" I swivel around to look at her. "You're a kid. Why talk about a husband? If you don't want Barbie, why dream about Ken?"

Her eyes tear up. For someone constantly being accused of being robotic by people whose intellects can't possibly understand the simplest of Sig's ideas, she is sensitive. Only shows it around me, of course, while I treat the world to my complete lack of anger management.

"I'm not *dreaming* about anyone. I was hoping we could have an intelligent conversation about something other than all the people you hate and all the numbers I can count."

Ouch.

For a moment, I want to hit her.

And then I remember that she's not like everyone else. She's my friend. My only friend. And she's right, sometimes, even when we're together, it's lonely.

"Sorry," I say, and she flinches with surprise. I'm not an apology slut.

I pick myself off the cold concrete, a seat I chose because it was hard and uncomfortable—self-inflicted punishment for having a friend. I've grown accustomed to misery. To discomfort. Physical and emotional. Angry is my baseline.

Sitting on the bench beside Sig feels dangerous. Vulnerable. Comfort is a sign of weakness.

It means I can be hurt.

She smiles at me. "Was that so hard?"

I slouch back, sinking into the curved wooden slats, my back thanking me. "You have no idea."

She sucks on her ring.

I slurp until brain freeze sets in. I can't even drink without inflicting pain on myself. When the daggers are removed from my eyes, I place the drink down, lean my head back and look up at the light green maple leaves above us. It's a kaleidoscope of overlapping, translucent green. "So. Ken."

"Do you know how many people are on the planet right now?" she asks. "Living?"

"Eight billion," I say, rounding down.

"Eight billion, four hundred million, seven hundred fifty-one thousand, three hundred and eighteen, nineteen, twenty, twenty-one..."

She rattles off the numbers so fast that she blurs the words together. She's not just being dramatic, but revealing the actual rate of population growth, and I realize this exponentially growing figure is ticking higher insider her head, all the time.

"Twenty-two, twenty-three, twenty-four."

When she stops to take a breath, I put my hand on her arm. Sometimes it takes physical contact to pull her out of the number stream. "I get it. What's this have to do with Ken?"

"In 2050, the human population is going to reach nine billion. In 2100, ten to twelve billion. And then, a large number of them are going to die."

"Uhh, okay. Morbid. And what does this have to do with Ken? Also, we're going to be old ladies, by then."

"Old ladies with kids and grandkids," she says.

Ahh, there's Ken. "Speak for yourself, Little Miss Optimism."

"I thought I was." A smile. "Even if all of humanity agreed to become vegetarian and every inch of the

3.5 billion acres of arable land was used for crops, producing 2.5 billion tons of grains per year, ten billion people is the absolute max that the planet can support."

"So in seventy-seven years, people will start starving?"

"People are already starving. Always have been. And that's assuming the world can convince places like Texas to give up steak. And we destroy forests for farms, and make the vast majority of other species on Earth extinct. And even then, crops will eventually degrade the soil to the point where nothing can grow."

"Rabbits on an island," I say with a nod.

Leave some horny bunnies on an island without predators, and within a few generations they'll have multiplied to the point where the limited resources can no longer sustain the population. The island would be stripped bare, and the rabbits—along with everything else competing for the same resources—would die. All of them. But in Sig's mind, humans are the rabbits and Earth is the island.

"But before we even get to that tipping point," she says, "industrialized nations aren't going to benevolently give up their chicken nuggets."

It's true. I love chicken nuggets.

"With enough data, I can see the future, Effie. And knowing history like you do, I think you can predict how the human race will react."

I take a slow drink of my Slurpee. Doesn't taste as good now. "People minus food equals war." It doesn't take a savant to do that math.

"Developing nations will be the first to suffer," she says. "And when industrialized nations fight over a plot of land, we all suffer. The human race, along with our children and grandchildren, will be bombed back to the stone age. Or worse."

"Is there a circuitous route back to Ken coming up?" I ask. "Because I think I'd rather talk about Barbie."

"That's the problem," she says. "*Everyone* would rather talk about Barbie."

"So a husband is an analogy for the future?"

She groans. "The only way the human race can possibly avoid destroying itself is if people like *us* come up with a solution."

I can honestly say that I had never considered the fate of the human race, a world without chicken nuggets or my role in solving problems bigger than myself. It's selfish. I'm aware of that. But it's also how I've survived.

"And it will take generations of people like us to solve the problems we're facing in the next seventy-five years."

"So, wait, you're saying that talking about future husbands and the children they will provide is really a discussion about our duty to produce genius offspring—"

"Superior intelligence in your case," she says with a grin.

"—whose minds can save humanity from itself?"

She pops the Ring Pop from her mouth. "Yup."

And just like that, Sig has somehow made a case for talking about boys, and husbands, and kids, and their names and our futures, that doesn't revolt me. We spent the rest of that day talking about our ideal mates. Their IQs. Their professions. Whether they would be good looking, strong and kind in addition to brilliant. What our kids would be like. How they would save the world. How we might, too. And for an afternoon, if you'd walked past that park bench, and heard our conversation, you wouldn't have seen anything special.

People say you see your life flash before your eyes in the moment before your death, but I see only that single moment in time.

That perfect day.

And then I see Quinlan's fist, in crystal clear focus, just inches from my head.

The world turns dark, my eyes squeezing tight. I hope I'll die fast enough to not feel it.

And then…

Clang.

The sound of a gong welcomes me into the afterlife. I open my eyes and am greeted to eternity by…

Hutch?

He's crouched down beside me, holding that big metal shield, pressed against it, gritting his teeth. A metal bar is wedged between the shield and the ground, absorbing some of Quinlan's blow, but some of it is buried, meaning some of that energy was transferred into Hutch.

"Run," he grunts before falling over.

When Hutch hits the ground, I do as he asked. I run. Out of fear? Sure. No one wants to be pancaked by a guy in a robot suit. But also because sticking around means making Hutch a target. If there is any chance he'll survive this now, it's not hiding beneath that shield with me—it's far away from me.

The trouble with the new plan, which really just involves me putting one foot in front of the other a bit faster than usual, is that a jolt of pain radiates from my side with each step. I've seen wounded animals run. On TV. Whether they've been hit by a vehicle, shot by a hunter or wounded by a predator, they all have the same kind of awkward gait. It doesn't always slow them down. Not at first. Not until they're overcome by the wound and drop down dead. But they all look a certain kind of ridiculous. Pitiful.

And I'm pretty sure that right now, as I look back over my shoulder, legs moving fast and uneven, arms flailing to stay upright, that I look worthy of pity.

But not to a man like Quinlan.

His roboticized voice laughs at me. Mocks me.

Without saying a word, he says, *I'm going to catch you and squash you, and all your frantic running is good for, is making me laugh.* The real problem with all of that is that he's not chasing me.

Because there is no getting away. Even if he stays put long enough to kill the others, even if Vegas manages to put up a fight, he'll still catch me. And when he does, there won't be anyone left to fight back or help.

They need time. To regroup. To escape through the hatch. Whatever. They won't be able to do any of it if Quinlan sticks around.

So I appeal to his brutish nature by stopping, turning around and laughing right back at him. "Are you seriously afraid of me?"

With his attention on me, he doesn't see Vegas creeping up behind him. But Vegas sees me, and when I give him a subtle shake of my head, he stops. He can't win that fight. We both know it. Their only hope is that Quinlan doesn't see through my astonishing ruse.

I back-pedal, keeping a steady pace, trying to hide my pain.

"I'm not sure why everyone is so afraid of you. I mean, yeah, the suit is kind of an unfair advantage, but you're obviously kind of a Nancy without it." Yeah, I know, calling boys a girl as an insult is kind of an insult to girls everywhere, but here's the thing: boys still hate it. Especially boys who are men with big muscles, rabid eyes and giant, robot, killing machines under their control.

I can feel his eyes glaring at me through the single red slit. My own personal Cyclops. If only I were a Greek hero with a giant sharpened stick... Not that a sharp stick is going to stop an ExoFrame. I'm pretty sure even the Cyclops wouldn't stand a chance.

When Quinlan bends his legs to leap, I turn and bolt. I hear the whir of his mechanical legs spring out, combined with a familiar hum—repulse engines. *If that thing has repulse discs in its feet, it can do a lot more than outrun me.*

A shadow slips past me, drawing my eyes up. The ExoFrame sails past overhead. He's going to land right in front of me and greet me with a hug. Maybe pop my head between his hands.

I cut hard to the left, heading deeper into the maze of huts.

I don't see him land, but I feel the ground shake.

I turn right, around a hut, hoping to stay out of his line of sight.

I can't fight him or outrun him, but maybe I can hide from him.

As I peel away from the hut, which is built around the trunk of a tall palm tree, the whole structure explodes. Wooden shrapnel peppers my back. The air fills with wisps of dry leaves. And the palm tree, severed near the base, topples over, crushing a second hut and sending a fresh beam of light down on the ExoFrame's body.

I nearly stop to call him an attention hog, but he lifts the palm tree up and hurls it at me. Strong as he is, his aim isn't great. While I round another hut, the tree punches through it, the top rushing past me. But the rest of the ruined hut pelts me, slapping my abused body. I'm forced to leap over the trunk, which slows me down, but I've got a solid lead.

Then I hear the hum of repulse discs again, and I look up in time to see him punch his way up through the canopy. A third beam of sunlight strikes the forest floor, filled with leafy confetti. He's coming my way, but I can't see him now.

I turn hard right, hoping he won't guess which direction I'm heading.

The canopy behind me shatters. Quinlan lands where I had been standing, punching the ground with enough force to stumble me.

But he's missed again, and it's making him angry. He pummels the ground, and for a moment,

I imagine what that fist would do to me. It's not pretty, and it fuels my flight.

But this time, my maneuvers have brought me to a wall of stone. Rusty debris is piled against the volcanic rock. I see old ExoFrame parts and newer transport parts mixed in with bits of history. Pieces of World War II bunkers. Ladders. Support beams. Assorted chunks of unidentifiable metal. It's a real mess, and a nightmare for anyone with a fear of tetanus.

I stop in front of the debris-covered wall. I'm out of hiding places, out of room and out of breath. With no place to go, I turn to face Quinlan, who is standing back up to his full height, which in the suit is about seven feet.

There's nothing snarky to say. He doesn't need to be egged on. He's going to kill me. There's no way around that. The best I can hope for is that he will be quick about it.

But then he stalks toward me, like he knows I'm trapped, like he might be rethinking the whole 'crush her like a bug' strategy. I lean away from him, my back leaning against the wall, my hand landing on a rough metal surface. I glance down at it, and then back at Quinlan.

And then I get it. This is why I'm a Point. This is what makes me different. This is the gift given me by a life of hardship. I can look at my own death and not feel fear, but anger. I can stare down a killing machine stalking toward me and say, "I have faced a good number of bullies in my short time on Earth, Quinlan, but you are, without a doubt, the most chicken-shit of them all."

Yeah, I broke my rule, but it seemed appropriate, and it works.

Quinlan breaks into a jog, which becomes a run, and then, just to make sure that every last bit of me is turned into juice, he kicks in those repulse discs in his feet, and he glides over the ground. Freed from gravity, he accelerates to an easy fifty miles per hour in just under three seconds, which is about the time it takes him to close the distance between us, and for me to lift up the six-foot length of rebar leaning against the wall behind me.

In my fragile state, I don't think I could hold the metal bar up for more than a few seconds, but I don't have to. Quinlan must see it, because instead of punching, he flails back, twisting his body as he tries to stop. His quick reflexes keep the bar from striking him dead center, but the rebar slides across the chest and finds the shoulder seam. With the metal braced against the stone wall, it punches straight through the weak point, and out the ExoFrame's back.

I can't tell if the bar has hit Quinlan inside the suit, or just the ExoFrame itself, but he screams like he's been hurt. Or at least like he's very, very angry. While he tries to tug himself free of the rebar, which has also become embedded in the stone, I duck down and crawl out between his legs.

Running feels almost impossible now. My side is warm and wet. The gunshot wound has opened up. My body feels ready to fall apart.

But Quinlan still hasn't freed himself.

Maybe I can get away.

Just push through it, I tell myself. *Hurt when you're safe.*

I flinch to a painful stop when Gwen and Vegas round a hut, armed with machetes and spears. The looks on their faces when they see Quinlan trying to pull himself free from the wall makes me wish I had a Featherlight to take their photo. But even if I did, there isn't time. Quinlan lets out a scream as he braces one foot against the wall and pulls.

"Let's go!" Vegas says, and the two of them help take my weight, leading me through the campsite and back to a winding valley of stone. The four foot gap of eroded stone would be hard for Quinlan to move through, but not impossible. And if it ends at a closed hatch...

We round a final bend and my heart sinks. The hatch is closed, and everyone is bunched together in an easy-to-slice package. One swipe of Quinlan's blade and everyone here is done. Only Hutch and Doli, who are sitting on the ground looking dazed, but happy to see me alive, would survive that first swing. Daniel, Gizmo and Sig are gathered by a digital lock beside a large metal door. Gizmo, Daniel and Duff are locked in a heated, high-pitched argument about how to unlock it. Sig is working the keypad, trying endless sequences of combinations.

She looks back at me and says, "There are too many variables. Too many numbers. It could be anything."

"Sometimes it's not about the numbers," I tell her, and then I turn to face the tunnel entrance, hiding a wince and ignoring the warm blood oozing from the reopened wound on my side and running down my leg. I can feel Quinlan's running feet shaking the ground. Vegas, Gwen, Ghost, Whitey and Berg join me. I glance at Berg, and he hands me one of his machetes. "We do what we have to, to survive."

"Sometimes it's better to die doing what's right," I tell him.

"Looks like we'll find out together," he says.

"Wait!" It's Sig. She's standing on her tip toes, reaching her hand up to what looks like one of three security cameras mounted into the metal frame above the lock. But she's not quite tall enough to reach the lowest of the three vertically spaced circles.

"The cameras are an extra layer of security," Daniel grumbles. "If someone were inside, they could keep the door locked even if the right code was entered."

"If there were anyone from Unity inside, they would have opened the door."

I'm not so sure, since those same people dropped us on an island populated by psychos, but I keep it to myself.

Daniel shakes his head. "But the keypad—"

"—is a decoy." Sig taps Daniel's forehead three times while she talks. "We have to assume this door was here for us to find. A keypad could take a century to crack." She looks at Gizmo. "And there is no way to access the insides and hack its hardware."

The small boy nods.

"So there would be a way for us to open it, even if—"

Hutch gets to his feet. Lifting her up in one arm. "Effie. Trust your Base."

He's telling *me* to trust Sig, who is pretty much the only person I trust? Then again, I am still standing here, waiting to be squashed. I push past Daniel and stand with them.

Base, Support, Point.

Unity.

Sig lifts her brand up in front of the lowest camera.

Hutch places his in front of the middle.

And I put mine at the top.

"See!" Daniel says when nothing happens. "I told you. The—"

A line of blue light traces our brands, flicking down and then back up.

"Effie," Gwen says, sounding nervous. I can hear the pounding of Quinlan's legs and grinding stone as he moves through the winding tunnel.

The blue light blinks, and with a clunk, the door unlocks and slides open.

"Inside!" I shout as Quinlan's shadow shifts just around the bend. His hand snaps out, reaching into our small hiding place and catching Whitey's head. There's a muffled scream. A crunch. And then Whitey goes limp.

"Inside, now!"

UNITY

30

After just a few days on the island, I feel like a Neanderthal who's been abducted by aliens and set loose inside a UFO. The modern, white hallway, pristine in a just-built way, is another world. Like a dream. A nearly forgotten place. For a fraction of a moment, I'm stunned by the well-lit hall and its perfectly octagonal shape, and the shiny floor, all lit by twin streaks of light emanating from within the angled portion of the wall. It's like the tunnel people talk about seeing when they die.

I'm shoved from behind, someone urging me inward, away from the ExoFrame grinding its way past the narrow rocky bend, just fifteen feet from the door. The rebar is missing from the shoulder, but the arm hangs like a dead weight, and blood trickles from the hole.

I pivot out of the way, waving the others past me. "Go, go, go!"

The simple act of waving my arm hurts. As much as I would like to distance myself from Quinlan, I'm not going anywhere fast. The trouble is, they're all overachievers. While Doli, Duff, Gizmo and Daniel retreat down the hall, Vegas, Gwen, Hutch, Sig and Ghost stop. Like they can help.

"Go!" I shout at Vegas. "Keep them safe. If there is something that can help us here, they'll find it."

To my surprise, he taps Ghost's shoulder, and the two of them chase after the four retreating Bases.

Gwen throws herself at the large metal door, trying to yank it closed, but it's not budging.

Outside, Quinlan pounds at the stone wall holding him back, turning it to powder and pushing himself slowly, but inexorably, through. He sees us watching from inside the hall, his prey nearly safe in the den. He roars at us, crumbling stone, nearly through.

"Effie!" Sig says. She and Hutch already have their hands positioned over three vertically spaced Unity brand sensors—not cameras. They mirror the three outside.

I place my hand above theirs, and will the blue light to scan them faster.

Gwen backs away from the door. "Guys..."

The blue light flickers.

Gwen leaps back with a shout.

The door slides shut, like a sideways guillotine.

Quinlan collides with the far side. I can hear the resounding impact, but can't feel it. This place was built to take a beating, even from something as powerful as an ExoFrame. He pounds on the door just three more times, venting his frustration. He knows he can't get through. Not without a Base and a Support. And what's left of the Diablos and Perseverantes are in here with us.

The moment I feel safe, my legs start to wobble. My vision blurs, as a kind of pressure moves from my head and down into my chest. For a moment, I'm lost in an unthinking void, and then I'm back and somehow still upright.

But not walking.

My arms are over Gwen's and Hutch's backs, and theirs are wrapped around mine. They're carrying me, my toes dragging over the floor. Sig is ahead of us, her tiny frame confidently leading the way.

We pass closed doors and branching hallways, but we stay on course, straight ahead. The walls are labeled in spots, revealing where we are in this subterranean Unity base. 'Mess.' 'Quarters.' 'Engineer-ing.' 'Labs.' 'Gym.' We pass them all—including a door labeled 'Medical,' which given the tacky warmth now covering my leg and my side beneath the black T-shirt, I'm going to need to visit, and soon. But we pass without stopping, heading toward the sound of voices, loud and excited—mostly Daniel.

"What is this place?" Gwen asks.

"I think we're about to find out," Hutch says. "But I'm pretty sure we're not going to like it."

The first open door we come across is labeled 'Armory.' But Sig doesn't slow her pace, and I get only a glimpse of what's inside. There are racks of guns, and armor, and other things I don't recognize. And there is also Doli, standing there by herself, taking it all in. As a Base, I can't imagine her being a gun lover, so I assume she's making some kind of mental inventory, filling her head with information that could come in useful later on. Not that I really know anything about her. She's been near catatonic since the moment I saw her.

Who can blame her? Especially now, after seeing what happened to Freckles. The rest of us are still mobile, still fighting and surviving, but sooner or later, the shell shock is going to hit. When the stillness of night and the darkness it brings returns, I doubt I'll be able to sleep. The horrors of the past days are going to replay through my mind's eye like a movie stuck on repeat.

As we approach the hallway's end, I find my feet again, taking some of the weight off Gwen and Hutch. But they don't let me go, and I don't want them to. The old me would have walked this hall alone, bound and determined to not show a hint of weakness. But I'm not that person anymore. Gwen and Hutch can carry me pretty much whenever they want, and I will never complain.

I've learned that depending on others isn't a sign of individual weakness, but of communal strength. And I really don't want to admit it, but I don't think I could have ever learned that lesson anywhere other than on this island. I'm not sure I would have even learned the lesson had we not crashed and been attacked by Los Diablos.

Would I change all that if I could? Absolutely. But I'd be a weaker person for it.

The hallway leads to an open space. The door, which looks like two thick metal plates, has retracted fully into either side of the hall. The wall to our right has two labels: 'Operations,' and beneath that, 'Hangar.' Sig glances at the words and then picks up the pace, nearly jogging through the opening.

The room on the far side is massive, and it reminds me of history-book photos of the old NASA control rooms. Three sets of computer terminals are arranged in an arc. Each station has a curved, touch-screen display, keyboard and some kind of headset that looks more like a rubbery mesh helmet than headphones. At the front of the room is a patchwork of large screens, all surrounding one massive display the size of a movie screen. The room has power, but the screens are dark. Nothing has been started up.

I have a hard time believing that Daniel and Gizmo wouldn't have already gotten everything up and running and made contact with the outside world, but they're gathered at the front of the room with everyone else, standing in front of a long row of windows positioned beneath the array of screens. From my point, higher up in the theater-style space, I can't see much through the windows, but the space beyond is vast.

"I have her," Hutch says, and Gwen releases me, heading down a curved staircase with Sig.

Sig gives me a look that asks, 'Are you okay?' and I give her a weary thumbs-up before she continues on her way.

"You're going straight to Medical after we see what's up," Hutch says.

"No argument here," I say, and I grunt as we clumsily move down the stairs. I glance at his face, so close to mine, and see a welt on his forehead. That's where the shield hit him. When he put himself between me and a giant robot fist. I'm not the only one who needs medical attention. I'm pretty sure almost all of us do. But it's nice that he seems most concerned about me. But is that because it's his job? Or something more?

"Thanks," I say.

He turns to me, our noses just inches apart. He doesn't ask, 'For what?' He's smart. He knows what he did and why I'd be grateful. He just says, "Any time."

And then he lingers there for a moment. Neither of us moving. Just looking at each other. Trusting each other. Sig earned my complete trust two years ago, but

I have partially trusted other women. Teachers. My most recent foster-mother. But I have never, not once and to any degree, trusted a man or boy, until now.

Gwen and Sig gasp in unison, pulling Hutch's attention a moment before mine. They've reached the windows, surprised by whatever they're seeing, but I don't become insatiably curious until I see them both lean to the side and look up.

Gwen actually smiles and says, "Holy geez."

"C'mon," Hutch says, and he helps me move down the staircase a bit faster. When we reach the window, I'm greeted by more than one smile. Even Vegas looks something near excited.

What in the world...

And then I see it.

The hangar.

And what's inside it.

The vast space beyond the window is circular and at least a half mile across. The size is dizzying, but I hardly notice it, because the five things standing inside the hangar are far more impressive. And like the others, I have to lean to the side and look up to the right to see the closest of them.

Standing at least four hundred feet tall is a sleek-looking robot, whose limbs don't seem thick enough to support its undoubtedly massive weight. It has the build, that in human terms, hasn't been seen since Bruce Lee. And it somehow carries that same lethal look, like it could strike in a blur, despite its size. The five robots have varying styles and paint jobs. The one closest to me has a body composed of stylish white armor with black joints. Red stripes run down the arms and legs, converging at a Unity triangle over its chest. The armor is covered in nearly imperceptible octagonal cells, like the ExoFrame. In fact, a lot of what I'm seeing is similar to the ExoFrame, but a *lot* bigger. Its head has a nobility about it, somehow also looking dangerous and wise. A facemask covers the lower half of its head, and above it, the two light green eyes are large enough to be windows. But I suspect they're actually filled with sensors. Something like this has to be a drone, controlled from here.

Hutch taps my hand with his, and then points to the robot's hand. He doesn't say anything. Doesn't need to. It's easy to recognize the massive hand we found in the cave. One of these things must have blown apart at some time, the hand crashing into the cave, or creating it with the force of its landing. Must have been one hell of an explosion.

Between each of the robots is some kind of vehicle. They're triangular in shape, but lack what I would call wings. Not that flying craft need them anymore, and it looks like there are at least six repulse engines on the bottom. The featureless curved hull gives no indication as to their purpose, but the symbol at the center of it gives a clue: Support.

"What *are* they?" Gizmo asks. I've seen commercials where kids open Christmas presents, warm by the fire, smiling parents nearby. The kids exclaim over the year's hot new plastic device. Gizmo sounds like that, like he can't wait to run out there and play with these monstrous toys.

I turn to Vegas. He's already looking at me. He raises his eyebrows, glances into the hangar, and mouths the word, "See?"

Right.

Aliens.

Unity defending the world from invasion.

I still think he's living in a twisted fantasy, but this does fit his conspiracy theory.

Flight simulator.

I look back at the mesh helmets around the room. *Psy-controls.*

"You can operate those...whatever they are... planes, can't you?" I whisper to Hutch. He and Gwen both turn to me, the surprised look on their faces is answer enough. Yes. They both can.

"Seriously," Gizmo says. He's beaming. "Who knows what these are?"

"Shugoten," Daniel says. He's at the far end of the line, forehead and hands pressed against the glass.

"Sho-what now?" Gizmo says.

Daniel makes eye contact with each one of us. Unlike Gizmo, and contrary to his typical personality, he looks almost sick. "Shugoten. It's short for Shugo Tenshi. Means Guardian Angels."

"How do you know?" Sig asks.

"Because I named them." He looks back out to the hangar, the first hint of a smile emerging. "I invented them."

"You *what?*" I'm so surprised that my voice rises to an octave so high that I'm not sure it was me who spoke.

"Well, I didn't invent *everything*. The psy-controls, the sensory mesh, the repulse engines. All of that already existed. Some of the tech is based on the old model ExoFrames, but I think they applied some of my advances to the model Quinlan was using. From what I can see, they used my visual design and load-bearing adaptations. I can only guess that a lot of what we can't see is also based on my design. Including the Support Striker."

"That the big curved triangle?" Gwen asks.

"They're much more than that," Daniel says, "and yes."

"How old were you when you came up with this?" I ask. Daniel is thirteen, and coming up with something like this seems impossible even for someone twice his age. But then, he wouldn't be here and be a Base if he wasn't brilliant.

He shrugs. "Eight when I started. Nine when I finished."

Geez.

"But I didn't *build* them," Daniel says. "I just worked out the science. And the math. And the designs. Unity built them. I think."

"*Why* did you design them?" Hutch asks. "Aside from them being awesome."

Daniel smiles at the compliment and says, "Uncle Jack asked me to."

"*Uncle Jack.*" Gwen sounds as dubious as I feel. Daniel's knowledge of these...Shugoten makes him suspect. Of what, I don't know. Of knowing more than he told us, I suppose. Though he does look just as surprised to see them as we do.

"He's not really my uncle. He's an old friend of my parents. I think they were in the military together. They didn't talk about it, though. Both of them work for Unity, but I'm not sure how. I thought the Shugoten design was like an exercise. A test."

"You spent a *year* on a test?" Gwen asks.

"I wanted to impress them," he says. "I was a kid."

Gwen grunts, confusion leading to frustration. "You still *are* a kid."

"He's more than that," Sig grumbles, just loud enough for me and Gwen to hear her.

Message received, Sig. If she takes him seriously, we should, too. Gwen squeezes her lips together, working hard to do the same.

"What are they for?" The question comes from Vegas, who looks neither amused nor confused. He's more interested than anything else, probably seeing the potential the robots possess while the rest of us marvel at their existence. Ghost looks ready to answer, but Vegas puts a hand on his shoulder. He wants Daniel to answer.

"I dunno," Daniel says.

Vegas makes brief eye contact with me and then looks down at Daniel. What he says next is for my benefit. He's proving a point. "Why did you design them so big?"

Daniel scrunches up his face. "Uncle Jack told me to imagine that massive..." His eyes widen. "No... no way!"

"Daniel," I say, my impatience skyrocketing into nuclear territory. "Spill it."

"I designed them to fight daikaiju. Giant monsters. Like Godzilla or Nemesis."

"What kind of giant monsters, exactly?" I ask.

Another shrug. "Size was the only criteria I was given."

"Can they get us off this island?" Duff asks, looking through the window with a kind of eager desperation. He has probably wanted off this island since the moment he set foot on it.

"Absolutely," Daniel says. "Although everyone would need to learn how to operate one, or a Support Striker. They're not transports. One operator in each."

"People *ride* in those?" I ask, once again peering up at the nearest Shugoten.

"*Operate* them. With psy-controls."

When I sense Hutch's attention, I give him a defensive, "What?"

"You're smiling," he says.

I don't feel it until he tells me, but part of me is definitely liking the idea of controlling a four-hundred-foot tall robot. But I've never used psy-controls. And I don't know what a neural mesh is. The odds of me not face-planting a Shugoten out of the gate are pretty slim. "Before we try anything that might result in death or the destruction of this facility, let's get things up and running. See if we can't contact the outside world."

Daniel, Gizmo, Sig and Duff are suddenly on the task. They each hurry to a different terminal. Within seconds, the room fills with the familiar whir of technology. The ambient glow of screens feels familiar and comforting. I hadn't realized how much I missed civilization.

"It's a typical Unity system," Daniel says. "Thirty seconds to boot. Another thirty to establish a satellite connection."

If there are any left, I think, and I'm sure Vegas is thinking the same thing.

Gwen and Ghost join the others at the computer stations, looking on as the four Bases work their fingers over the keyboards, each accessing one system or another. When I see Hutch looking back at them, I say, "Go ahead. I'm okay."

"I'll keep her upright if she needs it," Vegas says, eyes on the Shugoten.

Hutch looks unsure, but relaxes when I put a hand on his shoulder. "We're all okay now. You can let your guard down for a minute. And make sure Daniel and Gizmo don't start having wrestling matches with the giant robots."

Hutch smiles and nods before joining the others, sliding up next to Gwen and watching over Sig's shoulder.

I'm alone with Vegas.

"Still think they're for fighting aliens?" I ask.

"What else?"

"Besides people?" I say, thinking I'm stating the obvious.

"Unity doesn't attack people. It's contrary to everything we're about."

"Good to know," I say, feeling like a newbie once again.

"Eff," he says, and the familiar use of my name sounds strange coming from him, but also nice.

"Yeah," I say, relaxing as some of the tension drains from my battered psyche.

He taps on the glass twice, pointing to his left.

The Shugoten standing to the left of the operations center is structurally similar to the white one on our right, but it's painted in shades of gray and jet black with orange eyes and orange stripes, once again tracing the arms and legs and converging as a Unity triangle. But there's another splash of color, on the back of its right hand. A Point symbol, red on the top and black on the sides and bottom, which confirms that these mammoth machines are meant to be operated by people like me and Vegas. But it's what is below the Point symbol that blows my mind.

There are letters, written in a classic serial number style font.

F-B0MB-001

"What...the..." I lean closer, like I'll suddenly be able to see something different.

"Isn't that you?" Vegas adds.

"It's my nickname," I say.

"I think they made it your handle." Vegas is all smiles now. "A handle is—"

"I *know* what it is." I limp my way along the window, getting closer to the Shugoten that bears my name. My hand drags over the glass, squeaking, resisting the pull the rest of me feels.

"Greetings and congratulations." The voice is loud and newly familiar. I hobble back to look at the big screen mounted above me. My mother is there.

Seeing her again reawakens a nearly forgotten ache. I turn to Daniel, "Is this—"

He raises his hands in the air, understanding her significance.

Be safe.

Be strong.

Speak well.

Euphemia.

"It's a recording. It's playing on its own," he says.

"If you have made it this far, you have exceeded our expectations and proved yourselves worthy of advancement. The moment you entered the Unity Bunker, we were notified. A team of personal trainers has already been dispatched and will reach you within seven hours. Upon their arrival, your training with everything you see here will commence."

No mention of aliens. Nothing about saving the world.

"Until then, please enjoy the comforts of this facility. The mess, bunks and gym are all at your disposal."

There's no tapping. No secret message. There doesn't need to be. The letters stenciled on the Shugoten's hand are message enough.

Did she do that?

Did she rush me through the program, send me to this island and hope I would survive, find my way here and discover...this? *Sorry I abandoned you, here's a robot and a gym. Hope we're good now.*

Feeling manipulated and controlled, I'm starting to understand why Vegas and his people opted to hide from Unity. Being a puppet does *not* feel good. And when the person pulling the strings is someone who screwed up your life...it's even worse.

"Your future will be bright," she says, and it suddenly feels like she's talking to me again. "And the world will thank you for your service." She gives a nod, and the screen reverts back to a barebones Unity operating system.

"Who was that?" Sig says to me. "You look upset."

"My mother," I tell her, and I see all of my emotions reflected in her face. She knows what this means. How I feel. And now she's feeling it with me.

"Aww," says a mechanical voice. "Did I miss the family reunion?"

We turn around as a group, simultaneously gasping, as Quinlan steps into Operations. He's still wearing the damaged, but functional-enough ExoFrame, which is now decorated by two hands hanging from a chain around his robot neck. One is a Support and one's a Base.

What do you say when a psycho walks into a room, dressed in a robot suit, with two hands for decoration?

Nothing.

You say *nothing.*

Not out loud, anyway. If you're the praying type, you do that. No one can hear the whisper in your head, which if I were a normal person, would probably be something basic, like: *Please God, please God, please God.* I can see him sitting on a cloud, long white beard dangling, looking down and thinking, *Please what?*

But the words that fill *my* head are a question. A rhetorical question. The kind I loathe, but I'm sure God gets all the time: *Are you serious?*

I'm not even sure if the question is directed at a higher power, or just the best I can come up with.

We're weaponless. Most of us are injured. I'm *really* injured. And now we're trapped in a room with a killing machine, and there are giant robots, just out of reach, that could squash Quinlan like a bug. Granted, a punch from a Shugoten would probably kill everyone in this room, but at least we'd go out fighting.

Quinlan takes a step closer, extending the blade from his forearm. He's not going to waste time punching. He's just going to cut us up and be on his merry way. But it's worse than that. With us gone, he'll have access to the Shugoten, too. And then what? He'll become some kind of mad super villain? Stomp through some cities?

No, I think. Unity would have some kind of failsafe shutdown or self-destruct...

I try to hide my widening eyes as the idea takes root.

"Get him talking," I whisper to Vegas.

"Quin," Vegas says, stepping forward. While he moves, I move, inching my way closer to Daniel's station.

"I'm afraid there is no sacrifice you can offer, Vegas. You and your Point girlfriend are dead. Here and now."

The intent behind his words isn't veiled. He's planning on killing Vegas and me and enslaving the others. I'm a little surprised he didn't mention Berg—a Point. But Berg has been submissive from the start, acting out of fear. And maybe with Vegas dead, Ghost will fall in line, too.

Vegas stands at the bottom of the curved staircase connecting the bottom and top of the theater-style control room. It would take nothing for Quinlan to leap down and impale Vegas. But he holds his ground.

"You can kill me if you want, Quin," Vegas says, and the way he abbreviates Quinlan's name makes me think they were friends once. Maybe that's why Vegas is still alive? Maybe that's why Vegas survived all this time? "But I think you should see what's here first. See what we've earned."

I pretty much can't believe what I'm hearing. Is he being serious or simply buying time, like I asked him to? Either way, it's working. Quinlan is completely focused on Vegas.

"Duff," Vegas says. "Can you show him what's in the hangar?"

"Y-yeah," Duff says.

His breathing sounds labored. He must have thought he'd been freed from Quinlan. But now, the master is back. How bad will retribution be for him? Probably lethal, especially with several more Bases available to take his place.

The wall of screens behind me fill with security camera views of the hangar. The Shugoten are revealed in full, their size, style and design even more impressive when seen head to toe.

While Quinlan is transfixed by the display, I lean closer to Daniel and whisper, "Do the Shugoten have a remote override?"

His eyes ask a silent question, 'what for?' But then he nods.

"We don't have to hide anymore," Vegas says. "Don't have to fight."

"You said the ExoFrame borrowed from your design," I whisper.

His eyes go still, like he's suddenly worried about being caught. His fingers start moving over the keyboard, slowly, keeping the keys from tapping out a 'come kill me' code to Quinlan. But the big man seems distracted enough.

"Look at them." Vegas sweeps his hand up at the largest screen, showing a close up of the white Shugoten's face. Despite being masked and having green eyes, there's something in the furrowed brow that says the powerless Guardian Angel disapproves of Vegas's words. "Four hundred feet tall. The controls match the ExoFrames. The two of us could sink the Unity carrier together. We could be *gods.*"

"I have been telling you that all year," Quinlan says. The robotic modulation of his voice keeps me from hearing whether or not he's angered by Vegas's words, or relieved.

Quinlan raises the tip of his long blade up toward Vegas. "We could have all been Diablos."

Uh-oh...

"We could have found this place together." Quinlan takes a single step down, which for him is an entire flight. He could reach Vegas in three strides.

"Daniel," I say, trying to spur him on.

"Trying," he says through clenched teeth. "I don't have the access code."

"Try his name."

"I *did.*" He says this a little too loudly.

Quinlan's head snaps toward me. "And you." He glances at his wounded shoulder. At the limp arm. I did that to him. It's an injury he's never going to forget, in part because it will probably hurt forever, but also because he's a sexist and I'm a girl. "You're going to—"

The array of screens blink to a new image. Earth from high above. A satellite's view.

Before anyone can ask, or Quinlan can complain, Sig says, "I can't find any active communication satellites still working, but there are a number of spy satellites still locked in geosynchronous orbits." She sounds unruffled by what's happening around her, like she hasn't even heard the pre-slaughter banter. And maybe she hasn't. When she gets in her zone, the rest of the world slides away.

The blue-green image of Earth draws my attention. For a moment, I'm lost, but then I see the boot-shaped Italy, upside down at the top of the image. The satellite is over Europe. And even from this distance, I can see that something is wrong.

Europe is burning.

Columns of smoke rise from France, Spain, Germany and Italy, but the worst is the UK, which is hidden beneath a black cloud. It's like volcanoes have risen up across the continent, belching out soot.

To my surprise, it's Quinlan who asks the first question.

"What are those?"

At first, I think he's talking about the smoke columns, but then I notice an aberration in the image. There are large specks pocking the landscape, like the satellite's lens is dirty.

"Can you zoom in?" I ask Sig.

Her answer is seen on the screen. The image closes in on Germany, stopping miles above Berlin. We could probably get close enough to identify a single person, but there's no need. The thing above where Berlin is supposed to be is larger than the city itself. And there's no doubt about what we're seeing.

Vegas was right.

We've been invaded.

The black ship is miles long, hovering a mile above the ground, blotting out the landscape. Long spines extend from the front. Or is it the back? They look a little bit like something nature would create for defense. Like porcupine quills. But I think they're probably antenna of some kind.

"This—this isn't possible," Duff says.

Small black dots move in and out of the picture, some heading toward the city and others heading away. It's some kind of mothership.

"How many of these are there?" I ask.

Around the room, small fingers work keys. Several of the smaller screens around the room hop between various satellite feeds, shifting through different qualities, positions and heights. While the screens shift faster than I can think, Sig has her head raised, seeing it all.

"Fifty-seven," Sig says. "That we can see. There could be more, on Earth, or not."

Fifty-seven, city-sized, alien spaceships.

Alien.

Spaceships.

The one over Berlin wasn't a mothership at all, but just one of a fleet of carriers. This is an honest-to-goodness, old school invasion. Stephen Hawking was right.

I glance at Sig and say, "There are predators on the rabbit island now."

She nods like she was thinking the same thing.

Then the largest screen locks in place over a city whose coastline I recognize. San Diego. Home of Unity. Other than the coast, there is nothing about the city I recognize. There is no alien carrier here, but the view is perhaps more shocking. Resting at the center of a crater at the city's core is something like a fleshy seed that's been peeled open on one side. The crater must be a mile wide. The city beyond it has toppled away from the impact. Millions of people would have died.

My eyes drift to the coast. Some of the city litters the ocean, either blown there or dragged there by the retreating tsunami that would have rushed from the island to the U.S. coast the night we arrived here. Is that when they arrived? When all this started? We've been on this island playing native while the world was overrun by beings from another world.

I look for the Unity cruiser, expecting to see the massive vessel split in two and burning, hiding my real mother's corpse somewhere in its bowels. But it's not there. It's either sunk completely, or it's someplace else, but also probably sunk.

"That's what we saw," Gizmo says, eyes on the crater. "That's what crashed in the ocean. It was one of those."

I look at the giant pod again and realize he's right. The size and shape match, and they both fell from the sky.

"What are they?" Ghost asks.

"I think the more relevant question," Daniel says, "is what was inside them?"

The view onscreen zooms in a little closer. The revealed interior looks almost meaty, like it's still moist and oozing some kind of viscous gel. Padding for whatever was inside. A fleshy version of the rapid expanding foam.

"There's a trail," Daniel says, and our view shifts to the right, following a path. Though the entire city has been knocked over, forming a kind of sun design around the crater, there is a long streak of compacted rubble where something heavy passed by.

"What could have done that?" Gwen asks.

"Nothing good," Hutch says.

The path leads north, moving its way through the endless city that is the coast of Southern California. There are no crashed pods here. No carriers or small craft. But the destruction seems nearly as complete. Entire neighborhoods still stand, but the path of destruction meanders a bit. Whatever moved through there lingered from time to time.

And then, all at once, we see it.

For a moment, I feel like we're watching a cheesy, Japanese monster movie. What did Daniel call them? Daikaiju. But the thing on the screen is very real, and at the moment, it's wreaking havoc on a city south of Los Angeles. It's hard to describe what I'm seeing. The thing has four legs, I think. Or it could be walking on its hands and feet. Its dark gray body looks like it's covered in organic plating, like a rhino's dermal armor. From high above, it looks like it's trudging along, but its limbs are moving over, and sometimes through, buildings in a blink. A long tail sweeps out behind it, scouring the landscape. And its head, like a turtle's, topped with four red eyes, nudges its way through the buildings ahead.

Like its foraging.

But its size, speed and rugged appearance seem almost normal compared to its most disturbing feature. Red worm-like tendrils writhe from the thing's face, sides and tail, where the armor has pulled apart. Like whips, they snap out and withdraw, again and again, like each strand has a mind of its own. For a moment, I try to imagine the complexity of a brain capable of controlling that many appendages at once. Then I realize what it's doing and nearly fall to my knees.

"Closer," Hutch says. He suspects the same thing, but needs to see it. I don't want to, but I have to see it for myself.

The image drops down closer, revealing the rough texture of the monster's skin and twitching muscles the size of jets along its arms and legs.

The tendrils continue their barrage, burrowing into rubble, retrieving small things and then snapping back into what looks like an array of lesions before emerging again.

"Closer," Hutch says.

My stomach clenches. The gunshot wound throbs, leaking warm fluid, but I barely notice.

A tendril, close up and in clear view, pounds through the wall of a partially destroyed building. It emerges a moment later, its prize impaled on the end like a teriyaki stick. A human being. Dead or alive, I can't tell, but a moment later, a horde of frenzied tentacles penetrate the building, claiming more victims.

A small group of people burst from the side of the building and run in the opposite direction. I count seven. The giant turns toward them, watching, but it doesn't pursue them. It could catch them in a single stride, but it just lets them go.

And then it doesn't.

While most of the tendrils keep digging through the rubble, others jut out at the people fleeing, wriggling madly. Even though the wavering appen-dages fall far short of touching the group, all seven people hit the ground. Some fall flat on their faces. Others roll to a stop.

They writhe in the street like ants under a magnifying glass, tortured by something unseen.

The daikaiju takes its time, plucking them up from the pavement.

The tendrils retract inside the monster, re-emerging a moment later, seeking out more victims.

"Is it *eating* them?" Gwen asks.

I turn to Vegas, whose tough exterior has crumbled. He looks wounded. There are people in the world he cares about. He sees me watching and says, "Life is rare."

I nod. "It's valuable."

"Even more so when food—" he points up, "—out there, is scarce."

This isn't an invasion.

It's a buffet.

A heavy footstep makes everyone jump. We'd all forgotten about the very immediate and less massive threat to our own lives. Quinlan has taken another step toward Vegas, but his red strip of an eye is still fixed on me.

"Quin," Vegas says. "We have an enemy. We can fight them together. Don't you see? That's what the Shugoten are for. That's why we're here."

I can't see Quinlan's face, but I swear he's smiling inside that suit.

"The world is burning," Quinlan says, "And as far as I'm concerned, let it. I've never seen anything more beautiful. And this is the best seat in the house. I think I'll keep it." He cocks back the blade, lets out a battle cry and leaps down at Vegas.

The ExoFrame blade slides through the air, on a collision course for Vegas's head. As fast and as strong as he is, there is no avoiding it.

But there is something faster than Vegas.

A loud twang, like a loose guitar string plucked too hard, rumbles through the air. Through my body as a quiver. And then, through Quinlan's body.

Shards of metal explode out from the shoulder of the ExoFrame's functional arm. The limb goes loose, the blade no longer pointed at Vegas.

But the big machine isn't out of commission yet. Nor is its operator.

Vegas dives away as Quinlan lands on his feet, lets out a digital roar and kicks where Vegas had been standing just a second before. A computer terminal shatters from the kick's explosive force, spewing plastic debris and sparks. Had the heavy foot, propelled by small repulse engines, struck Vegas, his fate would have mirrored the terminal's.

With a fresh roar of anger, and maybe pain, Quinlan rounds on us. I get the sense that he's about to enter some kind of berserker rage, kicking everything and everyone he can reach.

But this time, he's stopped by a surprisingly loud and commanding voice from Operation's entryway. "Hey!"

Quinlan looks up at Doli. She's standing at the top of the stairs, pointing a weapon I don't recognize down at the mech suit. Her eyes aren't lost anymore. They're dangerous.

And so is she.

There is no victory speech or explanation.

And there is no mercy.

Doli pulls the trigger, unleashing another *twang*.

I'm not sure what kind of projectile the rifle fires, but its effects on the ExoFrame, and the man housed inside it, are immediate and brutal.

The small hole that punches through the armored chest explodes out the back as a metal-strewn mess.

Quinlan staggers back, arms dangling, managing a single digital gasp.

"Found it!" Daniel shouts, smashing his finger onto his keyboard's 'Enter' key, executing a command.

Quinlan moves to leap out of Doli's aim, a last ditch effort to save his life, but the suit freezes up, locked up by Daniel's override. And then he's shot again. *Twang!* The projectile must strike something impenetrably solid this time, because it doesn't punch through. It lifts the entire suit off its feet, toppling the now lifeless machine over.

There's a moment of absolute stillness in the wake of Quinlan's demise. I can't decide which is more shocking, that Quinlan is dead, that Doli killed him or that she used some kind of insane future tech weapon to do it.

Gwen is the first to move, hurrying up to Doli, who is starting to look a little glassy-eyed again. "You're okay," she says, gently taking the strange weapon away. "You're safe now. We all are, thanks to you."

Hutch joins Gwen, and they lead Doli toward the exit, Gwen speaking quiet platitudes the whole way. Hutch gives me a quick look before leaving, shifting his eyes from me to the satellite feed and back again. He looks worried. And while that makes sense—he *should* be worried—I can't help but feel disappointed in him. He's supposed to be my rock. My support. But if *he's* faltering, what does that say for the rest of us?

Nothing, I decide. Being a Support doesn't mean you have to be a superhuman emotional powerhouse. At least not all the time. With Quinlan dead and the newly discovered invaders thousands of miles away, this is probably the ideal time to be vulnerable.

A whir of robotic motors pulls my focus back to Quinlan.

So much for being vulnerable.

I start up the stairs, chasing after Hutch, intending to retrieve the weapon, but Vegas stops me with, "It's okay." I turn around to see Vegas crouching over the big robot body. The robot mask has lifted away from Quinlan's face. Blood trails from the side of his mouth, but his eyes are looking up at Vegas.

Still alive.

He's a tough one, I'll give him that. Too bad he was also off his rocker.

I step closer, listening to the conversation.

"You're all going to die." Quinlan's voice is strained. Wet.

"Probably," Vegas replies. "But that's always been part of the deal for people like us." He glances up at me. I'm part of the 'us.'

"Dying isn't the problem," Quinlan says, and I see for the first time that he's not the least bit afraid, even while the life drains out of him. I can see his face turning pale.

Ghost steps up beside me. Then Duff. One of them followed this man, the other was brave enough to resist him. But they stand with the somber faces of men losing a comrade. Long before this island, these men were brothers in arms. Maybe even friends. Berg stands beside me, arms crossed, looking indifferent.

"Dying for *them*," Quinlan says, and I think he's talking about Unity, "that's the problem. The men I killed. They died fighting for their lives."

Berg sighs and shakes his head. I think he's just here to make sure Quinlan actually dies.

"They died fighting *you*," Vegas says.

"On their terms," Quinlan says. "For something they believed in. Not for Unity."

"Unity was never about serving the organization," Vegas says. He looks up at me for the next part. "I've learned that now." Back to Quinlan. "We fight for each other. We fight for the *concept* of unity. It's the only thing that can stand in the face of that." He points up at the large screen, still displaying the image of a giant monster, yanking people out from their hiding spots, pulling them inside its body.

Quinlan laughs. Coughs up blood. "We never did believe them. Not really." Shakes his head. "*Aliens*. Shit. Too bad they were twenty years off about D-day."

He coughs more blood. Too much blood.

Vegas puts his hand on Quinlan's forehead, deeply sad for the passing of his friend turned enemy.

"Don't look so pitiful, Vegas," Quinlan says. "Hell has got to be better than this island. Just leave me in the grass with the others and I'll—"

Midsentence, his eyes go still.

Vegas lowers his head. Ghost and Duff do the same.

I can't tell if he's saying some kind of prayer or just reeling in his emotions, but when he looks up at Ghost, Hutch and Berg, his eyes exude a kind of fire. "We're down to four. Are you with me?"

Ghost replies without any hesitation. "Los Perseverantes."

Duff shuffles on his feet, avoiding eye contact. "There are other Bases to choose fr—"

"Chuck," Vegas says, revealing Duff's real name. "I won't allow division. Never again." I hear the not so subtle threat. Join up, or live on the island. Alone.

Duff hears it, too. "Los Perseverantes."

"The Devil has gone home," Berg says, eyes on the floor. "He nearly burned us all." He nods at Vegas. "Los Perseverantes. At last. And I'm sorry."

"Don't apologize," Vegas says. "Just make it right." He points at the three men. "You three are a unit now. Start living it."

After nodding in agreement, the three men move away, talking amongst themselves, leaving me and Vegas. "You don't want them to—"

"They'll trust each other," he says. "Work better together."

"And you?"

"Gwen and Daniel," he says. "If that's okay with you."

If it's okay with me? Why would the mighty Vegas need my approval?

His answer to my confusion takes the last of my strength. "Points are leadership positions, and only one of us has earned the respect of everyone here. The only one who has shown she'll do *anything* to keep her people alive. If we're going to do something about that—" He hitches his thumb to the large screen behind him. "—we're going to need leadership that no one questions."

"You can't be serious," I say. "I'm not a leader. Before we dropped onto this island, I had only one friend in the world."

"You don't need friends to lead," he says.

I lean back against a terminal desktop, feeling lightheaded.

"You just need to make the hard choices." Vegas takes a dirty bandanna from his back pocket and lays it over Quinlan's face. "With the right Support strengthening your heart, and the right Base guiding your mind, the pressure of leadership can never drown you. The fractures of war will never make you numb. Their fortitude becomes yours, and from what I've seen, you were born with an indomitable spirit."

He stands and looks at all the people in the room. "And that's what they need." He turns to the viewscreen. The carnage. "That's what we all need. I let Quinlan run this island."

"You resisted him," I argue.

"I avoided him."

"He had an ExoFrame."

"I should have died fighting him." He rubs his face, looking weary. "And I should have figured out how to get inside this place a long time ago. Your unit. Sig. Hutch. And you. You have the will to fight, but the brains to solve problems that violence can't. That's why Unity stopped recruiting soldiers. I will fight for you. I'll die if I have to. But I can't lead these people. I don't have the heart for it. Or the mind."

He puts his hand on my uninjured arm, his touch focusing us on each other, like he's just completed a circuit. "You're in charge, Effie. You're the boss."

And with that, I pass right the heck out from loss of blood.

34

Death greets us with a white tunnel of light and loved ones urging us on. That's what they say on TV. Uncle Bob is there. Maybe a grandmother, twice removed. *Somebody.* The problem this presents for me is that I have no family to greet me. Sure, I have ancestors, but I don't know them. If they'd come to greet me, I'd have run away. But still, there's the light.

The light is safe.

The light is love.

The light is home.

It's also painfully bright. And smells like a new shower curtain.

"Effie?"

"Sig?" I say. My voice sounds distant, like my own voice is on the other side of a wall. "Are you dead, too?"

That Sig is here to greet me makes sense, but why is *she* dead? How did she beat me here?

"Dead?" Sig says, sounding slightly amused. "You're not dead, Eff."

"But the light."

I feel someone touch the side of my head. A gentle pull. The light fades to dark, and for a moment I think I've lost my chance at a better afterlife. The idea of spending eternity in a place that mirrors my childhood makes me sick to my stomach.

Then the room comes into focus. I'm in a medical bay, looking at a line of empty beds, a bright white halo of light above each one. Killer on the eyes, but probably makes it easy for doctors to see wounded patients. Not that there are any doctors with me. Just Sig.

"Hi," she says.

"Hey." When my voice comes out all muffled again, I reach up to my face and feel a mask over my nose and mouth. I pull it away and the new shower curtain scent is replaced by the sterilized air of a doctor's office.

Sig is sitting beside the bed looking exhausted. Twigs and bits of leaves are still stuck in her long hair. Her eyes are ringed red. She's been crying. Not that I can blame her. These last few days have been hellish. Though I think her tears have more to do with my condition than our recent experiences.

"I'm okay," I tell her, though I'm still taking stock of the various pains pulsing through my body.

"You almost weren't." She leans forward. "You stopped breathing."

This is news to me. Maybe the white light really was more than just a white light?

"What happened?" I ask.

"You were talking to Vegas. And then you were on the floor." Tears well. "You were dead."

I reach out a hand, and she takes it.

"Vegas knew what to do."

"He gave me CPR?"

She nods. "You'll feel the broken ribs when the pain meds wear off."

I look down at my chest. I'm wrapped in something that looks like a tight black turtle shell. Someone, probably Hutch, has attached the Point badge from my go-pack to the front of the medical armor. My lower half is dressed in papery medical pants. My feet are bare.

"It keeps your ribs from moving," Sig explains. "So you can heal faster. Will help with the pain, too. Just don't take a deep breath."

The moment she says it, I try. How can I not? And I regret it. Whatever pain meds I'm on, they're working, but they have limits.

An IV is attached to my arm, which is bare except for the bandage wrapped around the bullet wound that Mack inflicted.

"Hutch sewed you back up," Sig says. "Arm, stomach and back. Covered the wounds in some kind of antibiotic glue. They shouldn't open again."

"Saved by Hutch and Vegas," I say, "the heart and the hunk."

Sig's eyes widen. She opens her mouth to say something, but I think the drugs are making me a little slap happy.

"Seriously, why can't there be one guy who's both a prime specimen *and* kind hearted? That's my Ken, Sig. I know, I know, you think he should be smart, too, but honestly, I don't really care. At this point, we just need to repopulate the planet, right?"

Sig is an ice sculpture.

"I mean, obviously, we have to fight. We weren't given gargantuan Shugerbombs? Shuguben? Shugoten. That's the one. We weren't given them just to admire, right? I mean, my *name* is on one of them. And my mother...my actual mother…she brought me here, but did she know? Did she know three weeks ago? About *them?*"

"Effie," Sig says, but I'm on a roll. I'm feeling good and a little something more and talking to Sig, just talking to her, this little person with a big brain who I trust more than anyone.

"Well, they knew, right? They told hunky Vegas. The Diablos knew. Mack knew. They all knew. Because of Mars. But they didn't know when. D-Day was sooner than they thought. That's what Quinlan said before he kicked the bucket. Twenty years. They thought they had another twenty years to turn us into soldiers. Shuger...Shugoten operators. Support Striker pilots." I make finger guns and shoot them at imaginary targets. "Peow, peow, peow."

"I think we gave her too many painkillers," Sig says.

I nearly respond with a joke, but it catches in my throat. For a moment, I'm confused, but then I remember my ribs. Laughing would hurt. But that's not why I stopped talking.

My mind claws up through the fog, and it finds purchase on two words.

'We,' and, 'her.'

Sig wasn't speaking to me.

There is someone else in the room.

Sig confirms my dreaded conclusion with a nod.

"Glad you're okay," Hutch says, clearing his throat. "And for the record, Vegas is definitely a hunk. That other guy is really kind of a jerk, though."

I whip my head toward the other side of the bed. Hutch is sitting back in a chair, looking casual, wearing a smug smile the way old men wear their pants too high—like it's their God-given right to give themselves wedgies and expose their wrinkly ankles to the world. The worst part is, he knows I can't do anything about it.

"You could have said something," I grumble. "That was a private conversation."

He holds up his hands, and I notice he's changed into a black flight suit with a pattern of orange stripes and dots that reminds me of the Shugoten bearing my name. But it's more than a simple flight suit, its closer to very thin, form-fitting armor. And the orange bits aren't just fabric, they're glowing, all of it coming together at his chest to form a luminous Support symbol. "I won't tell a soul. Doctor-patient privilege."

"I take back every nice thing I said about you," I say.

He makes an exaggerated quizzical face. "Does that include everything you said in your sleep?"

Sig snorts out a laugh, and I hate to say it at this moment—I hate everything at this moment—but the sound of her laugh makes me smile. "The moment I'm out of this bed, you're both getting punched."

"You'd never punch Sig," Hutch says.

I glare at him, but I'm unable to hide my smile. Stupid painkillers. "Then I'll punch you twice."

"Is she flirting with me?" Hutch asks Sig, on the verge of bursting into laughter, which he does the moment Sig lets out the loudest barky laugh I've ever heard.

"Good God, strike me down," I say, but I find myself chuckling, working hard to contain my building laughter. "This is *so* not fair. How about we talk about Gwen?"

"What about Gwen?" Hutch says. I can't tell if I misread the two of them, or if he's really good at hiding his emotions.

"Or Daniel?" I turn to Sig, and her smile is fading quickly. Oops. "Sorry."

"Daniel's a good guy," Hutch says, not losing an ounce of his good cheer, "but I think Duff is the man for you."

Sig fights her returning smile.

"So," I say to Hutch, happy to move past my faux pas, "You're just one of the girls, eh?"

He shrugs, unfazed by the crack. "I do have three sisters." As soon as he says it, his lightheartedness falls dead on the floor. He's quiet for a moment. "I hope I still do."

"I'm sure they're okay," I say, but he's equally unfazed by my platitude.

"I'm worried about my parents," Sig says. She's an only child. Not a lot of extended family in the States. But she's close to her parents.

I realize that the horror I felt at seeing the outside world torn apart and burning, as horrible as it was, was far worse for them. I'm not sure where Hutch is from, but Sig and I both lived east of San Diego.

"We are going to fight them, right?" Sig asks.

I try to push myself up, but Hutch puts his hand on my shoulder. "You need to rest. You lost a lot of blood. I had to give you a transfusion."

I'm about to ask from whom, but then I see the bandage in the crook of his arm. He gave me his own blood. Is that part of why they picked him for my Support? In case I was bleeding out and needed a fresh batch to keep me going? Are Supports seen as expendable? Are Points really that important?

Questions for another, more lucid day. "And now I need to punch you three times."

He sighs, but he helps support my back until I'm sitting up straight. I'm expecting it to hurt a lot, but the thing around my ribs holds everything in place.

"We're going to fight them," I tell Sig in my most serious, 'I'm not screwing around' voice. "We're going to fight them, and we're going to—"

An alarm sounds, like I'm on a game show and have just given the wrong answer. But then it repeats, over and over. A red light is flashing in the hallway.

"What's that?" I ask, but they're as clueless as I am. We all know it's an alarm, and probably not good, but what is it for?

"We'll be back," Hutch says, rushing for the door, Sig running to catch up.

"Hey!" I shout at them, flexing ribs, gasping from the pain. "Help me up."

Hutch shakes his head. "Effie, seriously, you can't—"

I yank the IV from my arm and ignore the trickle of blood that might be mine, or Hutch's. "The three of us are a unit now."

They both stare at me.

I point at Sig. "Base."

My finger slides over to Hutch. "Support."

I hitch a thumb at my chest. "Point."

"We don't have to do everything you tell us," Hutch says, speaking loudly over the alarm. "Especially if it's going to hurt you."

"Before I...died...Vegas told me I was in charge. Not him. Not either of you. Unless either of you think you can be a Point, I'm responsible for everyone in this place. Everyone who survived the past few days or longer on this island. I can't lead from a bed. Franklin D. Roosevelt was paralyzed from the waist down by Guillain–Barré syndrome. But did he say 'boo-hoo for me, let the Japanese have Hawaii'? 'Let Hitler have Europe'? No. He said, 'we will not only defend ourselves to the uttermost, but will make it very certain that this form of treachery shall never again endanger us. Hostilities exist. There is no blinking at the fact that our people, our territory and our interests are in grave danger. With confidence in our armed forces, with the unbounding determination of our people, we will gain the inevitable triumph. So help us God.'"

They just stare at me, dumbfounded, like they've never heard those words before. And maybe they haven't. So I elaborate for them. I point to the wheelchair folded up in the corner of the room. "Get the damn chair."

Hutch heads for the chair, but he doesn't look thrilled about it. As soon as he steps away from the door, Gwen slides into view, clutching the frame, stopping herself mid-run. She's out of breath. Afraid. And dressed in a white, armored flight suit with glowing red stripes that come together at a metal Unity badge on her chest. It looks like the badge

I found in my go-pack, but orange on the sides, and black at the tip and base. A Support badge.

She looks me in the eyes and delivers the one message I hoped she wouldn't. "They're here."

The two words are vague, but the message is clear enough.

They're here.

Them.

The enemy.

I don't know how wheelchair-bound people do it. Having your top speed limited by a motor or the person pushing you is frustrating. While even the fully mobile have a top speed, you can always improve it, or push against it, expand the limits a bit. But in a chair, being pushed, options are limited to sit back and enjoy the ride, or make the life of the person pushing you a living nightmare.

I choose the latter.

"I'm not someone's aging grandmama," I grouch at Hutch.

"You have broken ribs," he says. "Two bullet holes."

"One bullet hole. One bullet scratch."

"You *died*," he complains.

Is this what having a real mother would have been like?

"From loss of blood," I say, "which you gave back to me—thanks for that—and you've plugged all the leaks. This glue stuff will hold, right?"

During the alarm-whooping seconds of his non-response, Gwen and Sig round a corner far ahead of us. I slap both armrests. "Move it, Hutch, or I swear, I'm going to jump out of this thing and run."

"Hold on," he says.

My hair slides back in the breeze of our acceleration. As we approach the turn, I grasp the armrests. It takes a supreme, pride-fueled effort to not shout as we take the corner, the wheelchair tipping onto one wheel, nearly careening into the wall. When the chair thumps back to the ground, pain bursts through me, and I'm glad Hutch can't see my face.

The alarm goes quiet just before we reach Operation's entrance. Its shrieking call is replaced by the sound of shouting voices. Sounds like everyone beat me here, and no one knows what's going on.

Hutch slows us down as we enter the large control room. The first thing I notice is the people. Everyone is here. Vegas is wearing a white flight suit that matches Gwen's. Berg and Ghost are wearing armored flight suits, too. They're maroon and covered in a pattern of glowing yellow stripes that converge on their various Unity symbols. Where did they find them?

Then I see Quinlan's body is missing. They somehow got him, and the ExoFrame, out of here. The blood and debris has been removed, too, though I can still see a smear on the long hangar window, where someone hastily wiped it down. I must have been unconscious for a while. A few hours at least.

The third thing I notice is the wall of screens. Many of the smaller displays still show satellite views of the world in ruin. But the large screen shows a tropical ocean and something large moving just beneath the surface.

"Where is that?" I ask, but no one hears me. They're too busy shouting at each other about what to do.

"Hey!" I shout, and the pain caused by the lone word nearly makes me gasp. But I put on a strong face when everyone turns toward me. From the far side of the room, sitting at a terminal, Gizmo whispers, "Effie, thank God."

Thank God? For *me?* That's a first. I'm not sure how I came to be that person, whose presence can only be explained by divine intervention, thus requiring thanks to a supreme being—to Gizmo or anyone else. It's not something I ever wanted, or thought possible. And as views of the ravaged world glow around the room, the whole 'Why would God allow bad things to happen?' argument flits through my mind. It's the same question I've wrestled with all my life in regard to my parents. Why would loving parents subject their daughter to a life like mine?

As I push myself up out of the chair, my subconscious provides an answer: *To make you strong enough.* For what? To survive a life of abuse? Of solitude and confusion? Or to survive the horrors of an island my mother planned to abandon me on for a second time?

The back of a massive body rises through the water, creating a wake. I look from the screen to the hangar window below it, and to the Shugoten standing sentinel on the other side.

Strong enough for this.

I point at the large screen. "Where is that?"

"Three miles out and closing," Daniel says. "It triggered some kind of proximity sensors. The security system picked it up. Sounded the alarm. Has been tracking it automatically since."

"When will it get here?" I ask, and I think someone like Vegas might have said, "ETA?"

Daniel looks back at me. He's terrified. "Ten minutes."

I can tell he has more to say. "What?"

"It's approaching from the West. We already know these things hatch from the pods, and that they fell from the sky. I think this might be the one we saw crash that night. The one that caused the Tsunami. Since they seem interested in eating... people, there is no good reason for a pod to land in the middle of the Pacific. It being in this part of the world was probably unintentional. But it coming here, to this island, is not. Effie, it *knows* we're here. I don't know how it knows, but it does. And it's coming for us. To *eat* us."

Daniel's declaration sets the room abuzz once more.

"Quiet!" I shout, ignoring the pain a little easier this time.

With all eyes on me once more, I point at the hangar and ask Daniel, "You know how these work?"

"In theory," he says. "If they didn't change too much."

To Vegas. "And you can operate them?" To Berg. "Both of you?"

"If they work like an ExoFrame, we can manage." Vegas looks ready to charge out there and try. After seeing the state of the world, he seems ready for a fight.

"There's more to them than an ExoFrame, but the controls are similar enough," Daniel says. "Again, in theory."

I turn to Gwen, not wanting to ask anything of her, but I understand how this is supposed to work—even if I don't yet know the physical mechanics of it. "What about you? Can you fly one of those?"

Daniel pipes up again. "The Support Strikers should be identical to—"

"I asked her," I say.

"Yeah," Gwen says. "I aced the flight sims."

"This won't be a simulation," I tell her.

"I always assumed it wouldn't be someday," she says, and smiles. "And in case you haven't figured it out yet, it's our job to worry about *you*, not the other way around."

"Doesn't mean I have to like it," I say, turning to Ghost. "How about you?"

"I haven't flown one of those," he says, "but I passed the flight sim exam when I was fourteen. I'm more at home in the air than I am down here."

That settles it. "Vegas, Berg, see if you can get those things working. Ghost, Gwen. You're their Supports. Get in the air and back them up. Duff, Daniel, you're their Bases. Figure all of this out. Do what you can to guide them."

And just like that, everyone snaps into action. Vegas opens the hangar door at the side of the room, revealing a staircase leading down to the floor of the wide-open space. Berg and Ghost follow him out. Gwen isn't far behind, but I stop her. "Gwen."

She waits for me, as I hobble up to her. "I half expected you to jump in one of those robots yourself. You're showing strength and wisdom. I think—"

To our mutual surprise, I cut her short with a hug.

"Be careful."

She leans back, looking me in the eyes. "I will... but I'll also do what I have to."

I nod. "I know. Just come back alive."

She smiles, but makes no promises before leaving.

Daniel, Gizmo, Duff, Doli and Sig are all seated at consoles, working hard. I watch Doli for a moment and Hutch, the only other person left standing, notices.

"Killing Quinlan brought her back a bit," he says. "She hasn't said much, but she never really did. She's more at home in the digital world."

I watch Doli's curved screen, seeing only streams of text and numbers. "What's she doing?"

"Trying to make contact," he says.

"With who?"

"With anyone."

"Duff." Daniel leans back in his chair, looking past Gizmo to the older, chubby ex-Diablo. He holds up the strange white helmet connected to his system. It looks like some kind of sea creature—a jelly fish with holes and small sensors on the inside. "Have you ever used psy-controls?"

Duff nods. "Yeah, but we're not controlling anything from in here."

Daniel pulls the strange helmet over his head. "There are corresponding psy-controls in the Shugoten and Strikers. When all three are activated, we'll be able to communicate in real time, just by thinking. We'll also feel what they feel, so be ready for that. Just remember, we're inside a bunker under a mountain. We're safe. Our lack of fear can be a buffer for theirs."

"Unity," Duff says. "I know how it works."

And now I do, too. At least a little more than I did before. I had pictured the functions of Base, Support and Point as wholly external. Base supplied information. Support provided physical relief and emotional strength. Point led the way and did the dirty work. At best, it was all about trusting your team. But the three-person unit—mind, soul and body—merged through psy-controls, really could act as one. Separate, but unified.

And while that is kind of cool, I still don't really see the strategic advantage to simply having an army of Points in giant butt-kicking robots. When dealing with something the size of a daikaiju, brute force seems like a more appropriate response than the touchy-feely, 'let's share our feelings' Unity method.

But I suppose that's about to be put to the test.

"Copy," Daniel says, and I realize he's speaking to Vegas or Gwen. "Umm, I'm not sure."

"What's the problem?" I ask.

"Gwen can't figure out how to get the Striker running."

That's a bad sign, I think, but I keep it to myself. Then I ask what I think is the most obvious question. "Is there a place for a key?"

"Uhh," Daniel says. "Is there a place for a key?"

He waits, and then his face lights up. "Yes. Use that." He turns to me. "It's the badge," he says, tapping the center of his chest where the metal badge would be if Bases wore flight suits.

"Why are you guys even talking?" I ask. "I thought you were supposed to be—" I tap my head. "—mind-melded or something."

"Technically, it's called a psy-net, but it doesn't engage until the others are wearing their—" Daniel goes rigid, his eyes opening wide. He sucks in a deep breath, as a shiver rolls through his body. "We're connected."

"Us, too," Duff says from his console.

Motion through the hangar window draws me toward it. On the other side of the glass, two Strikers are lifting off the floor, held aloft by humming, blue repulse engines.

Light from above pours into the open space. Sunlight. Triangular sections of the circular ceiling lift up and separate, revealing the inside of the volcano's crater.

Is this really happening?

The Strikers rise straight up through the opening, and once they've cleared the top, the white Shugoten to my right and the maroon one next to it, step into the center of the room. Now fully powered, the pattern of stripes and spots covering the bodies glow; the maroon robot is covered in a luminous yellow pattern, the white one in red. As they move, a barely perceptible mesh of yellow hexagons appears and then fades.

The giants move with the fluidity of human beings, crashing through the uncanny valley—that uncomfortable feeling when humanoid robots creep you out—and stepping into awe-inspiring awesomeness.

Despite weighing untold tons, I can't hear or feel their movements. When they're both positioned at the center of the room, the floor rises beneath them, lifting the two giants toward the sky. Everything happens so smoothly that I think the four operators have done all this before. But then I realize they're being directed, without a spoken word, by Daniel and Duff, who are also fully present in this room, their fingers clattering over keyboards, their eyes scanning information, schematics and readouts.

"Here it comes," Gizmo says, and I turn to the big screen in time to see the daikaiju rise from the ocean and take its first monstrous step onto the island's tsunami-ravaged western side. Onto our island.

"Can they hear me?" I ask Daniel.

His fingers tap a few keys. "They can now."

"Vegas," I say.

"I hear you."

"Kick its ass."

36

Using the island and its trees for scale, I guestimate the creature's size to be around five hundred feet. And as big as that is, it's the least horrifying thing about the monster.

It emerges from the ocean on all fours, like the one we saw rampaging in Southern California. The dark gray skin of its vast armor plates glisten from the water. It's torn up a bit in places, but it looks more like scratched leather than any kind of real damage. Wounds from its rough landing, maybe.

Unlike the first daikaiju, this one is fully armored on all sides. Where most creatures on Earth would have a nose and mouth, this thing has folds of armor, like overlapping plates, speckled with blue. As the sun shines over its body, I see glimmers of light refracting off the water rushing down its coarse-textured body. If I hadn't already seen one of these treating San Diego like a smorgasbord, I might have been able to find some beauty in it. But I really just want to crush this thing under my heel. To stamp it into oblivion. Unfortunately, the opposite is far more likely.

The creature stops on the shore, its hind legs still in the ocean, its long tail cutting back and forth through the water. I imagine the force of that sweeping tail, the amount of liquid it's moving, and I can see these things pushing back the tide.

They're going to reshape our world. And they're going to start with us.

Since the human race figured out we were destroying the planet and instigating an extinction event on par with the asteroid that ended the Cretaceous Period and wiped the dinosaurs from the face of the planet, we've tried, and mostly failed, to undo the damage. But we've also romanticized what the planet would be like if people simply ceased to exist. The environment would rebound. Species on the brink would recover. New species would evolve. In short, life would go on without us, and in a few thousand years it would return to the pristine state it was in before the Industrial Revolution. But in all our imaginings, humanity never pictured the end like this, at the hands of colossal aliens with the power to leave our planet a lifeless husk. The human race was responsible for kicking off a mass extinction, but now we might be the only thing that can prevent a *final* extinction.

The daikaiju narrows its four yellow eyes. Then it flexes and stretches, the massive plates of armor shifting around, leaking sea water out from between the armor's fault lines. The body puffs up and expands, revealing an almost heart-shaped, reddish underside. The world's worst valentine. The armor covering its chest splits and separates, exposing more of the ruddy skin. Thousands of black holes covering the red flesh open and close, like mouths the size of cars, saying 'mop, mop,' and pushing out dribbles of fluid. The shell-like folds composing the creature's neck peel open to the sides, like big, spiky clam shells, revealing even more pores. The last bit to open is its mouth, which isn't really a mouth at all. What looks like armor covering the lower half of its face, snaps open like mandibles, revealing more of the pocked flesh. Then it shakes like a dog, spraying ocean water and some kind of viscous goo from its pores. The daikaiju's whole body sneezes the stuff.

I glance through the hangar window. The Shugo-ten are nearing the top.

Moving images appear on two of the screens, circling the giant at a safe distance. Video feeds from the Strikers.

"How are you doing, Gwen?" I ask.

"Like riding a bike," she says, "if you learned how to ride a bike on a simulator. I've got the hang of it, though. Daniel's teaching me how to use the weapons. The ones he knows about, anyway."

The lost look in Daniel's eyes reveals his level of concentration. It's like his consciousness isn't in the room anymore. There is just a hint of a smile on his face. But is that how he's feeling, or how Gwen and Vegas are feeling, their emotions filtering back to Daniel? *It's all three of them,* I realize, *but are they just geeking out or looking forward to a little old-school retribution?*

The main viewscreen shows the daikaiju from one of many hidden cameras mounted atop the volcano, tracking every one of the creature's movements. The alien invader flexes its three nubby fingers. When it brings them down, long hooked, retractable claws slide out, puncture the sandy beach and dig troughs, as they slide back inside their fleshy sheaths.

"Can they see the feeds?" I ask Daniel.

I'm not sure if he's heard me for a moment, but then he blinks, apologizes and says, "I can see them, and they're getting all that info from me. They knew about the claws the moment I saw them."

"They can't see through your eyes?" I ask, sounding more aghast than I feel.

He shakes his head. "Information I take in is passed on to them in real time. They don't feel it. They can't experience the flow of data. They just simply know things they didn't the moment before, like they always knew. There's nothing jarring about it." He sucks in a quick breath. "It's standing up."

I turn to the big screen and see the daikaiju rising up onto its hind legs. While Gwen and Vegas are knowing things through Daniel, he's also getting knowledge from them—in this case, from Gwen, who's still circling the monster.

I can't tell where its four yellow eyes are looking, but its face is upturned right toward the camera.

Toward the volcano.

And the rising Shugoten.

The clamshell plates on its face snap back down. Its body clenches from the inside out, and the armor snaps back together.

That's where it's weakest. "Tell them to attack the points where the armor comes together," I say.

Daniel smiles. "They already know. Vegas saw the same thing."

"Effie." It's Sig, sitting at a terminal, looking a little surprised.

I lean in next to her. "Yeah?"

"I just found a network of camera feeds around the island."

"More security cameras for the base?"

She shakes her head. "I think it's more than that. I'll put them up."

All around the room, the screens change to views of the island. Cameras aren't just atop or around the volcano. They're everywhere.

I guess Vegas only found some.

I recognize several locations. The landing pad. Several views of the river. Every single coastline. The Unity campsite with its hammocks. The Perseverantes campsite. A third campsite I don't recognize, but assume belonged to Los Diablos.

They knew.

She knew.

About the island's real dangers. And they sent us here anyway, knowing full well that some of us, maybe even all of us, would die. They clearly hoped that wouldn't be the case, that we would rise to the occasion and overcome hardship, but they were willing to risk all our lives.

One of the video streams catches my eye, and it has nothing to do with the daikaiju. It's a beach, devoid of everything but a strip of sand separating ocean and jungle. I reach for my chest pocket, which is no longer there. "My photo," I say, speaking to myself, but Hutch answers.

"I took it from your flight suit," he says, digging the dented rectangle from his pocket and handing it to me.

I hold the photo up beside the screen in question. On the left, I see empty beach. On the right, my parents embracing on the very same beach. They were here, even back then, on this island. *Is this where I was conceived? Where I was born?*

Vegas snaps my attention from the confusing past, and back to the horrible present. "We're going in."

His words are for the benefit of those who aren't connected via the psy-net. From a variety of views around the room, the action unfolds like some kind of immersive movie experience.

Moving with surprising grace and speed for their size, the Shugoten slide down the mountainside like surfers catching a wave. But there is no rumble inside the mountain. Onscreen, the trees beneath them simply bow away before springing back up. They're not actually touching the ground. The repulse engines in their feet keep their weight off the ground, allowing them to move without relying solely on mechanical muscles.

The two Shugoten separate halfway down the mountain, carving the invisible wave in opposite directions, putting them on either side of the daikaiju. Vegas's white Shugoten reaches the ocean first, and I expect it to plunge in, topple and sink to the bottom. But it slides out over the water, kicking up twin streams of water behind its feet. Flaps in its back open up, revealing two more repulse engines that kick in with a flash of blue light, pushing the giant robot forward, even faster.

Berg mirrors Vegas, bringing his maroon Shugoten around toward the monster's other side.

The daikaiju seems confused, pulled in two directions, unsure which side to defend.

But it doesn't back down, either. It's not afraid.

It should be.

Blades extend from both robots' forearms.

They close the distance, spraying arcs of water out behind them.

I'm so captivated by the impending collision that when a cloud of rockets hit the monster's back, I hiccup in surprise. When two Strikers punch through the rising ball of fire, spinning before pulling up over the island, I let out a cheer that is joined by a, "whoop!" from Gwen in her Striker.

But the pitched-forward monster still moves within the cloud of smoke, rising back up.

Not fast enough, I think, as the Shugoten close in, leading with their blades and aiming for the seams between the armored plates.

Just when the collision seems inevitable, the daikaiju moves with surprising speed, leaping off the ground, reaching out and spinning. Berg misses his mark completely, sailing beneath the monster, which hooks its claws into the robot's back and throws. At the same time, Vegas leaps up over the daikaiju, flipping upside down, hundreds of feet in the air, and swiping his blade across the monster's back.

The monster continues its spin, swiping at Vegas, but it falls short. The robot lands on its feet and is carried out of range by the repulse engines.

Vegas cruises in an arc, out into the ocean, coming back around. Berg climbs back to his feet and turns to face the creature. He's not moving quickly though, and I think his repulse engines have been damaged.

Sig looks up at me from her station, pointing at the scrolling information on screen. "They're going to hit it with rockets again, from Berg, Gwen and Ghost. Vegas is going to hit it from behind."

Sounds like a good enough plan, but I think they're underestimating it. It's faster than I thought possible. Vegas's first strike scratched the armor, but nothing more. And he's headed straight toward the creature's monstrous tail. I want to say something, but in the time it takes me to voice my concerns, the attack will be over.

Large flaps on Berg's shoulders snap open, revealing rocket pods.

Vegas cocks his blade back, aiming to impale rather than cut.

The two Strikers descend from each side, ready to unleash rockets before narrowly missing each other and flying away in opposite directions.

It's a carefully timed and coordinated attack, all thanks to the psy-net. But will it work?

The daikaiju answers the question even before the first rocket fires.

No.

The armor covering the thing's sides peels open. The face opens up. The tail rises from the ocean, its many segmented shells pulling wide to reveal softer flesh. For a flash, it appears to be taunting us, daring Vegas to strike its exposed flesh. Then its pores open up, unleashing a wriggling mass of red tendrils, and along with them, our darkest, most vile fears.

"Euphoria." The voice, followed by a slamming door, brings tears to my eyes. The house is too small and sparse to hide in, so I hide my tears instead. He finds me sitting on my bed, eyes on the floor. I see the colorful construction paper and scissors I stole from school—I was cutting the paper into the sun and planets—and his grime covered toes poking out from his worn down sandals.

"Euphoria," he says. "Hey."

I don't look. I don't dare. But he's not going to give me a choice. Never does.

"Hey!"

"That's *not* my name," I say when I look up. I'm not sure why I said it. I'm seven years old and smarter than most twelve year olds. I know that I shouldn't even talk to this man, let alone mouth off to him.

"Your name is whatever damn name I decide to call you, *Shithead*. And that's with a capital S. You know what that is, right? A big S before hithead, which is what I'm gonna do, if you don't—"

My legs and mouth move on some kind of auto-pilot, like I've been possessed. I stand up and level a finger at his face. "You're not my father."

He smiles at this, revealing what I'm sure are wooden teeth. "Your father ain't your father."

"I'm going to tell him about you."

"Are you now?" He pushes the door open all the way and steps into my room, stepping through the force field I've always imagined, but never had. A six pack of beer dangles from two of his fingers. The cans are unopened, but his breath says it's not his first for the day. "You think my brother gives two turds about you, other than the money the state sends him?" He holds up the six pack. "Keeps us fully stocked."

"My mother will—"

"She's not your mother," he says, stepping closer. "And today is Friday."

Friday.

Two days to heal.

The slap comes fast and hard, knocking me back onto the bed.

I hear the front door open and close again. Howard ignores it. His predator eyes are locked on me.

"Howie?" It's Jenny, his girlfriend. Like Uncle Howard, she's an addict. Her escape of choice is a white powder that sends her somewhere else. But when she is here, she's nice.

My uncle ignores her, but the smack of his back-hand, across the other side of my face, can be heard throughout the house. The first slap stung, but the knuckles of his back-hand shake something loose in my mouth. I taste blood.

"Howie, what the *hell?*" Jenny stands in the doorway behind him, heavy purse weighing down her shoulder. She looks like a vampire in serious need of a drink, dressed in a cheetah skin top and very short shorts.

"Take a hike, Jennybird." He glances back at her. "Mirror's in the living room."

"Howie..." Jenny looks unsure. "If she gets too hurt, they'll—"

Too hurt. She only cares about me the way a trucker cares about his truck. I'm a means to an end. I'm money for their various addictions. And like a truck, I can be broken.

Howie's retort is another hand against my cheek. I fall to the side, seeing stars. I'm too hurt to cry, in part because of the very real physical pain, but also because I know that come Monday morning, the yellowing bruises will be easily covered up by make-up that I'll be too afraid to wash off. Or they'll just keep me home again.

"You dumb, sonuva—" The sentence ends in a mumble somewhere else. She's stormed away.

"Atta girl, Jennybird," Howie says, with a hacking chuckle. "You go fly away." He turns back to me. "We're all just gonna fly away."

Right there is where this foggy memory had always ended for me, patched together in a quilt of pain made from a year of my life. It's been almost ten years since then, and all I've remembered about that time is shattered fragments.

Until now.

Memories reverse like a broken stained-glass window, divergent shards pulling back together in a mosaic suddenly made whole. The picture is complete. The now-me screams. I can hear myself in the memory of past-me. But there is no escaping. No looking away.

All I can do is watch.

But it's worse than that. Because I'm not watching. I'm *reliving.*

I've heard the sound of a shotgun being pumped enough times to recognize the sound without actually seeing the source. Howie knows it, too, and he turns around like he's expecting danger. Then he sees Jenny and relaxes. "Gah-damn, Jennybird, you..." He snarls at her. "You testing me, girl?"

Jenny takes one hand off the weapon to point at me and the barrel sags toward the floor. "We need her, How. Ain't no point in roughing her up. There are plenty of other people in the world you can—"

Howie's hands snap out, clutch the shotgun and twist. The weapon turns Jenny's arm until she cries out and lets go. Before Howie can turn the weapon around on her, she lunges, scratching at his face. Screaming. She's gone mad. Like a feral cat set upon another.

Red streaks appear on his cheek.

Howie stumbles back from the assault, mumbling a string of curses together. Then he spins the butt of the shotgun around and catches Jenny in the side of the head. She falls hard, striking my thin mattress and the sheet of plywood holding it atop four milk crates.

He points the shotgun down at Jenny.

I know what's coming next. He'll do the dance. The one he always does when things get nuts. When they lose control. He'll shake around to music only he can hear, then stop and shout, "Pow!" making everyone jump. Then Jenny will get up and leave, and we'll be back on course, except things will be even worse for me now.

He does the dance.

Jenny looks at me. She doesn't look afraid now. More relieved. "Don't run," she says. "You can't."

I'm crying now. Jenny knows this is different.

So do I.

"You have to fight, Effie," she says. "You have to—"

"Pow," Howard whispers, and then he pulls the trigger.

Fight.

There isn't enough left of Jenny to speak the word, but I hear it.

Fight...

"Euphoria."

I blink. *What?* Jenny is gone. My project is on the floor. The scissors.

"Euphoria. Hey."

"Hey!"

The memory repeats. I relive it again.

It cripples me.

"Don't run. You can't."

"You have to fight, Effie. You have to—"

Pow.

"Euphoria."

I crumble inward, gripped by despair.

"Hey!"

No...

"You have to fight, Effie. You have to—"

Fight!

The memory trembles. I hear my mock name called again, "Euphoria," but the reset fails.

The memory continues.

I see Jenny, who isn't even a person now.

Howard is laughing. Pumps the shotgun. Turns it to where I was, but am no longer. Pulls the trigger.

My mattress explodes.

Something bigger than myself propels me. Faster than I can think. Faster than Howard can move.

He pumps the shotgun again, but that's as far as he gets.

That's where his life ends.

My last memory of Howard is him looking down at the scissors in his chest, and then falling over on top of them.

I gasp out of the memory, curled in a fetal ball on the floor of Operations. Hutch lays beside me, twitching, eyes rolled back. Sig is slumped over her console, whimpering, shaking. Every single person in Operations has come undone. The enemy is crippling us with our worst fears, projected into our minds. That's why all those people stopped running.

And there is no escaping it. On the display screens, I see the Strikers, spinning away. They're not crashing, but they're not being controlled, either.

Berg's Shugoten is on its back in the sand, motionless.

Vegas is in the water, fallen to his hands and knees, shaking, perhaps fighting, but losing.

And then there is the daikaiju, tendrils writhing, stomping a path straight toward Vegas's Shugoten. The robot has its head bowed down, ready for execution.

I feel the memory slam back into my head, trying to restart, but failing.

The monster made a mistake.

My worst fear isn't some imagined phobia, it's a memory, walled up by my seven-year-old subconscious until just now. But it's also the day I discovered my strength, the reason I don't wait to be punched first, why I could kill Mack and Bear and why I could stand up to Quinlan. By showing me Uncle Howard, the monster outside simply revealed its true self to me, and reminded me that I'm strong enough to stand and fight in the face of abject terror.

I push myself up with shaky arms, defying the fear.

Fighting my past.

I rebel against it, beat it down and climb to my feet again.

I look up at the daikaiju, name it Howard in my heart, and think, *I'm coming for you.*

Then I turn to Hutch and say, "And you're going to help."

Denying fear's cold grip is one thing, but pushing past very physical pain is another. There are very real limits that no amount of determination can push you past. Bleed too much, you die. Hurt too much, you pass out. Look at an injury, you go into shock. These are biological functions no person can overcome by strength of will alone.

But I'm trying anyway.

Hutch is heavier than he looks, and in his limp, twitchy state, he's not helping at all. I've got him under his arms, pulling him through the broad hangar, his heels squeaking against the metal floor. His weight pulls on my arms and core, straining my vast array of wounds and putting Hutch's assurances—that the glue will hold and the wrap around my chest will keep my ribs in place—to the test. Without the armored flight suit recovered from a locker that had *'F-BOMB'* stenciled on it, I don't think I would have made it this far. The suit is a perfect fit, probably made in the past few weeks during my Unity training. Like Hutch's, it glows with power, the pattern of stripes converging at my chest where there is a luminous Point symbol. While it's not really a mechanized battle suit, I can feel it augmenting my strength and stabilizing my body. Unfortunately, it's not dulling the agony of my injuries.

The pain pushes tears from my eyes.

My legs weaken.

You're almost there, I tell myself. *You can do this. You have to do this.*

Then I look and nearly fall to my knees.

I'm only halfway across the hangar, with several hundred feet still between me and Hutch's Striker. My bare feet slap the cold floor as I stumble, catching myself and Hutch at the last moment. The pain nearly drops me. My arms quiver from the effort. And then I feel it. A gentle squeeze on my hand.

I look down at Hutch's upside down face. He's covered in sweat. His jaw trembles. But his eyes, for the moment, are lucid. He looks up at me, freed from his nightmare long enough to say, "You...can make it."

He glances back at the Striker. At the Shugoten. Without our minds being connected by a psy-net or any words spoken between us, he knows what I'm planning. "You are our strength, Euphemia."

His use of my full name has a strange effect. I don't want to punch him. I want to embrace him. To save him. To stand at his defense and shout into the raging tempest consuming the world, 'You cannot have him.'

I have never felt these things before. They confuse, but also empower me.

Hutch. Sig. Gwen. And all the others who have now become my friends—my family—are going to die if I can't push past this pain.

Hutch squeezes my hand again, tighter this time. "Hurry—"

His body seizes. Eyes roll back. He's trapped in the daikaiju's psychological prison once more.

But his brief visit galvanizes me. I drag him, grunting and screaming until we reach the Striker. When we approach the front of the vehicle, the badge on his chest glows for a moment and a hatch opens up, lowering to the floor, mocking me with its many steps. But I'm not about to stop now. I haul him up one step at a time, sounding like an aggressive tennis player. The space inside the Striker's cockpit is limited, and I struggle to get Hutch in the seat. But his unconscious state lets me shove him around and manipulate his limbs until he's seated and strapped in place. I get his psy-control headset in place and...what next? The Striker sits quietly.

How do you start one of these things?

Then I see it. A triangle shaped depression on the console, the same size as the Support badge on

Hutch's chest. I pull the badge free and hold it over the console, feeling a magnetic pull. When I let it go, the badge snaps into place and the console lights up. The hum of electronics fills the cabin, and a vibration tickles my feet. It's the hatch, retracting. I hurry to the still-open hatch and half stumble down the stairs, while they're pulled back up inside. At the bottom, I have to jump the final four feet to the solid floor.

I land on my feet, but my knees buckle. My fall ends with my hands on the floor, like I'm bowing, prostrate before some god. But when I look up, there is no deity, just *F-B0MB,* the black and orange Shugoten, standing nobly and impossibly tall, awaiting its Operator.

Once I'm inside, the weakness of my body won't matter anymore. Psy-controls mean that even a quadriplegic could operate one of the giant robots. I just need to reach its head...four hundred feet above me. One shaky leg at I time, I get back to my feet and hobble to the lift that rises up toward the ceiling. There's only one button, so I give it a punch and am carried aloft. The rapid ascent twists my stomach for just a moment, and then I'm four hundred feet up, telling myself not to look down. The catwalk clangs against my feet, sounding not nearly solid enough, but then the side of *F-B0MB*'s head opens up, and I forget all about the height, and my pain.

I step over the threshold and into another world. The cockpit, if that's what it can be called, is sparse, but very different from anything I've seen. There's a chair, but it's not attached to the floor. Instead, it's held in the center of the dodecahedron-shaped space by a network of shock absorbers. Will I even feel the robot moving?

A psy-control helmet hangs down over the chair, and that's about it. No manual controls. No gauges. No lights. No view through the robot's eyes. Just a flat console with an empty spot awaiting the placement of a Point's Unity badge.

My Unity badge.

Will this Shugoten work with anyone's badge? I wonder, and I pull the Point symbol from my chest. It was in my go-pack from the beginning, its purpose unclear at the time. But I was always meant to find myself standing here, with this badge. It wasn't fate that brought me here, it was my mother. Who left me. Who risked my soul, and then my life. Who in her very hands-off way, allowed me to endure tortures that gave me the strength to make it this far. And if she hadn't? What then? Would I be out in the world, dying with the rest of them? With my parents?

Despite the anger I have for the woman I met via Featherlight recording, I hope she and my father are alive. I have questions for them. Things to say.

But that's only going to happen if I survive. And that's only going to be possible, if I focus. So I push thoughts of my parents and the entire outside world—past, present and future—from my mind. I hold the badge out over the console. It snaps into place, and I feel the Shugoten come to life beneath me. It doesn't move, but I can feel its powerful potential. And it brings a smile to my face.

I turn around as the chair lowers to the floor. *F-BOMB* is offering herself to me. And I accept, sliding into the cushiony chair. I look for straps as the chair lifts back into place, but find none. Instead, they find me. Hard, padded restraints snap out from the backside of the chair, wrapping around my waist and chest, slowly tightening until I can't move, but not enough to hurt my broken ribs. When that's done, the same thing happens to my arms and legs in two places. When it's done, I'm completely immobilized. I'm seized by a moment of panic, which nearly lets the daikaiju back inside my head, but then the psy-controls lower down over my head, and my consciousness is set free. I can no longer feel the chair beneath me, my body's pain or the straps holding me in place.

I feel a tingling, like I've bent over for five minutes and stood up too fast. And then, nightmares.

Two of them.

One involves spiders.

The other features me, dead.

I can't tell whose nightmare belongs to whom, but I know I'm feeling what the daikaiju is doing to Sig and Hutch, thanks to the psy-controls I put on both of them. Our unit is connected, which means they can feel me, too.

So I invade their nightmares.

I lend them my strength.

The spiders scurry for cover.

And dead me stands living and unharmed.

Can you hear me? I think at them.

Effie? Sig replies. *How?*

Psy-controls. We're all together now. And then no explanation is needed. They know what I know and I know that they know. Information flows freely between us, our minds networked.

Hutch is already lifting off.

Through Sig, I know that the daikaiju has nearly reached Vegas.

I need to get out of here fast, I think, and then I know the solution, information on how to operate the Shugoten appearing in my mind like I've always known it, like memories recalled in perfect clarity.

And then, all at once, my body returns. I can feel and see and hear the outside world again. But everything is sharper. Layered. And...smaller. The once enormous hangar now feels like it's closer to a school gymnasium. I lift my hands, my strong, metal hands, and I understand. I'm experiencing the world through the Shugoten. Through its sensitive microphones. Its high-def vision that strangely has a perfect clarity and a one-hundred-and-eighty degree field-of-view. I can even feel the temperature of the air. I place my right hand on my left wrist and trace my fingers across the network of octagonal cells. I can feel the touch, like it was my own arm.

F-BOMB is not a robot I'm controlling.

I *am F-BOMB.*

Knowledge flows to me from Sig. I can't see through her eyes, but she must be speed-reading everything Unity has on the Shugoten, because I suddenly know how to extend the blade. How to fire its rocket pods. Control its repulse engines. And...I look down at my hips. They open to reveal halves of a large weapon, like an oversized version of the gun Doli used to kill Quinlan.

A railgun. It fires tungsten rounds accelerated by electromagnets. The 18-inch-long, 23-pound projectiles fire at 5600 miles per hour, with an effective range up to 250 miles, and they deliver a kinetic punch comparable to a five ton bus moving at three-hundred-and-twenty miles per hour.

I leave the weapon parts inside my legs, which feel completely normal when they open and close. The knowledge of how everything works and how my senses are integrated into the Shugoten's makes all of this feel, well, normal. Even though I know it isn't.

Hutch's Striker rises up in front of me, slowly spinning around, so we're facing each other. I can't see him. Can't even see where the cockpit is. But we're connected, and I know he's watching me, just as I'm watching him.

Want to see what you look like? he thinks, and then I'm seeing things through his eyes...or sensors ...or whatever. *F-BOMB* is alive with color, orange lines tracing a complicated course around its body, merging at the Point symbol on its chest. The pattern of hexagonal cells shifts over the body as I move, revealing active sensors. The Shugoten looks powerful, and deadly. If I'm honest, it projects the kind of image I've worked hard to cultivate for myself, the kind of look that says if you mess with me, pain awaits you.

I like it.

Are you ready? he thinks.

Not quite born ready, I respond, *but made ready, yeah.* I step forward as he flies back and up, our movements effortlessly coordinated.

The Striker rises up through the open Volcano and peels away, heading around the mountain, where the daikaiju can't see him. I stand atop the circle of the hangar floor that can rise up beneath me and carry me to the surface. But I saw how slow it moves, and we don't have that kind of time. The daikaiju has reached Vegas. It's lifting its massive arm to strike, claws extended.

Eyes turned to the sky overhead, I jump, shoving first with my limbs and then with the repulse engines in my feet and back. The Shugoten can't fly, but it sure as hell can jump.

In the time it takes me to rise several thousand feet in the air, the daikaiju brings its arm down.

No time.

There's no time!

'Five thousand six hundred miles per hour.' The reminder comes from Sig, along with her instantaneous breakdown of the numbers. Five thousand, two hundred and eighty feet in a mile. Twenty-nine million, five hundred sixty eight thousand feet per hour. Eight thousand, two hundred thirteen feet per second. Vegas is three point seven four miles—nineteen thousand, seven hundred forty-seven point two feet—from the exit. It will take a railgun round just 2.4 seconds to reach the daikaiju, a full second before its downward swing removes Vegas's head. If my aim is right.

My thighs open as I rise, giving me access to the rail rifle stored inside, in two parts.

I lift the weapon's two halves in both hands, slamming them together, activating the weapon, its barrel crackling with energy. I take aim at where I know the target is standing, thanks to knowledge fed to me by both Sig and Hutch. When I crest the top of the volcano, emerging like expelled magma, I pull the trigger.

Despite all the knowledge appearing in my mind, on how to use everything from the Shugoten to the massive rifle in my hands, it's still possible to overlook simple things, like physics. The Shugoten can fire a railgun, no problem, but like a human being with a high powered weapon, you have to lean into it so it doesn't knock you back. You also need to have your feet on the ground.

When the projectile launches from the front of the rifle at 5600 miles per hour, a lesser but still powerful force pushes the rifle back. My amazingly strong arms absorb the jolt, but the energy is transferred into my body. I flip through the air and fall, all of my weight coming down on the mountain-side, crushing a swath of jungle and shaking the hidden base's interior.

I feel the impact and the small amount of damage it caused, but it mercifully doesn't register as pain. I can be shot, or have an arm torn off and feel it, but not in a way that cripples me.

The daikaiju stumbles away from Vegas. I can't see it, but I know. It seems surprised, searching for what shot it. Then Hutch sees the impact site. There's a crater in the armor on its back. The round could punch through a row of sky scrapers, but it didn't penetrate this thing's armor.

So, I think, *shoot it in the same place until it does.*

Ten shots.

The information appears in my mind. Ten shots per minute max or I risk melting the gun. *F-BOMB* wasn't loaded for combat. I'm assuming that's because Unity's plan went out the window, and we were all supposed to be trained on these things before fighting an actual enemy. So I also don't have ammunition to reload. Ten shots in a minute. Ten shots total. Check.

I return the weapon's halves to my thighs and push myself up. Once I'm on my feet, the repulse discs kick in. I lift off the ground, weightless and stationary.

Time to build up some speed.

Using Vegas's trick, I let gravity give me a kick start, sliding down the mountainside, never touching the carpet of trees. I feel like I'm on a skateboard again. As confidence and adrenaline surge, I see the luminous stripes on my arms glow brighter, reflecting my inner strength. I nearly flinch when I reach the water, but I don't even register the difference when moving from land to water. With a thought, the flaps on my back open up. The twin repulse discs kick on, pushing me forward, toward the speed of sound.

Hutch is closing in from the far side, descending from above.

Let it know you're there, Hutch, I think, and my plan filters out to him and Sig. Executing it requires no more thought, and each moment, the minutia of it is refined by Sig's mind, taking it all in on the viewscreens, breaking down the numbers and supplying us with real-time tweaks.

There are seven classical maneuvers of war used by great leaders and generals throughout history. We're trying one of the more commonly used techniques: the indirect approach.

Hutch descends in clear view of the monster, opening fire with a cloud of rockets. Many of them will miss, but there is no way to escape all of them.

I cruise around the island, moving into the open ocean and then around toward the daikaiju's back. While this is the same tactic employed by Vegas, a second Shugoten and two Strikers, I'm making one big change. Pushed forward by the repulse engines, I reassemble the rifle from my legs, lean into it and take aim.

The daikaiju bends forward just before the rockets hit, absorbing the attack with its thick hide, and showing me its back. Sure, it's not the most noble attack, but this is war, and there is nothing noble about war. Killing this thing is all that matters. If I have to fight dirty to do it, so be it.

I fire the railgun, but am prepared for the kick this time. The round strikes the monster's back before I'm even done pulling the trigger. An armor plate bursts, but I've only managed to create another fifteen-foot-wide crater. The daikaiju lurches forward from the impact, and my second shot sails over its back, landing in the ocean hundreds of miles away.

When I fire my third shot, Hutch flies overhead, arcing around for another pass.

The daikaiju rounds on me, thrusting its tendrils out further. I feel a momentary pang of fear, of Howard the human monster, spiders and my dead self, but I push back, seeing the alien invader but mentally transposing Howard's face on it.

Fueled by rage at monsters of all forms, the missile pods on my shoulders snap open and fire. A hundred snaking trails of smoke swirl out ahead of me, breaking the sound barrier, while I creep up toward it.

I can't see through the cloud of smoke trails, but I don't need to. Thanks to the two extra sets of eyes linked to my mind, I know exactly where the monster is. I fire one more time with the railgun, striking the monster's armored chest. It pitches back and is then slapped by a hundred rockets. I'm not sure if they're enough to kill it, but I hear the thing let out a wail. Wormy tendrils fall free, landing in the ocean.

We hurt it.

'Effie, look out!'

The thought comes from Sig. I was so distracted by my minor success that I missed what she was seeing on her screens. The creature's massive tail, nearly as long as it is tall, hidden beneath the ocean, rises up beneath me.

I give the repulse discs in my feet a surge and spring off the ground, but the tail rises up faster than I can, slamming against my back and damaging the repulse discs. I aim down at the daikaiju's writhing face, but before I can pull the trigger, a squirming mass of tendrils shoots out of the tail and engulfs my arms and body. Using my own momentum against me, the tail lifts me up and over Howard and smashes me, face down, into the beach. Even with the sand compressing beneath me and the shock absorbers dulling the impact, I feel the first twitch of real world pain in my chest.

Then I'm airborne again, pulled backward and slammed down into the ocean. Water engulfs my field of view, and I hold my breath despite being able to breathe just fine.

Above me, the monster snaps its tendrils back inside its body and raises both clawed hands in the air, ready to dig them into my metal gut.

The moment those tendrils shrink from view, the disabled Bases in Operations start groaning. Outside, Vegas's Shugoten is shaking its head, mimicking what its Operator must be doing. Berg starts to sit up. If we can keep this thing busy long enough, we might get some help.

But I don't have much time.

I can feel its brutal arms, crushing *F-BOMB*'s body, rending the limbs. I have just seconds before I'll be torn apart and filled with seawater, which is when the real me will also fill with seawater and drown.

But there is hope.

The plan is Hutch's.

He swoops in, skimming the ocean surface, facing the creature head-on once more. He unleashes another fusillade of rockets. They're not intended to hurt the monster this time, just add a little more kick to mine. I lift my legs as the rockets close the distance, and when they hit, I give the repulse discs everything they have.

The daikaiju holds on, its mighty body vibrating from the strain. And then I'm free again, a four-hundred-foot torpedo. *F-BOMB* bends at the waist and I emerge from the water like I've been baptized. Energized. Possessed by something greater than myself.

And the monster sees it, too, taking a single step back before holding its ground.

I've lost the railgun in the waves. The shoulder rocket pods are reloading, but they need another thirty seconds. There is one weapon I haven't used, though.

With a quick pump of my arm, the large two-sided blade slides out. The front is a razor sharp, segmented blade. The back side is red hot and probably able to melt through anything the front side can't slice.

This is what I do best, I tell myself.

This is how I'm strongest.

How I will survive.

With a boost from the repulse rockets in my feet, I dash forward, cock my brightly glowing fist back and plunge the blade toward the monster's chest.

This is the twisted, but happy ending when the abused girl overcomes her oppressor and puts a blade between his ribs. That's how it worked when I was seven. That's how it will work now.

Only it doesn't.

The daikaiju catches my fist and stops the blade before it can strike. I try to throw a punch with my other hand, but I'm ensnared by the tail once more, lifted back and tossed.

F-BOMB tumbles through the air. I try to right myself, but I don't engage the repulse discs at the right time. I only manage to spin myself higher before falling to the beach in a tumble that takes me back into the ocean.

But maybe it was enough? Gwen and Ghost have turned around. Vegas is standing up. Berg is about to fire his rocket pods.

The massive alien stomps its foot on the ground and roars at me. Its plates of armor burst open again, and the warbling tentacles whip out. Berg pitches back. Vegas drops completely beneath the waves. And both incoming Strikers are once again spiraling away.

I feel looming defeat.

And then hope.

"I got you," Hutch says, even though it's not necessary for me to 'hear' him. For a fraction of a second, I wonder what he's doing.

But I already *know* what he's doing. In the last five seconds, Sig uncovered a Shugoten function that is both new to Daniel's original design and untested.

Now, I think, and I leap. The repulse engines carry *F-BOMB* several hundred feet into the air, directly into the course of the incoming Support Striker.

The Striker turns nose up and nearly passes by above me, but doesn't. Not completely. And that's the plan. Massive magnets pull the two machines into place, the Striker locking onto the Shugoten's back.

There is a moment of equilibrium as the Striker struggles with the massive amount of extra weight, but four more repulse engines kick on, in time with the engines on my feet. We lift off together, rising to two thousand feet, where a kind of metamorphosis occurs.

The Striker's underside opens up and folds around *F-BOMB*'s arms, legs and torso, providing an extra layer of armor and a jolt of power, super-charging the machine. Hutch's missile pods rise up over my shoulders, adding their number to mine. The armor on my left arm unfurls into a sharp-edged shield that could just as easily be used like an axe. While the Striker's repulse engines fire from my back, its broad wings separate into six airfoils, each able to rotate individually, providing us with a freakish amount of maneuverability for something so large.

The best part about this conjoined formation, officially called 'the marriage' by someone with a bad sense of humor, isn't the newfound power, speed, armaments or even the fact that I'm flying. It's that I'm no longer alone. The back of *F-BOMB*'s head merges with the Striker, and Hutch's control chair slides in above and behind mine.

I shift my vision back to my real eyes for a moment, and I see the blank interior of *F-BOMB*'s head. I look up at Hutch as his chair is locked in place, held by a framework of shock absorbers, and his body locked down tight. He smiles down at me. "See? I got your back."

"Literally," I say.

Then I slip back into my robot body and a funny thing happens.

I take control. It's not a conscious choice. It just happens. One moment, I've got a body that in many ways is humanoid. But now...I've got wings. I can fly. And for a fleeting moment, I just want to fly away. But like Icarus, I won't make it far. There is no escaping the monster waiting for me, so I don't use the wings to run, I use them to fight.

After climbing another two thousand feet, I stop, let gravity pull me in the other direction and then dive.

The sound barrier comes and goes with a thunderous boom of breaking pressure.

I swoop in low, cutting a wake of thirty foot waves into the ocean. Shield raised, blade cocked back above my fist, I turn myself into a missile, making no effort to hide myself from the daikaiju.

It turns to face me, pulling its tail back to strike.

Two hundred rockets streak out ahead of *F-BOMB*, launched simultaneously from the shoulder pods and Striker pods.

I lose sight of the daikaiju, and it loses sight of us.

But I still know where it is. What it's doing.

I roll to the right, raising my shield in time to block the tail strike. Then, as I continue rolling, I cruise beneath the creature's left arm, swiping up with the blade, severing hundreds of tendrils.

The monster shrieks.

The writhing mass of red flesh pulls back inside the creature's body and the plates snap back into place.

Past the monster, I flip over, and push the repulse engines to their limit, kicking up a small mountain of sand and creating a new bay, as my supersonic flight is stopped within a thousand feet, and then reversed.

What happens next is the most natural thing in the world for me: I punch the daikaiju in the face, knocking it back.

But it's not done.

It's a monster, after all.

A clawed hand rakes across my chest, peeling away metal shielding, but thanks to the Striker's additional armor, it doesn't reach anything essential. And the blow leaves the creature open. I bring my left hand down, thrusting the shield's edge down onto, into and then through the creature's arm.

Another shriek, as the limb falls away.

I pound my right hand, and the long blade extended above it, at the monster's chest. It chips the armor, but can't get through. I punch harder, again and again, knocking it back, screaming now, seeing Howard and seeing red.

Claws streak by my face—by *F-BOMB*'s face—raking three gouges into the lower facemask.

I kick the creature in the gut, adding a boost from the repulse engines, knocking it back. Then I unload our final batch of rockets. The force of the explosion knocks the alien back, but has the same effect on *F-BOMB*.

But I recover faster, stabbing at the thing's chest over and over, chipping away at the seam in front.

And then, with a final thrust, the blade finds a chink, slips through the tightly clenched armor and slides into monster Howard's chest.

The daikaiju goes still.

Its four yellow eyes stare at me. Empty and unblinking.

Then it moves.

The daikaiju's still-whole left arm swings around and catches *F-BOMB*'s right arm in the elbow. Held tight between the robot's shoulder and the blade buried in the monster's chest, the elbow bends inward and shatters.

I feel no real pain, but suddenly losing all control of a limb is still jarring.

I flinch back, pulling the blade from the creature's chest, cursing myself—and Hutch and Sig, whose knowledge I share, for assuming its vital organs would mirror that of a human being's. This thing might not even have a heart.

The tail sweeps around behind me before I can recover, and it takes out my legs. The repulse engines on the Striker reduce the fall's impact, but I go down just the same.

Subdued.

On the defense.

About to be impaled by the tail's sharp tip, and crushed beneath the daikaiju's massive, rising foot.

And that's exactly what we want it to think.

Lying on my back, I lift my left hand up, raise a single finger and do my namesake proud.

The first shot strikes the end of the tail, where flesh tapers and becomes a spike. Vegas's marksman railgun shot removes the tail's lethal tip and sends the daikaiju reeling back on one foot. Before it can recover, a cloud of rockets, three hundred strong, fired by Berg, Gwen and Ghost, knock the giant forward onto its knees and lone hand. Its back smolders. Blood, as red as ours, pours from its severed arm and tail. And yet, those glowing eyes haven't lost any of their hateful glare.

The face plates burst open, unleashing the tendrils once more. Up close, I can see a mouth, unleashing a defiant roar.

It loses its voice—and its head—a moment later when *F-BOMB*'s repulse discs launch me to my feet and I bring the shield-turned-axe down on the back of its neck.

Headless, the body goes slack.

The armor plates open up.

Limp tendrils spill out.

And the whole thing drops down at my feet.

I take a moment to catch my breath and then ask, "How many of these things are on the planet?"

The question goes out to all Unity teams, and it's Daniel who answers. "Best guess, upwards of ten thousand."

Sig, Hutch and I all wince in unison, but the hopelessness is shoved back a moment later and replaced by my words, “Well then, one down, ten thousand more to go.”

Three days have passed since the beast's destructtion. But we found no peace in it. The world far beyond us is still in shambles. We can watch the horrors from high above, witnesses to the end of civilization. Of humanity. And every other species on Earth. The daikaiju invaders aren't particular about what they eat, as long as it's flesh and blood.

Sig has done the math—she can't *not* do the math—and says we have just six months.

Six months and everything larger than a raccoon will be wiped out.

Consumed.

The insects will inherit the Earth. And rodents. In a thousand years, the planet *could* be covered in rabbits, leading to the next great extinction.

And in six months, when they've eaten everything, will the daikaiju move on?

Will they find this island?

If not, will *we* be all that's left?

There have to be other nooks and crannies of the world that they'll overlook.

No, I think, *they can sense us.* The daikaiju that crashed in the ocean came here because it knew we were here. The monsters turning the mainland to ash might not feel us now, but when we're the only ones left...I'm not sure there is anywhere on Earth we could hide.

And I don't want to hide.

I want to fight.

We all do. But what can three Unity teams, Shugoten or not, do against ten thousand daikaiju? We narrowly survived an encounter with just one of them, and that was only because I managed to overcome my greatest fear nine years ago. Vegas, Berg and all the others are still susceptible to another psychological attack, and we don't even have a shrink on hand to help them work past their phobias or past traumas. Despite having Shugoten on hand, I'm the only one who can take them into battle without turning into a pile of mental mush. Well, me and Hutch.

He's been quiet since our victory—we all have been—but our friendship is now rock solid. The trust that exists between him, Sig and me is like nothing I've experienced. We have felt each other's worst fears and have overcome them together.

"You're drifting," Sig says.

I smile at Sig and lean back, watching the sunset. We're sitting at the edge of the Unity campsite's cliff, feet dangling over the precipice of doom, just like the rest of the planet. Some of the hammocks behind us have been replaced by graves. Mandi is there, visited once every day by Hutch. While everyone is quiet for their own reasons, Mandi is his. And if I'm honest, a large part of mine. Freckles is there, too, along with the rest of the Unity bodies we could recover from the crashed transport.

Quinlan, Luiz, Bear, Whitey, Twig and even Mack, have been buried in the field by the landing pad. We buried the long-dead skeletal remains of those slaughtered by Quinlan, as well. I was surprised that Vegas wanted to honor Quinlan's final request, but despite being a hardened soldier, he's shown a great capacity to forgive. "Some people break easier than others," he said after shoveling the final bit of soil over his old friend's body. "Sometimes even the best of us. I'll miss who you were, buddy, and try to forget who you became." He looked at me then and said, "Overcoming an enemy is just the first step. Making peace with them, that's the hard part."

For a moment, I thought he was suggesting there was some way for us to come to some kind of peaceful agreement with the invaders, but that would be like lions making peace with zebras. Sure, the zebras would be all for it, but the lions...they need to eat. And so do the daikaiju. We might just be one stop on some kind of intergalactic migration. Maybe some of us will live, and in a million years, they'll be back for more. Maybe they've been here before?

Visions of the slain daikaiju flit through my head. It invaded my dreams that first night, but I've managed to not think about it since we put it under the ground. That was the first body we buried, using Shugoten to dig a massive grave where the tidal wave flattened the jungle—where we first washed up on Unity Island, as we now call it. We didn't bury the creature out of some kind of respect for our slain enemy. We just don't want it to be noticed. We're not ready to face another of those things, let alone have a bunch of them come to find out what happened to poor old Howard.

"Still drifting," Sig says. "You do that a lot now."

"There's a lot to think about now."

"There has always been a lot to think about," she says. "It's just unavoidable now."

"Thank you, Socrates." A twitch of movement pulls my attention down to her hand. A spider creeps along her skin, toward her knuckles. "Spider on your hand."

I say the words casually, but her reaction is big. She snaps her hand up, flinging the arachnid away.

But even after it's gone, she keeps shaking. "Where did it go? Where did it go?"

I've never seen her in such a panic, and in that moment, I know the fear of spiders I felt while connected to the psy-net, belonged to her, not Hutch.

"Is it in my hair?" she asks, shaking her head.

I point at the small spider, scurrying away. The size ratio between Sig and the fleeing creature is comparable to a daikaiju and a human. "It's right there." I point at it. "See? I don't think it's going to mess with you again."

She catches her breath for a moment, relaxes again and leans her head against my shoulder. I place my cheek against her smooth hair and close my eyes to the sunset, drifting once more.

This time inside the mountain.

Daniel, Gizmo, Duff and Doli have set themselves to the task of repairing the damaged Shugoten. There's a repair bay with an army of robot arms capable of disassembling the giant machines, fixing damage or replacing parts. There are also forty-seven perfectly functional Shugoten standing idle in the hangar bay's sublevels, including `F-B0MB-002` and `F-B0MB-003`. But the Bases seem more interested in the damaged machines, taking them apart, seeing how they work and exploring how they can be made better. Seeing their excited faces, as they peel back plates of armor the size of buildings, reminds me that they're just kids.

Kids turned soldiers.

It's tragic, but a common occurrence in conflicts throughout history. Industrialized nations cry out against the practice when warring African nations recruit the young, often brutally. But those same nations take eighteen-, seventeen- and sixteen-year-olds into their militaries, sending them out into combat from which there is no return.

The First and Second World Wars were full of child soldiers, on both sides, the youngest being an eight-year-old boy. The Hitler Youth served the Nazis, while at the same time, Jewish youth resisted the Nazis in the Warsaw Ghettos. Kids in the allied nations, as young as twelve, fueled by national pride, signed up for active duty.

Part of me wants to be aghast that it has happened again, that Unity took a bunch of kids and thrust us into this war. Made us killers. Made *me* a killer. Again. But I'm having trouble staying angry at them. Unity believed that we had twenty more years. And the alternative, in this situation, would have been to sit back, do nothing and let us all die.

But like New Hampshire's John Stark once said, 'Death is not the worst of evils.' Though I doubt he ever pictured being eaten alive by a daikaiju. As the words sift through my thoughts, I find myself feeling connected to America's revolutionaries. 'Live free or die.' Also Stark's words. The point is, living in fear of losing your life is worse than fighting for it, and losing it. To die fighting is an American cliché, but it still rings true with anyone who has ever been oppressed, humiliated or abused.

Don't run.

You can't.

You have to fight, Effie.

That advice saved my life nine years ago, and again, three days ago.

And I intend to follow it again.

I'm just not sure how. Guerilla warfare works, but I can't recall a situation in history where just eleven people, age eighteen down to nine, fought off an army of ten thousand, never mind an army of ten thousand five-hundred-foot-tall daikaiju from another world.

The situation is hopeless. The realist in me knows that. But it will be better to die fighting. *And take as many of them with me as possible.*

"Mind if I sit down?" Gwen's voice startles me out of my glum determination.

I look back at her. She's dressed in a white flight suit that matches Vegas's and shows off curves I would have never guessed she had. I see Hutch behind her, kneeling at Mandi's grave, hands gripping the cross that marks it. They came here together, probably not expecting company.

I pat the solid cliff edge beside me, inviting Gwen to sit, which she does.

After a moment of silence, Sig says, "Are you drifting, too?"

"What's that mean?" Gwen asks.

"Means you're not really here," Sig says.

Gwen leans forward, looking past me. "Who's not really here?"

I raise my hand.

"Well, there *is* a lot to think about," she says, making me smile and Sig laugh.

"Always has been." I give Sig a little nudge.

"S'pose," Gwen says, and we all fall silent again.

Hutch joins us in the sun's setting glow a moment later, sitting down beside Sig and putting his arm around her.

I've never had a family, but I think it would have felt something like this.

It's a perfect moment.

And that's as long as it lasts.

The stone beneath us shakes. Not violently. But it feels like the whole island is quivering.

"Back from the edge," I say, pushing myself away. Then I take hold of Sig and drag her with me.

When we're far enough away from the cliff, we stand on shaky ground and move back further, past the campsite and into the jungle, some primitive instinct telling us to hide.

I search the view before us for some sign of an approaching daikaiju, but the only monster in view is the one we buried far below.

"What is it?" Sig asks, but none of us has an answer.

Crunching leaves turn us around. I'm expecting some kind of attack, but it's just Vegas and Ghost, shirtless and buff, out for their run.

"What's happening?" Vegas asks, addressing me.

"No idea."

"Have you asked Operations?" he asks.

We keep one person in Operations at all times, monitoring the situation around the world, keeping watch on the island's perimeter, ready to sound the alarm. Right now, that's Gizmo. And the nine-year-old is probably freaking out right now, trying to reach the person in charge—which is somehow still me—and failing. I had shut my comm off to enjoy the sunset. To connect with Sig, the way we used to. A sacred moment.

But nothing is sacred anymore, it seems.

I tap the comm unit on my black flight-suit collar and Gizmo's high-pitched voice fills my ear. I can't understand a word of it.

"Gizmo!" I shout. "I can't understand you. Gizmo!"

He stops talking, breathing hard. "Effie?"

"I'm here."

"I couldn't reach anyone. I thought they got you."

"Who?" I ask, not really wanting to know.

"*Who?*" He says it like it's the stupidest question I ever asked. "Look *up*."

I turn my head up, but all I can see is the jungle's canopy. The leaves overhead are shaking, filling the air with a loud *shhh*, but it's not being caused by the rumbling moving through the ground. There's something above them.

I run back through the campsite, past the crosses and hammocks, sliding to a stop before careening over the cliff. I look up again, and see it.

A massive object, perhaps a mile across and miles long, cruises past—flying, not falling—high in the atmosphere, but still looking way too close. Its surface is black and jagged. Long black spines protrude from the front of it. It makes no sound as it flies past, but the effect of its passing can be seen in the trees, and in the rippling ocean.

A cloud of smaller objects buzz around it. They look like black sea urchins, spiked on all sides.

This is how the daikaiju got here, I think. But did they *pilot* this thing, or were they *passengers*?

From their altitude, miles above us, I would look like nothing more than a fleck of dust on a boulder seen from a hundred feet away. But I duck back anyway, sure I'll be spotted. "Back," I tell the others. "Back inside. Now!"

When no one moves, Vegas rounds the others up and herds them toward the nearest hatch, all of which are now programmed to open for any single brand. But I linger, watching the massive ship head toward the horizon. Vegas returns for me, gripping my arm when I don't reply to the three times he says my name.

A shadow falls over us, the setting sun blotted out.

Vegas steps in front of me, my eyes at hardened pec level. He puts a hand under my chin, lifting my eyes toward his.

"What are we going to do?" I ask.

"We have before us an ordeal of the most grievous kind. We have before us many, many, long months of struggle and of suffering. You ask, what is our policy? I can say: It is to wage war, by sea, land and air, with all our might and with all the strength that God can give us; to wage war against a monstrous tyranny..."

I smile, despite the—for lack of a better word—mothership, framing his head. "Did you just quote Churchill at me?"

"Sig says you're a history buff. I considered Patton, but that guy had a potty mouth. Sig also said you're trying to clean up your language. So, did Churchill help?"

I look around his big shoulder. The ship and its gnat-like fleet of smaller vessels continues toward the horizon, not interested in our tiny dot of an island or the people hiding on it. There wasn't a single moment of World War II, with all its horrors, that looked this bleak. "Not really."

"I'll use Patton next time," he says, and he motions to the jungle with his square jaw. "You should get back. They're going to be scared if you're not there."

I'm about to argue. That other people could gain strength from my presence still doesn't feel right. I get how it worked with Hutch and Sig, connected through the psy-net, but I'm not some kind of great leader. I was just lucky that my past was worse than anything the daikaiju could conjure.

"*I'll* be scared without you," he adds, catching me off guard. "We'd all be dead, if not for you. You're stronger than any of us. You'll need to fight. There's no doubt about that. But you also need to come home alive. If you die, our hope dies with you."

"Great. No pressure."

He grins. "The point is, get your ass inside before I pick you up and carry you."

I turn my back on the impossible view, forced smile fading away. I start through the jungle, each step either carrying me closer to the end of mankind or our rise from the ashes.

EPILOGUE

The only time it's quiet in Operations is at night. People talk. Noise from the hangar—drills, machinery, grinding—filters in. Computer systems chirp and chime whenever a new event is detected around the world. But at night, with all the alarms shut off, the only sound in the room is the gentle shush of cooling fans. It's why I volunteered for the night shift.

I'm not shirking my duties or ignoring the world outside, I'm just maintaining my vigil like a monk, watching in silence, as one person after another is plucked from the ground. They writhe in some kind of nightmare, before being pulled inside the daikaiju... and what? Are they killed? Are they slowly digested?

Questions I never really want answers to. Whether the end comes quick or long and torturous, it comes just the same. The moment those people are trapped in their own nightmares, they're dead.

I watch it happen all over the world. In Japan. Siberia. Iceland. Brazil. Hawaii. The monsters wade through cities, moving slowly out into less populated areas, following the scent, or something, of fleeing people. The assault is organized, like archeologists working a grid, making sure nothing is missed. Only the smallest of islands, like ours, seem to be out of the current game plan. Maybe we're just too far away? The energy it would take to reach us greater than the benefit of consuming us? Maybe that's how humanity will survive?

Mind numbed by the thousands of murders I've watched from a distance tonight, I dig the photo out of my pocket and look at the two smiling people standing on this same island, sixteen years ago. *What were you doing here? Why did you take me away from here?* The list of questions has grown longer. While I've seen my mother and know she's alive, and aware of me, I still don't know her name. Or her place in all this. Or if she's even still married to my father—or ever was.

The only real change is that I'm no longer angry at her.

The choice she made sixteen years ago nearly destroyed me.

But in the end, it saved me.

And everyone else in this base.

Was my abandonment sage foresight, cowardice or circumstantial necessity? Beats me. But if I had to go back and change it, I wouldn't. The only thing it would really change is the quality of my life up until this point, at which time I'd be dead and eaten, or soon to be.

A chuckle rises from my core. And I've discovered the answer to my own question.

Why would God allow bad things to happen?

Because they make us—or those that survive us—stronger for when things get worse.

All of my pain and fear and loneliness were a forge, melting me down and remaking me into something stronger and sharper.

Suffering is a teacher that cannot be ignored or forgotten.

But does that still apply if there's no one left to live the lesson learned?

Will we—the human species—be remade fast enough to survive?

"Too many damn questions," I say to myself, and I lean back in my chair, feet up, fingers massaging my temples. I turn my eyes to the ceiling, seeing through it, the volcano above, the atmosphere and stars, to whatever creator it is that hides behind a curtain of dark energy universe glue. "A little hope would go a long way. You know, if that's something you still do."

The only answer I get is the tap, tap, tap of bare feet on the hard floor. I lean back a little further and tilt my head, watching an upside-down Daniel walk down the stairs.

"Feet off the console," he says, rubbing his eyes.

When I don't budge, he pushes my feet off and takes a seat. He's bleary-eyed, yawning and stretching.

His exhaustion is contagious. I find myself yawning, tired and annoyed. I look at the time. 2:15 am. Ghost is scheduled to relieve me at 3:00 am. "Your shift doesn't start until nine in the morning."

"I had a dream," he says.

"Most people go back to sleep after having dreams." And I'm one of them. I've been plagued by nightmares since arriving on Unity Island.

"Most people don't dream inventions," he says, "or in this case, solutions."

His screen blinks on. I can't follow the streams of code that flow down multiple windows. His finger scrolls over the screen, tongue wedged between his lips. "Uh-huh. Hmm. Yes." He taps the touchscreen with his index finger and declares, "There it is! I can't believe we didn't think of this before." He turns to me. "Well, not you, but the—"

"I get it," I say. "It's a Base thing."

He snaps his fingers and points at me. "Exactly."

Then he's back to work, tapping the keyboard like a mad scientist.

"Have you seen Sig much?" The question stumbles his fingers, and he smashes the Backspace key until the error is erased.

Typing again, he answers, "Not much."

It's been four weeks since the motherships arrived. We've counted twenty-five of them around the world, but Sig insists there would need to be three times that number to contain all of the daikaiju. And even then, it would be a tight fit. Daniel has spent the majority of that time with the Shugoten. Day and night. Meals. This is the first time I've seen him up close in two days.

"We need to make sure the Shugoten are really ready for—"

"No point in fighting for something you've already given up," I say. He's smart enough to know I'm talking about Sig, not the world.

He stops typing and turns to me, trying to hide a half smile. "Point taken. But..."

"But, what?"

"I get results," he says, and he hits the Enter key.

I wait patiently for the big reveal, but nothing happens. Daniel looks momentarily concerned, but then picks up a headset and says, "Uhh, hello. This is...Unity Island. Is anyone out there?"

"I thought the communication satellites were down."

"They are," he says, staring at the screen, though I don't think he's actually reading anything on it. "But the island also has cables laid out into the ocean. I don't know where they go, but—"

"Hello?" The voice is young, feminine and completely unfamiliar, speaking with a Chinese accent.

Daniel and I share a wide-eyed glance. "This is Lijiang, China. Is someone there?"

I hold my hand out to Daniel and he gets the message. "Can we get video?" I ask, taking the headset from him and putting it on. He goes back to work, and I respond. "Hello, uhh, hi," I say, sounding dumb, "This is Unity Island. Who am I speaking to?"

"Shen Jia," she says, "but my American friends call me Pickle."

The big screen at the front of Operations turns on. I see a room that looks very similar to the one we're in now, occupied by a girl, no older than eleven, staring straight at us. She's wearing a plain black flight suit, the kind we were wearing when we crashed.

"Who are you?" she asks, looking back and forth at the screen on her end.

"Daniel Chen" He points his thumb at me. "This is Effie."

"Your hand," she says to Daniel. "You're a Base?"

He nods, and she shows us the back of her hand. "Me, too."

I lean in closer to Daniel to make sure she can see me. "Pickle, listen, are we the first people you've talked to?"

She shakes her head. "Oh, no."

"How many others?"

"People or—"

"Bases," I say. "How many?"

"Fifteen," she says, looking annoyed. "Each with thirty kids. That's four hundred fifty people total, in case you wanted both numbers. But there might be more. We make contact with a new group every few days."

"And none of them have tried fighting yet?" I sound more aggravated than I am, but it would be nice to know if someone else was having any success.

Pickle's annoyance fades. "I'm sorry. I neglected to subtract the deceased. Four hundred and thirteen. Several Points have tried to repel the invaders, but were subdued with little or no fight. We're not sure why they can't fight back."

Four hundred and thirteen, plus our eleven. Against ten thousand monsters, twenty-five to fifty motherships and untold numbers of smaller, spiky craft. A bit closer to the odds Leonidas faced against the Persian Empire at Thermopylae, but still, they all died.

"Can we network with that many people?" I ask Daniel.

"Yes," Pickle says. "We can. And we do."

"Good," I tell her. "Get them on the line. Now."

The girl squints at me. Whoever is in charge on her side of things must be a little more diplomatic. "Who are you again, Effie?"

I lean in close to the camera, holding up my right hand so she can see the Point symbol. "Listen to me closely, Pickle. We have lost a lot of people. We have watched the destruction of our homes. And we have engaged and *killed* our enemy." The girl's eyes go wide, and I know this is a message she has never heard before. The Points who tried to fight the daikaiju must have done so alone, vulnerable to the psychic attacks. "You want to know who I am? I'm the person in charge."

I lean back, satisfied that the girl is impressed. I glance at Daniel and nearly laugh when I see his surprised expression mirroring the girl's.

"Now. Both of you. I want everyone in on this call in fifteen minutes. We have a planet to take back."

I stand and say, "I'm going to get the others." I leave the room without another word, heading down the hall, the weight of it all slowly bending me forward until I lean my head against the wall, and weep. I'm not crying for the people we've lost, here and around the world, but for the four-hundred-and-twenty-four people who I'm probably going to lead to their deaths.

My sadness lasts about as long as it normally does—just a few seconds. Then it's replaced by my old standby emotion. Defiant anger. I grit my teeth and punch the wall, letting the repressed me slip out for just a moment. If this is to be Earth's Alamo, then we're going to make Davy Crockett proud, and go down fighting—sans the raccoon hat. I punch the wall two more times, shake out my hand and head for the mess. Our counterstrike will start soon enough. Until then, we're going to regroup, repair, heal and eat chocolate pudding. A lot of chocolate pudding.

ACKNOWLEDGMENTS

While I poured my heart and soul into this book and Effie's character, this book was not created by me alone. I have to thank several people, starting with Liu Junwei (aka Shark) who not only created the amazing cover for Unity, but also labored over the character, robot and daikaiju designs. His input had me going back to rewrite scenes several times, as his amazing designs shifted the story's details. For a behind the scenes look at Shark's work, check out the art gallery at the back of the book.

As always, I must thank Kane Gilmour, whose edits once again help my writing shine, and Roger Brodeur, whose proofreading ads polish to the shine. Roger was also joined by a small army of advance readers and proofers, who catch all the stuff we miss. So a big thanks to Kelly Allenby, Jen Antle, Lyn Askew, Heather Beth, Julie Carter, Liz Cooper, Jamey Lynn Cordery, Dustin Dreyling, Donna Fisher, Dee Haddrill, Becki Laurent, Sally Ross and Jeff Sexton.

ABOUT THE AUTHOR

Jeremy Robinson is the international bestselling author of over fifty novels, including *Apocalypse Machine,* and *Project Nemesis,* the highest selling, non-licensed kaiju novel of all time. He's known for mixing elements of science and mythology, which has earned him the #1 spot in Sci-Fi and Action-Adventure, and secured him as the top creature feature author.

Robinson is also the bestselling horror writer, 'Jeremy Bishop,' author of *The Sentinel,* and the controversial novel, *Torment.* As 'Jeremiah Knight,' he is a bestselling post-apocalyptic Science Fiction author. Robinson's works have been translated into thirteen languages.

His series of Jack Sigler / Chess Team thrillers, starting with *Pulse,* is in development as a film series, helmed by Jabbar Raisani, who earned an Emmy Award for his design work on HBO's *Game of Thrones.* Robinson's original kaiju character, Nemesis, was also adapted into a comic book through publisher American Gothic Press in association with *Famous Monsters of Filmland,* with artwork and covers by renowned Godzilla artists Matt Frank and Bob Eggleton.

Born in Beverly, MA, Robinson now lives in NH with his wife and three children. Visit Jeremy Robinson online at www.bewareofmonsters.com.

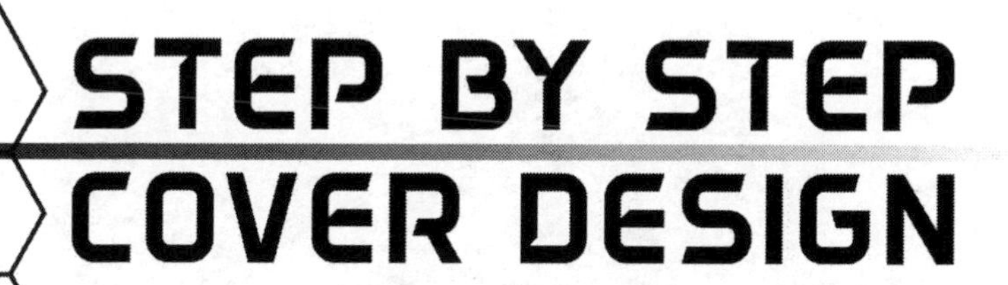

STEP BY STEP COVER DESIGN

LIU JUNWEI (AKA SHARK) CREATED THE FANTASTIC COVER, AND CHARACTER DESIGNS, FOR *UNITY*. THE FOLLOWING PAGES CHRONICLE HIS PROCESS. CHECK OUT HIS WORK AT: SHARKSDEN.DEVIANTART.COM

EFFIE DESIGN

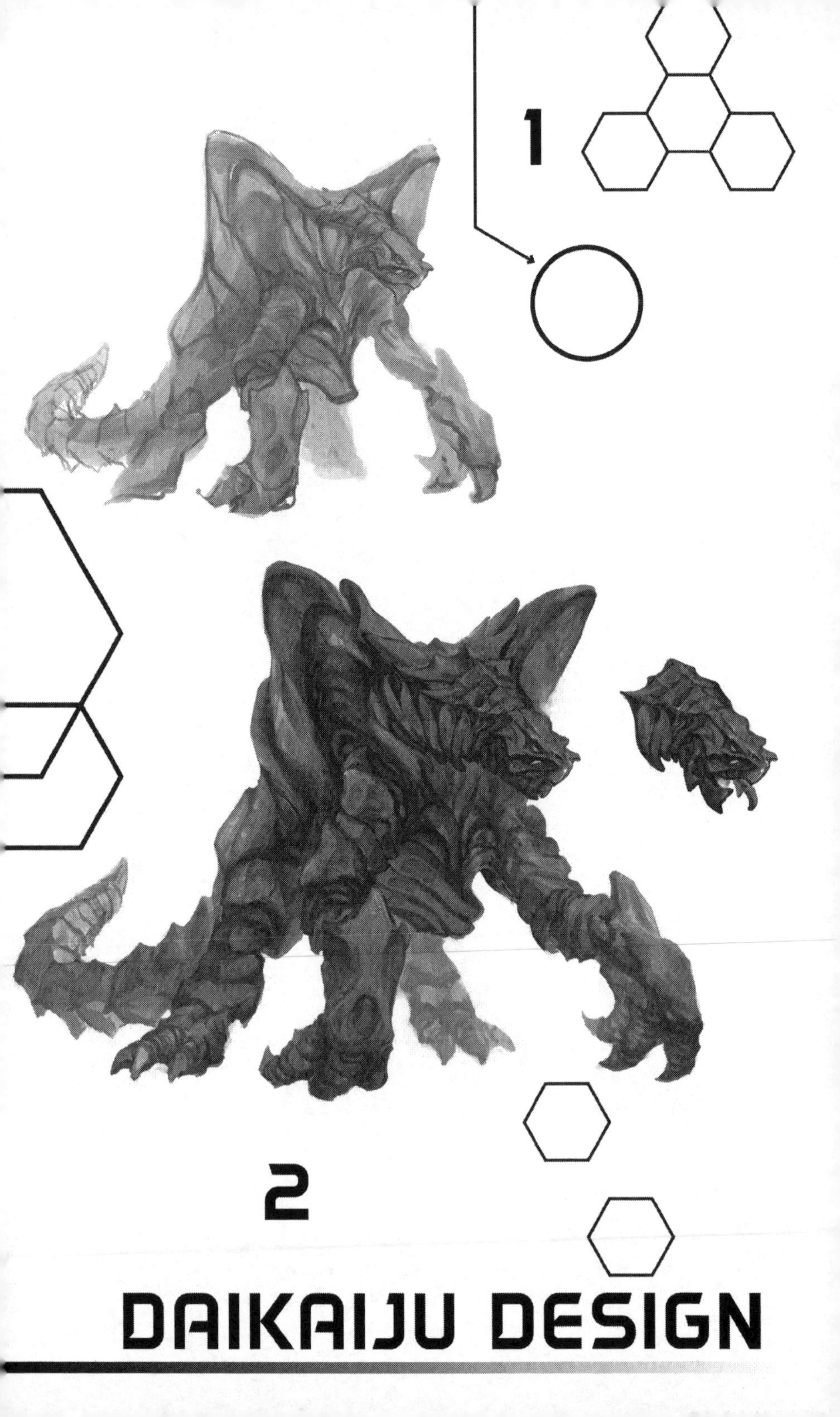
1
2

3

F-BØMB DESIGN

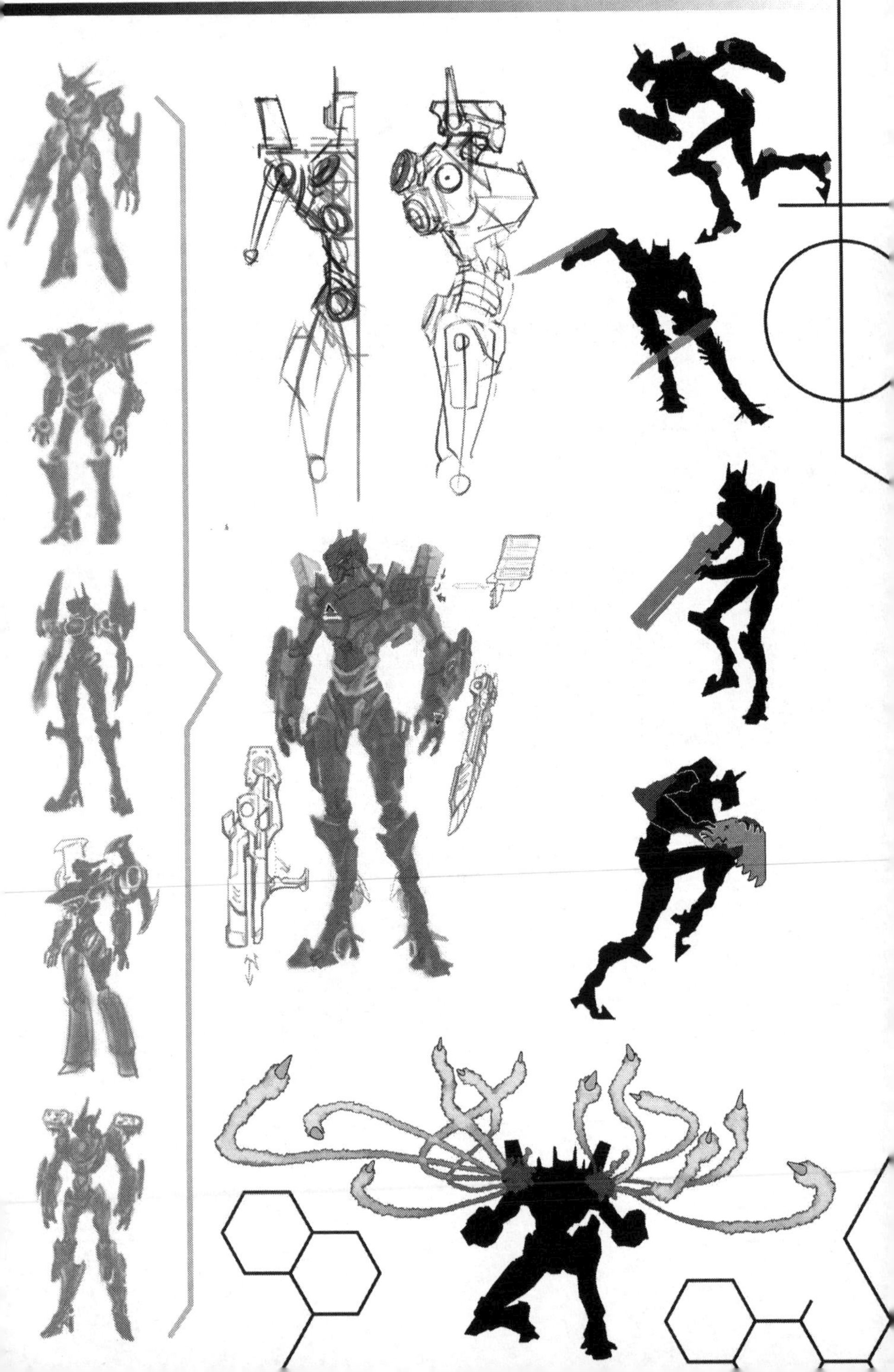

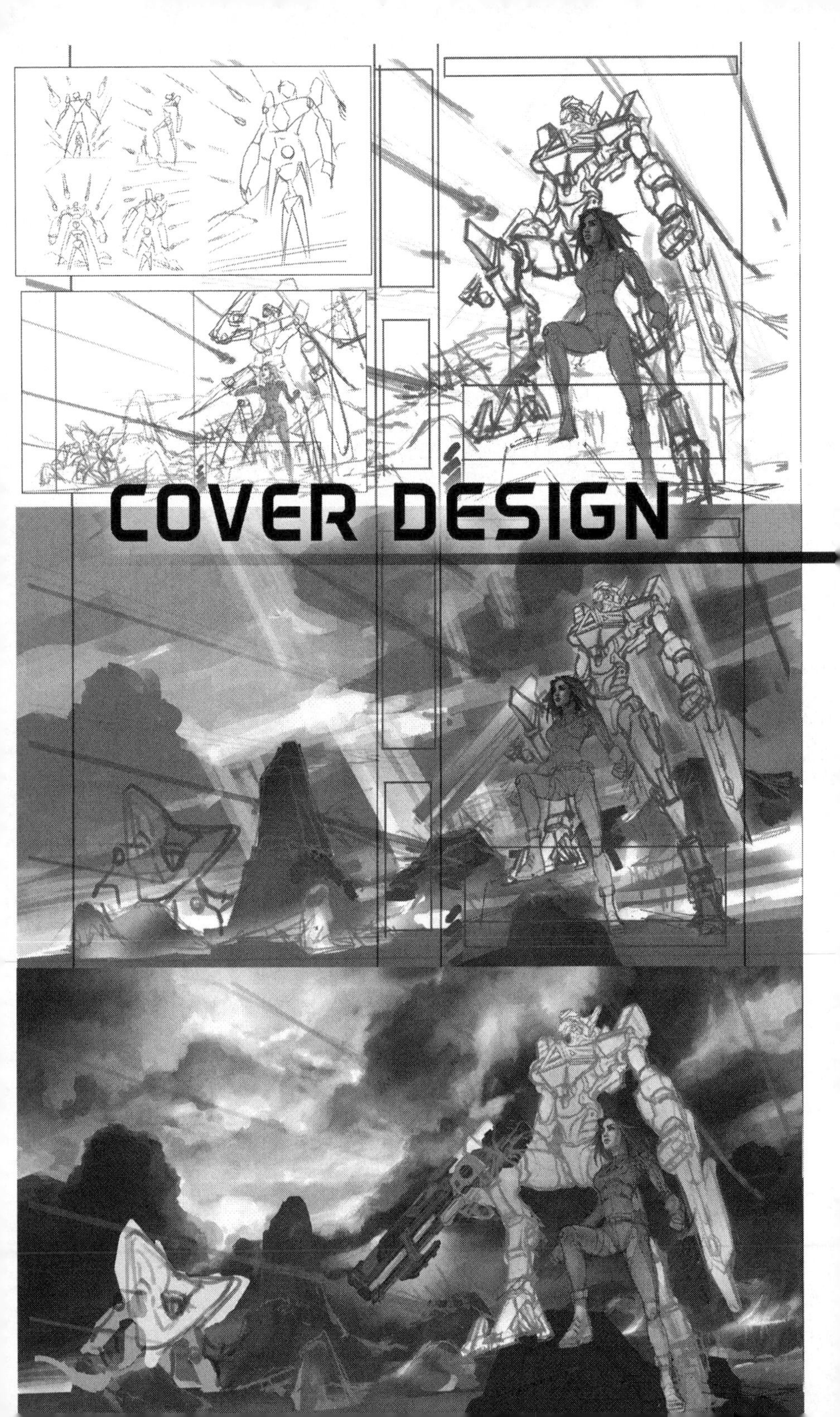
COVER DESIGN